RUNNING
IN THE
SHADOWS

RUNNING
IN THE
SHADOWS

A Lizzie Crane Mystery

Skye Alexander

LEVEL BEST BOOKS

Historia
ESTABLISHED 2019

First published by Level Best Books/Historia 2024

This novel is entirely a work of fiction. The names, characters and incidents portrayed in it are the work of the author's imagination. Any resemblance to actual persons, living or dead, events or localities is entirely coincidental.

Skye Alexander asserts the moral right to be identified as the author of this work.

Author Photo Credit: Anne Schneider

First edition

ISBN: 978-1-68512-706-0

Cover art by Level Best Designs

This book was professionally typeset on Reedsy.
Find out more at reedsy.com

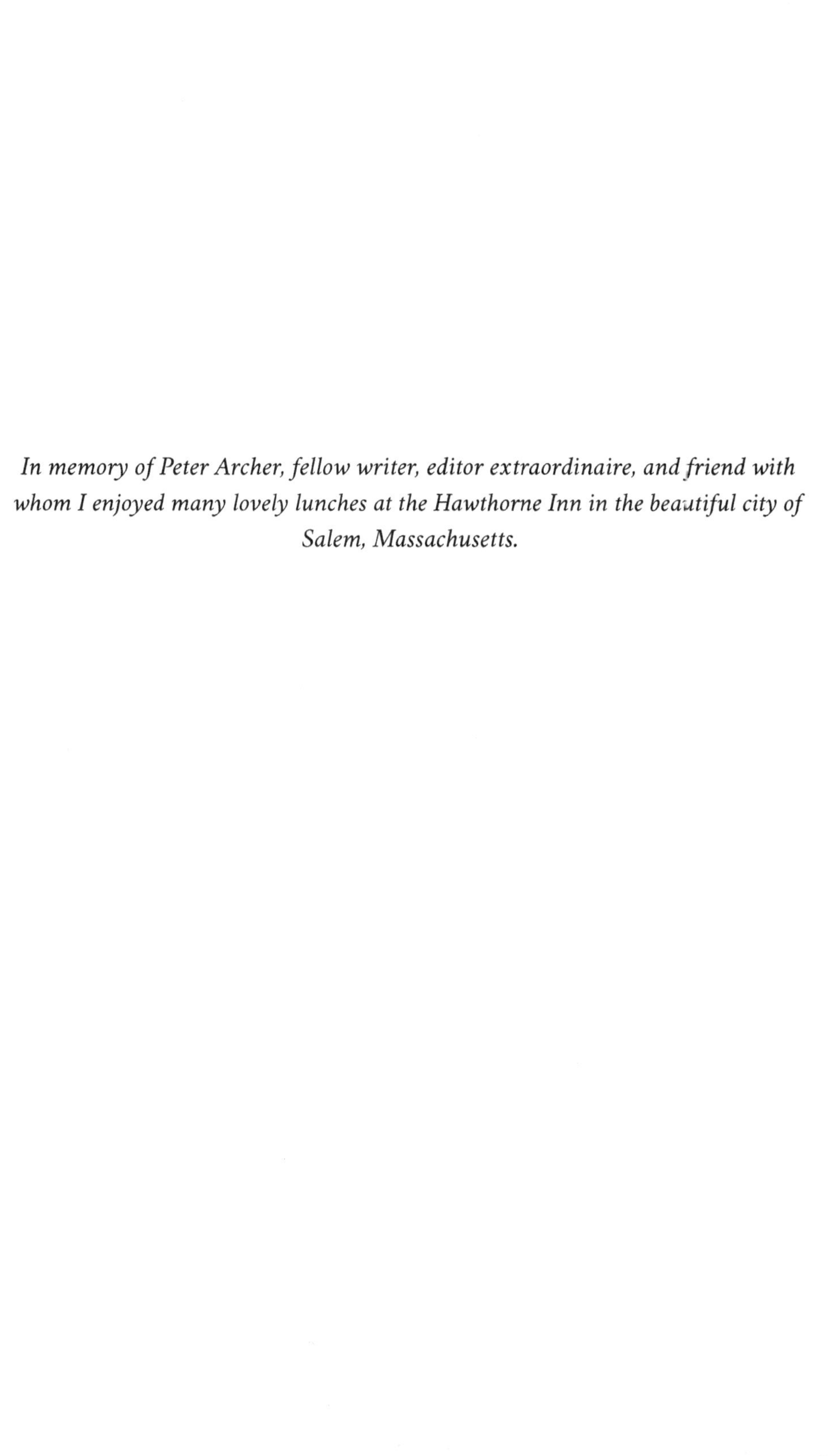

In memory of Peter Archer, fellow writer, editor extraordinaire, and friend with whom I enjoyed many lovely lunches at the Hawthorne Inn in the beautiful city of Salem, Massachusetts.

Praise for Running in the Shadows

"The Roaring Twenties, elaborate parties, fabulous fashion, jazz…and murder. *Running in the Shadows* has it all. What more could you want from the latest intriguing mystery from Skye Alexander, starring that sultry songstress, Lizzie Crane?"—Laraine Stephens, author of the Reggie da Costa Mysteries

"Lizzie is a likeable heroine, and her character is drawn with depth, particularly with respect to her musicianship and relations with her bandmates. The plot unfolds with many suspenseful scenes and is well-researched as Lizzie encounters aspects of Salem's history. Dialogue is tinged with a pleasing amount of period slang. An enjoyable historical mystery for fans of the flapper era."—Brodie Curtis, Historical Novel Society

"A great book. So much fun to read." — Guns, Knives, and Lipstick

"A delightful mix of mystery, romance, and the Roaring Twenties set against the background of coastal New England during Prohibition. In actress and singer Lizzie Crane, Alexander has created a refreshing heroine, whose charm and keen understanding of human nature make her an amateur sleuth to watch. Highly recommended."—Paula Munier, *USA Today* bestselling author of the Mercy Carr series

"Alexander captures perfectly the zeitgeist of the era, drawing upon her evident and impressive knowledge of the history, music, style of dress and argot of the jazz era…a thoroughly enjoyable read that will appeal to everyone who enjoys well-written and accurately represented historical mysteries.

I recommend it wholeheartedly."—Gregory Stout, author of the Shamus Award-winning Jackson Gamble series

"Alexander skillfully captures the milieu of the Roaring Twenties, Prohibition, motorcars, and the Jazz Age. [Her] characters are realistic, intriguing, and filled with adventure. Fortunately for readers, it's only the beginning of more thrills for Lizzie Crane and her admirers as the series continues."—Susan Van Kirk, author of the Art Center Mysteries

"The Golden Age of Mystery is alive and well in Skye Alexander's clever and charming Lizzie Crane novels. Agatha Christie fans: You've found your next great read."—Lori Robbins, author of the On Pointe and Master Class mystery series

"Skye Alexander…vividly recreates the Roarin' 20s through her depiction of the architecture, fashion, literature, and language. She's also created a smart and sassy heroine in Lizzie Crane with a supporting cast that's the 'bee's knees'."— Kevin Kleusner, author of *The Killer Sermon* and *The Killer Speech*

"Alexander brings the period to life with a twisting tale of murder and mayhem that will satisfy any fan of historical mystery."—Edith Maxwell, Agatha-winning author of the Quaker Midwife Mysteries

"Alexander's protagonist, Lizzie Crane, is a ball of fire. You'll love her talent, her courage, and her clothes."—Kate Flora, award-winning author of *A World of Deceit*

"Alexander drops the reader into the glamour and vibes of the Roaring 20s, the Prohibition Era, and a Gatsby-style backdrop in which Lizzie Crane operates as elegantly as the smooth jazz she sings. Richly steeped in delightful period details, *Running in the Shadows* delivers on romance, intrigue, gorgeous women, rich men and a heck of a twisty mystery."—Chris Keefer, author of *No Comfort for the Undertaker*, a Carrie Lisbon Mystery

"Travel back to the Roaring 20s, where the jazz is hot, the company cool, and the Champagne flows like a golden river—despite Prohibition. Lizzie Crane, the chanteuse with a knack for solving crimes, is back. This time, she's turning her skills to murder in the art world and the realm of forgery, where nothing—paintings or people—is what it seems. Pour yourself a drink-ski, fire up the Bix Biederbecke, and treat yourself to this well-written and entertaining mystery."—Liz Milliron, author of the Laurel Highlands Mysteries and the Homefront Mysteries

"In *Running in the Shadows*, the enthralling fourth offering in Skye Alexander's Lizzie Crane historical mystery series, the lively and intrepid chanteuse is once again up to her feathered boa in intrigue and murder. This time, the action unfolds when Lizzie's Troubadours are asked to entertain at a gala in the mansion of a high-rolling art connoisseur. The champagne flows liberally from the ballroom fountain, as soon will flow the blood of one of the attending artists.

"Alexander's sensitive portrayals of her characters are as profound as a chiaroscuro painting, and the intricate plot offers more twists and turns than Charles Lindberg's daredevil airplane performance. The author's vivid evocation of the Roaring Twenties and Jazz Age is so palpable it will make readers yearn to have lived during those dazzling times.

"Whether you're new to the Lizzie Crane series or a fan, this book will hold the reader spellbound with its magic."—Carolina Dow, author of *Scent of Murder*

Chapter One

"Men and girls came and went like moths among the whisperings and the champagne and the stars." — F. Scott Fitzgerald, The Great Gatsby

March 1926: Salem, Massachusetts

Isaac Roman's gaudy ballroom looked just the way Lizzie remembered it. The size of a basketball court, it resembled a lavish Parisian bordello rather than a room in a century-old Federal-style brick mansion in the historic and rather staid city of Salem, Massachusetts. Red-flocked wallpaper covered the walls. Half a dozen chandeliers dripped crystal tears. Louis XV settees, chairs, and bombé chests arrayed along the walls left plenty of room for dancing, and numerous gilt-framed mirrors allowed guests to view themselves everywhere they went.

In the center stood the fountain. Three human-sized marble nymphs in all their naked glory, hands held aloft, poured champagne into tiers of shell-shaped basins. They reminded Lizzie of the Three Graces in Greek mythology. Beautiful couples dressed in beautiful attire strolled by the fountain and dipped their glasses into its shimmering waterfall. Watching them, she recalled the words of the seventeenth-century winemaker and Benedictine monk Dom Pérignon, who claimed that when he put a glass of champagne to his lips, he was drinking stars.

Lizzie stepped down from the stage nestled in one corner of the ballroom and made her way toward the fountain to refill her own glass. Before she reached it, however, a tall, formidably built man with shoulder-length white hair and wearing an impeccable white tuxedo intercepted her. Amid a sea of black evening suits, he shone like an angel. Except Lizzie knew he was anything but.

Isaac Roman. Her host. Art collector and alleged thief.

Next to Roman stood a strikingly handsome man in his mid-thirties with intense brown eyes and wavy dark hair that brushed the collar of his starched white shirt. Instead of the usual bowtie he wore a purple ascot knotted at his throat. Although his broad shoulders and chest gave him the appearance of an athlete, his pale skin and full reddish lips brought to mind Thomas Gainsborough's foppish "Blue Boy." A fashionably thin woman with a chic blond bob, perhaps a few years older than Lizzie's twenty-six, grasped his arm with a proprietary air.

"Miss Crane, I want you to meet my friend Sebastian Amory," Roman said. "He's a marvelous artist."

"Pleased to meet you, Mr. Amory," she said, holding out her hand. "Might I have seen any of your work?"

"Possibly, although you wouldn't have known it if you did. I'm not exactly a household name."

"Lizzie Crane is our lovely diva, which no doubt you've already ascertained," Roman said, fingering a diamond stickpin on his lapel. "She and her three friends have driven all the way from New York City to play for us this weekend."

"I hope you've enjoyed our music," Lizzie said to Amory.

"Uh, yeah. It's swell."

"Are you fond of jazz?"

"Well, sure, I guess so." He shrugged. "Actually, I don't understand it at all."

"Don't try to understand it," Lizzie told him. "Just feel it. Jazz speaks to the heart, not to the head."

The woman at Amory's side waved her hand as if hailing a taxicab. "Hello everybody! Joan here. Remember me?"

Roman laughed and patted the top of her blond head, as if she were a puppy. "And this is Sebastian's wife, Joan. I can't even begin to describe her many charms and annoying quirks. Can you, Sebastian?"

"Hardly."

"But you adore me anyway, don't you?" she asked, pushing Roman's hand away.

The woman looked up at Sebastian, waiting for a response, but he'd turned his attention back to Lizzie. The singer was accustomed to men sizing her up, captivated by her hourglass figure and arresting beauty. This one, though, studied her dispassionately as if she were an object to be painted, not a flesh-and-blood woman. She might as well have been a bowl of fruit.

"Are you an artist too?" Lizzie asked Joan, recalling her meeting with Edward Hopper and his artist wife Josephine during the Christmas holidays.

"Good heavens, no. One in the family is more than enough."

Sebastian's intense, dark eyes continued scrutinizing the singer, making her feel like a specimen under a microscope. "Will you model for me, Miss Crane?" he asked.

"I'll only be in Salem for a few days, and Mr. Roman has me booked solid the whole time," she answered, surprised by his blunt request. Regardless of how good a painter he might be, the thought of him staring at her for extended periods of time gave her the creeps.

Joan Amory jabbed her husband with her elbow. "You just want to get her between the sheets."

Roman laughed. "Or at least see her nude."

"Time for me to go back to work," Lizzie said, eager to get away from them. "Mr. Roman's paying me to sing, not socialize."

Her host smiled and bowed dramatically from the waist. "Indeed."

To Sebastian and Joan Amory, she said a polite "Nice meeting you both." Then she swung by the Three Graces fountain and filled her glass before returning to the ballroom's stage.

Lizzie's longtime friend, Sidney Somerset, played the first notes of "Davenport Blues" on the grand piano, and their colleague, Bert Halley, joined in on cornet. Melody Fitzgerald, the fourth member of The Troubadours, whose flute and violin didn't figure into Bix Beiderbecke's sultry song, retreated to the back of the stage.

When the last chords echoed through the vast room, Lizzie stepped up to the brand-new microphone at the front of the stage. She motioned for Melody to join her. Together, they launched into a lively rendition of "Sweet Georgia Brown," with Melody grabbing the spotlight on violin. Bert's sax and Sidney's piano backed them up. From there, the musicians eased into a repertoire of jazz favorites, show tunes, and blues numbers. Lizzie's strong, clear soprano soared above them, like the voice of a siren who, the old myths said, drove sailors wild with delight so that they crashed their ships onto rocks and drowned in their delirium.

Many of the younger guests danced. The rest meandered about in their elegant gowns and tuxedos, chatting, flirting, preening, munching canapés, and drinking champagne as if they believed the marble fountain would supply them indefinitely. *Perhaps it will,* Lizzie thought. Since the party began, it had spouted a steady stream of sparkling gold liquid, seemingly drawn from an endless reservoir that existed solely for their pleasure.

As The Troubadours finished their performance and took a final bow, a man Lizzie would never have noticed in the crowd approached the stage. In his middle years, he was neither tall nor short, stout nor slim, handsome nor ugly. His hair was cut short, brown fading to gray. His tuxedo, though well-tailored, was indistinguishable from most of the others in the room.

"Miss Crane, I understand you have an interest in art," he said.

"I visit the Metropolitan Museum in New York occasionally, but I can't claim to be knowledgeable about art. Why do you ask?"

He handed her his calling card. "My name is Hugh Franklin. I own a gallery in Boston."

"That explains why you're here at Isaac Roman's party, but I still don't know why you've approached me. I'm not an artist, nor can I afford to buy fine art."

Behind her, Lizzie's friends snapped their instruments into cases and gathered up their belongings. Sidney, the quartet's business manager, stood a few feet away, waiting for her to finish talking to the nondescript man.

"I understand you've seen Isaac's art collection," Franklin said.

Before she could answer, the clip-clop of horse's hooves rang out. Shrieks and howls of laughter erupted from Roman's guests.

"What the hell?" Sid said.

Astonished, Bert exclaimed, "That lady's starkers!" Then he burst out laughing.

Lizzie spun around to see a young woman with waist-length, chestnut-colored hair falling over her shoulders riding a dappled gray horse. As the horn player had noted, the lady was stark naked. Men's cat-calls followed her while she circled the ballroom. Even some of the women applauded and cheered her on. Bert joined in, whistling enthusiastically through his gapped front teeth.

"Is this part of the entertainment?" Melody asked Lizzie.

"Haven't the foggiest," Lizzie said, as surprised as the rest of them. If this act was part of the night's festivities, their host hadn't clued her in.

After making a complete circuit of the room, the young woman pulled her horse up beside Sebastian Amory and stopped. "Are you coming with me?" she asked.

The artist paused only a moment, before slipping his foot into the stirrup and hauling himself up onto the horse's back. He settled in behind the naked woman, the tails of his tuxedo spread out over the horse's rump. She laid the reins against the gray's neck, and they trotted to the back of the ballroom, where a servant opened a door for them to exit.

Joan Amory's face blanched. Her mouth opened and closed again and again, as if she wanted to speak but couldn't get out the words. Lizzie searched the crowd for Isaac Roman and spotted him amid a group of his guests, grinning enthusiastically.

I hope she's stashed a cloak someplace; it's below freezing out there, Lizzie thought. Despite the fact that "Lady Godiva" had stolen some of The Troubadours' thunder, Lizzie couldn't help but admire the brazen young woman's panache. *I guess that's one way to get a man's attention.*

Chapter Two

"Everything we see hides another thing." — *Rene Magritte*

Lizzie sat in a chair upholstered in gray suede with bentwood arms stained almost black. "Nice digs you've got here," she said, glancing around the spacious and well-appointed bedroom Sidney had been given for the duration of their stay at Isaac Roman's home. "Straight out of last year's Paris Art Deco Exhibition. You've even got a radio."

The Troubadours' contract stipulated that, in addition to their performance fee, hosts must provide room and board for the group during the term of their employment. That clause, however, was subject to broad interpretation. Once Sidney had been installed in a barn with stable boys and grooms, while Lizzie and Melody slept in a sweltering attic with the housemaids. The luxurious accommodations at Isaac Roman's mansion were the swankiest the musicians had enjoyed yet.

Still dressed in her midnight blue flapper dress, studded with hundreds of tiny crystal beads that looked like stars strewn across a night sky, Lizzie kicked off her shoes and stretched out her shapely legs. Slowly, she sipped the warm, peaty scotch Sidney had poured for her, letting it help her unwind after the night's excitement.

Sidney loosened his tie and removed the jacket of his tuxedo, then lowered himself into a matching chair. "Now *that* was an entrance," he said, referring to the naked horsewoman's display of theatrics. "You might give it a try sometime, Bearcat."

"I don't know how to ride a horse."

"Alas, a loss for mankind."

"Guess I'll have to rely on my singing to get attention."

"Which you did splendidly tonight, by the way." He fitted a cigarette into an engraved silver holder that he used not only because he considered it stylish, but to prevent the nicotine from staining his long, pale fingers. "The fella Lady Godiva made off with…I noticed you talking to him earlier in the evening."

"An artist friend of Roman's. His name's Sebastian Amory. He asked me to pose for him, but I told him I didn't have time."

Sidney blew a series of smoke rings at the ceiling. "Good-looking chap."

"He made me uncomfortable," Lizzie admitted. "He just kept staring at me."

"In case you haven't noticed, men stare at you a lot."

She shook her head. "Not that way. He wasn't being lascivious. It seemed more like I was a statue on the auction block, and he was trying to decide how much I might be worth. Honestly, it felt, well, dehumanizing."

"Who's the horsewoman who swept him off his feet?"

"No idea. Melody wondered if Roman hired her as part of the night's entertainment. The blonde the fella was with earlier, though—the one you saw me talking to—is his wife." Lizzie sipped the last of her scotch as she recalled how Sebastian had virtually ignored Joan Amory.

"After tonight's spectacle, *was* his wife may be more accurate." Sid stood and plucked her empty glass from her hand. "Want some more-ski?"

"Sure-ski. Then I suppose I should get some shut-eye. What time is it anyway?"

"Ten 'til two." He refilled their glasses from a bottle of Lagavulin he'd brought up from the City and handed Lizzie's back to her. "What's on our schedule tomorrow?"

"More decadence and debauchery after supper. We're free until then. I'm planning to have tea with my friend Cora Delaney in the afternoon. I want to thank her—if she hadn't introduced us to Mr. Roman, we wouldn't have gotten this job. Maybe I'll do some sightseeing. I never got to see the inside of the House of the Seven Gables the last time we were here. Want to come along?"

"Pass. How about taking Melody with you? She tends to hibernate unless somebody drags her out of her lair."

"Her days of peace and quiet are numbered," Lizzie said. "This time next year she'll be married, pregnant, and living in Connecticut with her insurance exec husband."

Sidney sighed dramatically. "The Troubadours will be infinitely poorer without her. What *are* we going to do without her?"

"I don't know. I can only hope we'll find someone to fill the vacancy. Not take her place, but do the job and do it well." She held up her crossed fingers. "Hey, we found Bert after Henry died, and he's the bee's knees, right?"

"True. We lucked out."

"So, I'm going on the assumption that everything will turn out okay. It's better than the alternative."

"You're right, Lizzie. As always."

* * *

The clock on her nightstand said quarter to eight. "Too early," Lizzie groaned and pulled the eiderdown comforter over her head. But after fifteen minutes of trying without success to go back to sleep, she gave up. Tossing the covers off, she swung her legs over the side of the bed and shuffled into the *en suite* bathroom. After washing her face and running a comb through her bobbed, chocolate-colored hair, she pulled on a French blue crepe dress with a low waist and pleated skirt. She rubbed rouge on her cheeks and painted a red Cupid's bow on her lips. Then she made her way along the second-floor hallway of Isaac Roman's mansion to the staircase that swept down to the foyer.

Housemaids scurried here and there, tidying up after last night's gala. None of her fellow Troubadours or any of Roman's houseguests appeared to be roaming about at this early hour, however. Following the seductive scents of coffee, bacon, and cinnamon buns, Lizzie found her way to the kitchen at the rear of the mansion. There, she asked a kitchen maid for a cup of coffee. The girl filled a delicate porcelain cup that might have come to Salem on a clipper ship from the Orient seventy years ago and handed it to her.

Trying not to spill coffee on the waxed wooden floors, Lizzie meandered through the first level of her host's house. Despite the busy ministrations of the household staff, the three-story brick mansion on Salem Common seemed relaxed and peaceful after last night's raucousness.

Avoiding the garish ballroom, she turned down a hallway that led behind the kitchen and into a glass-walled solarium illuminated by gray morning light. Flowering trees filled the space with evocative scents. Birds flitted about, trilling their songs. White wicker furniture invited her to stop, sit a while, and let herself be transported into a lush tropical world, even though wet snow splattered the solarium's panes of glass. Brick pathways wound through the copious vegetation. Lizzie followed one of them, past a pair of squawking parrots and a koi pond.

At first, she didn't register what she saw—it was too bizarre and too horrible.

A pale young man, naked to the waist, was tied to a tree. A slew of arrows pierced his torso. Dried rivulets of blood streaked his chest and stomach. A wad of purple cloth hung from his mouth.

Lizzie clamped her hand over her own mouth to keep from screaming. It took her a moment to recognize Sebastian Amory, whose lifeless eyes stared back at her. *Who had those eyes seen in his last moments on earth?* she wondered.

Gathering her wits, she choked back her initial reaction to retch and stepped closer. Gingerly, she touched his arm and found it cold. The dead artist reminded her of Botticelli's fifteenth-century painting of the martyred saint by the same name.

She hurried back into the kitchen and hailed one of the maids. "Please summon the housekeeper. It's an emergency."

"Yes, ma'am," the girl said and scurried away.

A few minutes later, a stout woman wearing a simple black dress with a starched white collar strode into the kitchen, trailed by the curious young maid. She shooed the girl back to her tasks and asked Lizzie, "I am Mrs. Nutley. What's this about an emergency?"

"One of Mr. Roman's friends is dead. He's in the solarium, tied to a tree. Would you please telephone the police? And let Mr. Roman know?"

"And may I ask who are you, miss?"

"Elizabeth Crane. I'm with The Troubadours. We're entertainers from New York City. Mr. Roman hired us to perform for his guests this weekend."

"Yes, of course. Now, before I bother the police, let's have a look at this man who has ostensibly died in our greenhouse." The skeptical expression on her long, plain face suggested she'd witnessed more than a few pranks during her employment at Isaac Roman's home.

"Oh, he's dead all right," Lizzie said. She'd seen lifeless bodies before, but none as grotesque as this one. "Come, see for yourself."

The housekeeper followed Lizzie down the hallway behind the kitchen and into the glass-walled garden. A parrot shrieked as they followed the winding pathway through the foliage. Mrs. Nutley shrieked even louder when she spotted Sebastian Amory's lifeless form, perforated by more than a dozen arrows.

"Now, please, go and telephone the police," Lizzie said.

Chapter Three

"Revenge may be wicked, but it's natural." — William Makepeace Thackeray

The policeman seemed composed entirely of sharp angles, like a Cubist interpretation of a cop. He stood as straight as a ladderback chair. His long, pointed nose jutted from his face like a chunk of granite. His square jaw might have been cut with a saw. The creases in his uniform were so severe it seemed they'd slice the fabric of a chair if he chose to sit. But Sergeant Richard Darcy didn't look like the type who spent much time sitting.

"You're the one who discovered the body?" he asked Lizzie.

"Yes, sir," she answered, glad he'd arranged for the artist's body to be removed and taken to the morgue.

"How did you know Sebastian Amory?"

"I didn't. I only met him last night. We talked for a couple minutes. That's the extent of it."

She sat on one of the solarium's white wicker chairs, sipping strong black coffee as she watched the policeman. He stood with his back to the tree where the artist had been tied and sighted a line through the foliage, in the direction from which the arrows would have come. Step by careful step he made his way toward a spot where the archer might have stood. His eyes scanned the brick floor of the greenhouse, the bushes and potted plants, searching for clues.

"The woman he rode away with on horseback. Do you know her?" Sergeant Darcy asked.

"Never saw her before. I don't even know her name."

"Dorothea Gallagher goes by Thea. Her father is an executive at the Pequot Mills."

Sid's going to have kittens when he hears about this, Lizzie thought. *Another murder at yet another one of our stints. That makes three in seven months. What are the odds?*

"Looks like she and Sebastian Amory were having an affair," Lizzie said. "Have you talked to her yet?"

"She's on my list," Darcy answered.

"More than one fella's gone to his grave for adultery. Maybe Mrs. Amory killed her cheating husband."

"Maybe."

Lizzie thought again about Botticelli's painting of the Christian martyr. "Poor guy, he died just like his namesake, Saint Sebastian."

"Saint Sebastian survived being shot full of arrows by his fellow soldiers," Darcy corrected her. "He was beaten to death later."

The policeman stopped to pick up something, using a handkerchief so as not to taint potential evidence. He dropped it in his bag, before moving on. "I understand you're from New York City, Miss Crane."

"Yes, sir. Isaac Roman hired my colleagues and me to entertain his guests this weekend."

"Is this your first trip to Salem?"

Lizzie shook her head. "No, we were here a few months ago to celebrate the twelve days of Christmas."

"Unless we manage to wrap up this case quickly, I may have to ask you to remain in Salem beyond this weekend." He didn't ask if such a change in plans was convenient. To Lizzie, it sounded more like a demand than a request.

"My friends and I didn't have anything to do with Mr. Amory's death."

"Right now, we don't know who had anything to do with Mr. Amory's death. We're treating this as a murder case—obviously, people don't accidentally die or commit suicide by shooting themselves with arrows when so many more convenient methods are available." He knelt to get a different perspective and closed one eye. "You were here on the premises last night, correct?"

"Along with at least seventy-five of Mr. Roman's close personal friends, not to mention the staff."

"Were you here all night?"

"I haven't left this house since we arrived in Salem yesterday afternoon," Lizzie answered, trying not to reveal her nervousness at the direction his questioning had taken. "Am I under suspicion, Sergeant?"

He stood up, his knees snapping noisily into place. "Until we have more information, everyone's under suspicion. Do you have an alibi that would exonerate you?"

"After we finished performing, I went upstairs to bed."

"Alone?"

Yes, unfortunately. Her thoughts shifted to the Boston Brahmin who'd recently become her lover. "That's a rather personal question, don't you think?"

"Miss Crane, your personal life is of no interest to me unless it has an impact on this case. Now, if you'll excuse me, I have other members of Mr. Roman's household to question." He handed her his card. "The telephone number of the police station is on it. If you happen to recall anything else, please contact me. In the meantime, until we know more about what happened here, I must ask you not to leave Salem without my say-so."

* * *

Lizzie knew Sidney would be upset. It was too early in the morning. The news was bad. And neither of them could do a thing about it.

She'd brought him a blueberry muffin and a cup of coffee—cream, two sugars, the way she knew he liked it. It didn't do much to ease the anxious look on his face when he opened his bedroom door, though.

Sidney tied his paisley smoking jacket over his pajamas and motioned her inside. "What's up, Bearcat? This better be good."

"'Fraid not." *Just give it to him straight,* she decided. "Remember that artist fella who made off with the naked equestrian last night?"

"How could I forget?" He took a bite of the muffin she proffered.

"Well, he's dead," she said, lowering herself onto one of the room's gray suede armchairs.

"Dead? How?"

"Somebody shot him full of arrows."

"This is the twentieth century, Lizzie. People don't go around shooting other people with bows and arrows. Where'd you hear this bushwa?"

"I'm the one who found him, tied to a tree downstairs in Roman's greenhouse. He looked like a human pincushion."

Sidney sat in the matching Art Deco chair, the color draining from his face. As if he still didn't believe her, he asked, "Why were you prowling around Roman's greenhouse at this hour of the morning, pray tell?"

"Couldn't sleep," she shrugged. "It seemed like a peaceful place, full of flowering plants and birds—"

"And a guy some archer used for target practice." He frowned and sipped his coffee, trying to assess the situation. "Do you think Roman knows?"

"If he doesn't, he will soon."

"Have you told Melody and Bert?"

"No, I came straight here after talking with the police."

"You talked to the cops?"

"Cop, singular. To wit, one Sergeant Richard Darcy of the Salem Police Department. I found the body, so naturally he wanted to ask me a few questions. Did I know the guy, did I know the woman on the horse, that sort of stuff." She decided not to mention what Darcy said about the group sticking around after this weekend.

"But you don't know either Amory or the woman he rode off with."

"Which is what I told the cop. I'm guessing Amory's wife did it. After being humiliated publicly like that, she'd want revenge, right?"

"She could've just murdered him at home and saved the rest of us a lot of bother."

Lizzie feigned a yawn. "Boring. Besides, this way she makes everyone who was at the gala last night a potential suspect. Including Lady Godiva."

Sidney set down his coffee cup and plate, then lit a cigarette and blew out a stream of smoke. "Lizzie, why do people keep dying wherever we go? First our man Henry, then that woman in Gloucester. And now this. Are we jinxed?"

"Applesauce. It's just a coincidence," she said, waving off his question. "None of us had any connection to Amory or any reason to want him dead. Unless you can shoot a bow and arrow, we're in the clear."

But the same thought had nagged at her since she first laid eyes on Sebastian Amory's lifeless body. Being linked with yet another murder in less than seven months wouldn't look good on The Troubadours' résumé, she realized.

Sidney drummed his fingers on the chair's bentwood arm. "Bearcat, there's something I have to tell you."

"You can shoot a bow and arrow?"

"I know—knew—Sebastian Amory."

For several moments, Lizzie stared at her longtime friend, stunned, before asking, "When? How?"

"In the Village, years ago. He was trying to make a go as an artist. I was playing in clubs." His features softened, and he cast a forlorn gaze out the window as he remembered a time from his past. "We were lovers."

"Jeepers creepers, Sid. Do the police know about this?"

"Probably not. At least not yet. But if this Sergeant Darcy is worth his salt, he'll ferret it out."

"Well, he won't hear it from me," Lizzie promised. "I'm pretty sure Salem doesn't use torture anymore to force people to incriminate their friends."

Questions raced through her mind, tumbling over each other before she had time to sort and examine them. *Sid and I have known each other for eight years—why didn't he mention this relationship before? Did he know Sebastian would be here this weekend? What will the cops think when they find out?*

"What about Sebastian's wife Joan? And the naked equestrian?" she asked.

"I've never met either of them." Sidney stubbed out his cigarette in a glass ashtray and lit another. "Sebastian worked both sides of the street, at least back then."

"Did his wife know about your relationship? Or the horsewoman?"

Sidney shook his head. "No idea. Do you think Roman will cancel this weekend's events?"

"Haven't the foggiest," Lizzie answered, still trying to process Sid's startling revelation. "Amory was a friend of his, so Roman may be grieving. Or he may consider it in bad taste to go on with the party when a murder has just taken place under his roof."

"I guess we'll simply have to wait and see."

She studied Sid's handsome face, trying to see through the mask he'd put on, but he'd closed himself off to her. "How are you feeling? This has got to be a terrible shock for you."

"I don't think it's registered yet," he said. "Will you tell Melody and Bert?"

Although Sidney was The Troubadours' business manager and twelve years Lizzie's senior, when problems arose, the group usually looked to her to handle them.

"About the murder, yes. About your connection with the deceased? Well, let's leave that for another time. I hope Melody doesn't panic when she hears about this. It's really quite grotesque, don't you think?"

"Medieval evil," Sidney agreed. "So other than Amory's wife, who else might have wanted to kill him?"

"I guess that's the question everyone's asking right now. Let's hope Sergeant Darcy doesn't think it was you."

Chapter Four

"The job of the artist is always to deepen the mystery." — Francis Bacon

After giving Melody and Bert the bad news, Lizzie returned to her bedchamber and wrote a note to her host on thick, creamy paper that she found in a drawer in the room's dressing table.

Dear Mr. Roman,

I hope you'll accept my most sincere condolences regarding the death of your friend, Sebastian Amory. As I'm sure you know, I had the misfortune of discovering his body in your solarium this morning. I can't begin to imagine the disturbing effect this sad incident must have had on you.

Please let me know what role, if any, you would like The Troubadours to fulfill during this unsettling time. We will stay on, as per our original contract, or return to New York, according to your wishes.

Sincerely,

Elizabeth Crane

In the hallway, she found a maid whose dark curls peaked from beneath her white cap and asked her to deliver the note to Isaac Roman.

"Certainly, ma'am. And thank you," the girl said when Lizzie handed her a coin.

"Is there a telephone I can use to call someone in Boston?"

"Yes, ma'am. There's one downstairs in the entrance hall."

Lizzie hurried down the sweeping staircase with its graceful balustrade and found a Bakelite unit on a table at the rear of the foyer. She dialed the operator and asked to be connected to Alan Peabody's home.

A housemaid answered. "Mr. Peabody is at his office, ma'am," the girl said after Lizzie identified herself. "Do you want me to ring him for you?"

"No, thanks. I have the number." But his secretary had the weekends off, so on this dismal Saturday, no one answered Alan's business phone. After ten rings, Lizzie hung up. "Drat."

She'd planned to have supper with her lover this evening at Salem's handsome new Hawthorne Hotel before The Troubadours performed for Isaac Roman's guests. Now, in light of the murder, everything had changed. Roman might cancel the rest of their stint and send them packing. "Drat," she said again.

Lizzie hadn't seen Alan since Valentine's Day when he came to New York to spend the weekend with her. As she replayed memories of that weekend in her mind, a familiar tingling began coursing through her body. She glanced at the mahogany grandfather clock in the hallway: half past ten. After she heard back from Roman, she'd try to telephone Alan again.

In the meantime, she had a few hours to herself. Lizzie had planned on having tea this afternoon with her friend Cora Delaney. She'd met Cora at an extraordinary and disastrous event five months ago in nearby Gloucester while celebrating the fiftieth birthday of an eccentric occultist. She also wanted to get in some sightseeing. Depending on how things played out, this might be her last chance to do those things.

She grabbed her rubber rain slicker and cloche hat. *Tomorrow's the first day of spring. I should be donning my linen frocks instead of wearing these winter woolies,* she grumbled to herself. But March in Massachusetts was rarely balmy, and tomorrow promised to bring even colder weather. Lizzie wondered if that might spoil the egg hunt Roman had scheduled for the afternoon, assuming her host decided to go ahead with the game.

She knocked on the door to Melody's bedroom. "It's Lizzie. Open up."

The flutist answered, still wearing her flannel nightgown and chenille robe, her blond hair tied up in rags to curl it. Lizzie entered the room furnished with delicate Sheraton antiques and floral fabrics. Apparently, each guest chamber in Roman's mansion featured a different décor. Her own was done in the graceful Queen Anne style, and she suspected all the pieces were genuine.

"Get dressed, Mel," she told her friend. "We're going to see one of the most famous houses in American literature."

Being the eldest in a family of seven children, Lizzie had slipped easily into the role of matriarch for The Troubadours. Her younger colleagues, Melody and Bert, accepted her judgment and direction—even Sid deferred to her in most matters, except those involving money.

Melody set aside the crossword puzzle she'd been working on. Earlier this morning, when Lizzie broke the news about the murder to her friend, Melody had cried "No, no, no, no," and started shaking like an aspen. She'd retreated to her bed where she cowered under the blankets. But true to her mercurial nature, she seemed to have recovered during the past couple hours and now appeared in control of her emotions.

"You mean the House of the Seven Gables?" she asked.

"Right," Lizzie said. "Sid gave me the keys to the breezer. That copper Darcy is interrogating everyone he can round up. If we leave now, you may be able to escape his annoying questions."

"Why would he want to question me? I don't know anything."

Lizzie shrugged. "Nor do I. But you don't want to talk to him if you don't have to. I doubt anyone's ever described Darcy as charming, congenial, or even tolerable company. Just brush out your hair, put on some clothes, and grab your coat. We're in one of the most historically significant cities in the whole country, and we have a perfect opportunity to take in the sights. Besides, it'll get our minds off the murder."

* * *

The Buick's wipers smeared rather than cleared the wet snow that fell on the windshield as Lizzie motored east toward Salem Harbor. On this dismal Saturday, no pedestrians strolled along the waterfront. She turned onto Derby Street and drove to the side road where Nathaniel Hawthorne's fabled House of the Seven Gables perched at the edge of the ocean.

"Why would somebody use a bow and arrows to kill a man?" Melody asked.

"Maybe because it's quieter than a gun," Lizzie suggested, picturing the purple ascot jammed in the artist's mouth that would have muffled his screams.

Now that Melody had adjusted to the idea of Sebastian's murder, the macabre crime seemed to perplex rather than horrify her. "But why not just strangle him?"

"Sebastian Amory looked like a pretty strong, robust young man. If the person who killed him was smaller, old, or less physically fit, strangulation might not have been an option." *But if that were the case, how did the killer manage to tie his victim to the tree? Lizzie wondered. Wouldn't Sebastian have been able to fight him off?* "Besides," she continued, "strangulation's nowhere near as colorful. I suspect the murderer was going for dramatic effect."

"Do you think the naked lady on the horse had anything to do with it?"

Lizzie parked the auto and turned off the engine. "Possibly. She certainly knew how to grab people's attention. My money's on the wife, though."

"A woman scorned?"

"Right."

They paid their entrance fee and followed a tour guide through the seventeenth-century house that had recently been renovated—not to its original state, the docent explained, but to suit Nathaniel Hawthorne's description of it. They followed their guide through shadowy rooms with worn pine floors lit by narrow, diamond-patterned windows and heated by brick fireplaces large enough to roast a whole pig. Secret staircases and cramped attic rooms hinted at mysteries unsolved, even after all these years. By the time they finished their tour, the morning's wet snow had melted, and a weak sun struggled to climb out from behind a bank of clouds.

"I'm glad I didn't live here. It's so dark and creepy," Melody said as they walked around the kitchen gardens that wouldn't begin to bloom for several more weeks.

"But look at this amazing view." Lizzie swept her arms in a wide arc to embrace the expansive harbor. "Wouldn't you like to wake up to this beauty every morning?"

Although Salem's harbor had lost prominence to Boston and New York's deeper waters, it once welcomed clipper ships bearing precious cargo from the Orient to the New World. Imported tea, spices, silk, porcelain, exotic wood, ivory and jade—as well as opium—had made Salem one of the richest ports in America during the nineteenth century.

They motored back along streets now dotted with shoppers who'd emerged as the temperature rose and the clouds parted. Children scampered about the Common under the watchful eyes of their mothers and nannies. Tomorrow, if Roman's original schedule prevailed, servants would hide colored eggs around the city's park for guests to find.

She parked the Buick near the carriage house behind their host's elegant brick home. "I'm having tea with Cora Delaney this afternoon," she told Melody. "You're welcome to join me if you like."

"Do you think she'd be offended if I didn't come? I know she helped us get this job, and I don't want to seem unappreciative…"

"But you think she's weird, and you'd rather not. Poor little bunny, don't worry. She won't hold it against you." Lizzie knew Cora's practice of reading tarot cards made Melody uncomfortable, and she decided to tease her friend. "Besides, we can talk about secret stuff if you're not around."

"What sort of secret stuff?"

Lizzie ran her fingers across her lips as if to seal them. "If I told you, it wouldn't be secret, would it?"

Chapter Five

"The true Tarot is symbolism; it speaks no other language and offers no other signs." — Arthur E. Waite

Lizzie hung her damp rain slicker in the narrow hallway behind the kitchen, intending to retrieve it later after it dried. The hallway led to Roman's solarium, but she couldn't bear even to look in that direction. As she entered the mansion's tastefully appointed foyer, she heard a woman's voice, high-pitched and angry, coming from the formal parlor. She paused on the staircase just outside the parlor and listened.

"If it weren't for you, Sebastian would still be alive," the woman accused.

A voice that Lizzie recognized as Isaac Roman's replied, "Understandably, you're upset, Joan. But just because he died in my home doesn't mean I'm responsible for his death."

"All he ever wanted was to be recognized for his own work as an artist."

"The world is full of starving artists," Roman said. "This is a difficult time for all of us. Don't you have someone who can be with you now? Family? Friends?"

"I thought *you* were a friend," Joan snorted. "Guess I was wrong there. Guess I was wrong about a lot of things."

"Let me have one of my staff drive you home."

"I have my own car. I don't need any more of your patronage."

Not wanting to be caught eavesdropping, Lizzie scurried up the stairs as her host, and the murdered man's widow emerged from the parlor. She

"

pressed her back against the wall on the second-floor hallway, far enough away from the balustrade that she couldn't be seen from below, as Isaac Roman held the front door open for Joan Amory to depart into the cold, gray, painful morning.

* * *

She'd barely had time to remove her wet shoes and set them beside the radiator to dry when she heard a knock on her bedroom door. Lizzie opened it to a red-cheeked housemaid whose golden-brown hair escaped in rebellious wisps from the braid that ran down her back almost to her waist.

"Mr. Roman would like to speak with you, ma'am," the girl said.

"When?" Lizzie asked.

"Now, if it's convenient, ma'am."

"All right," Lizzie said, pulling a pair of pumps from the wardrobe in which she'd hung most of her clothing. "Lead on."

The maid showed her to an office on the mansion's second floor, adjacent to the private art gallery Roman had invited Lizzie to view during her last visit to Salem. Her host sat behind a gargantuan desk piled high with paperwork. Unlike the flamboyant attire she was accustomed to seeing him wear, he was dressed in a conservative charcoal gray suit and could have passed for a banker or attorney, except for his shoulder-length white hair.

He stood when she entered. "Thank you, Miss Crane, for your note of condolence."

Roman motioned for her to sit in one of a pair of Wassily chairs designed by the Bauhaus artist Marcel Breuer. To her untrained eye, their tubular steel arms and legs seemed to clash with the rest of the room's antique furnishings. *He's going to send us packing,* she thought; then, *What if he knows I overheard his conversation with Joan Amory?*

"I'm sorry for your loss, Mr. Roman."

"And I'm sorry you had to be the one to find Sebastian. It must have been quite a shock."

The image of the handsome young artist's body pierced by a dozen arrows flashed in her mind's eye. "Yes, it was."

"Given the circumstances, I understand you may wish to leave us and go back to New York. But your note suggests you might consider staying on."

"We'd like to complete our engagement here, if that's what you want and feel is appropriate."

"It's what I want. I don't know what's appropriate—no one's ever been murdered in my home before. I do know that your music will distract my friends and me and keep us from dwelling on this horrific incident. Miss Crane, I'm counting on you to shine a bright light during this dark time."

"We'll do our best, sir."

He stood, abruptly ending the discussion. "Until tonight, then."

Lizzie let out a sigh of relief as she made her way down the hallway to Sidney's bedchamber. Roman wanted them to stay on. That meant they didn't have to return the hefty fee he'd paid for their services this weekend. But as she knocked on her friend's door, a sense of foreboding gripped her. Remembering a time a few months ago when police had placed The Troubadours under house arrest during another murder investigation, Lizzie thought, *maybe we should leave now, while the getting's good.*

* * *

Now that the wet, mushy snow had stopped falling, Lizzie decided to walk the half-mile to Cora Delaney's home. She knocked on the mustard-colored front door of the card reader's Federal Period house, eager to see the woman with whom she'd remained friendly since the tragic gathering that brought them together last October. Although Cora was only a dozen years older than Lizzie's twenty-six, she seemed infinitely wiser and more self-confident, perhaps because she came from old money or because, without a husband or any living family, she had only herself to rely on.

A housekeeper with a deeply lined face and gray hair tucked beneath a starched white cap opened the door. "Good morning, Miss Crane. Please come in. Miss Delaney is waiting for you in the parlor."

The woman took Lizzie's coat and led her into the handsome room furnished with Queen Anne antiques. A crackling fire chased away the morning's damp chill. Cora rose from her mahogany secretary desk and held out both hands to greet Lizzie.

"It's wonderful to see you again," Cora said. "How are things going with our friend Isaac Roman? I hope you're getting along."

She doesn't know, Lizzie realized as she sat in one of the wingchairs near the fireplace. Even though the *Salem Evening News* wouldn't have reported the story yet, word traveled quickly through the city's grapevine. Lizzie had assumed Cora's attorney friend, Karl Blume, would have heard the news by now and told her about it.

"Actually, there's a bit of a problem..."

Cora asked a housemaid to bring them tea and sat in the matching wingchair. "What sort of problem?"

"A friend of Roman's has been murdered."

"Murdered? How awful! Who?"

"An artist by the name of Sebastian Amory. I only met him briefly at the party last night. Do you know him?"

"No, the name doesn't ring a bell. Roman knows so many artists. He's a collector, but of course, you know that. You're one of the privileged few to have seen his private museum." She smoothed the already perfect skirt of her moss green woolen frock. "What happened?"

Lizzie recounted the story of the naked horsewoman, Thea Gallagher, trotting through Roman's ballroom and whisking Amory away. "This morning, I found Sebastian dead in Roman's greenhouse, tied to a tree with a dozen arrows sticking in him."

"You mean someone shot him with arrows?" Cora sounded incredulous. "That's crazy. Who'd do such a thing, especially in this day and age?"

"That's what the cops are trying to figure out. I agree, it's pretty bizarre."

The maid brought a tray with tea and a plate of gingerbread and set it on a mahogany piecrust table. "Will there be anything else, ma'am?"

"Not at the moment, thank you," Cora dismissed her, then asked Lizzie, "How are you doing? It must have been awful seeing him like that."

"Yes, it was. I'm still having a hard time believing it—it seems surreal. Like something from a bad dream." *Is that how Sid sees it?* Lizzie wondered as she stirred a spoonful of sugar into her tea. "Do you know anything about Thea Gallagher?"

"I've never met her, but I've heard stories about her and her family. She's the rebellious youngest daughter of a wealthy businessman named Paul Gallagher. He's a big muckety-muck with the Pequot Mills now, but supposedly, the family made its money in the Triangular Trade more than a century ago."

"What's the Triangular Trade?"

Cora took a sip of her tea before answering. "Beginning in the seventeenth century, distilleries proliferated in Massachusetts and Rhode Island. Rum was traded for slaves in West Africa, and the slaves were sold in the West Indies to work on the sugar plantations. Those plantations provided sugar and molasses to New England's distilleries for making rum, thus completing the triangular relationship."

Lizzie had never thought of Yankee businessmen being involved in the slave trade—she'd connected slavery with plantations in the South. She bit into a piece of gingerbread and considered the matter. Although families like the Gallaghers may not have owned or worked slaves in their fields— New England didn't have vast plantations that relied on abundant, cheap labor—they were equally complicit in the tragedy of human trafficking.

Turning the conversation back to the present, Lizzie asked, "Do you think Gallagher knows about his daughter's Lady Godiva act last night?"

"I'm sure he does. That piece of juicy gossip would spread as fast as the 1914 fire that destroyed half of Salem."

"I guess it's pretty embarrassing for him," Lizzie said as an idea popped into her head. "Do you know anything about Thea's relationship with Sebastian Amory? Might Papa Gallagher have been angry enough to kill Amory? To keep him, a married man, away from Thea?"

Cora shrugged. "I can't say. I've never met any of them, so my thoughts are pure speculation."

"Do you think the tarot could provide insight into the situation?"

Several times in the past few months, Cora had done tarot readings for

Lizzie. The singer found the whole idea of oracles baffling yet fascinating. According to Cora, the tarot cards could tell the future. Sometimes, they prompted a person's unconscious to pay attention to signs that offered meaningful insights and information. Yet mysterious and strange as it seemed, Cora's cards had always revealed the truth—even when the truth was disturbing or unwanted.

"I don't know, but it's worth a try."

Cora took a deck of cards wrapped in a piece of silk cloth from one of the drawers in her two-hundred-year-old desk. For a moment, she closed her eyes and held the cards to her chest, as if communing with them. Then she motioned for Lizzie to join her at a game table beside one of the six-over-six windows that looked out onto Federal Street. Ochre sunlight spilled onto the table's surface.

"Shuffle," Cora said and handed the deck to Lizzie.

Lizzie mixed the seventy-eight illustrated cards with both hands, then passed them back. Cora cut the deck and laid the first card face up on the table. It showed a skeleton in armor riding on a white horse: Death.

"This represents the present," she said.

"I guess that's no surprise, given the situation," Lizzie said.

Cora laid a second card beside the first. On it, a young man held a tall staff, but the card was positioned upside down. "This one, the Page of Wands reversed, suggests a creative person who's naïve about a situation and has unrealistic expectations. He's out of his league and should use caution."

"Sebastian Amory?" Lizzie asked.

"Yes, that's my first interpretation. How old was he?"

"Mid-thirties, maybe."

"Hmm. Usually, a page refers to someone younger than that. Can you think of anyone else who might fit that picture?"

Lizzie shook her head. "Too bad Sebastian didn't ask your advice. He might still be alive if he had."

The next card depicted a man wearing a crown and seated on a throne. He held a golden disc with a five-pointed star on it. "The King of Pentacles signifies a successful man in the business or financial world," Cora said. "He's someone Sebastian knew, perhaps an employer, friend, or colleague. Maybe a backer, or a person to whom he owed money."

Could the card represent Isaac Roman? Lizzie wondered as she sipped her tea. Cora's description—a rich man and associate of Sebastian's—clearly fit her employer. Did the artist owe a debt to Roman? And if so, was that a factor in his death? But she didn't want to imagine her colorful, charming host as a killer and shook her head to chase away the thought.

"The Ten of Swords," Cora said as she turned over a card that pictured a man lying face down on the ground. Ten swords punctured his back.

Lizzie had seen this one before, in a reading Cora did for her a few months ago. "Deception," she said, thinking about the arrows that killed Sebastian. Were there ten of them? She couldn't remember.

"It can also mean exhaustion, but in this case, I think you're right," the card reader agreed.

Lizzie's thoughts turned to Joan Amory. Her husband had deceived her by taking up with another woman. Last night the lovers had flaunted their infidelity, disgracing her in a most outrageous way. Then there was his former affair with Sidney, and perhaps other men as well. Did Joan know about that side of her husband?

Cora laid down the final card in the reading. It showed a man holding five swords as he hurried away, casting a worried look over his shoulder. Behind him, two swords stuck upright in the ground.

"The Seven of Swords, reversed," she said. "Another indication of deception. It can also mean gaining through underhanded means or taking advantage of someone else." She fingered the strand of good pearls she always wore, as if they were worry beads. "I'm not sure, but this might be a message for you, Lizzie, to separate yourself from a dangerous situation."

Six months ago, Lizzie would have pooh-poohed Cora's warning. But recently, she'd unwittingly gotten swept up in a series of events that had threatened her life in ways she never could have imagined. As a result, she'd become more wary. And more trusting of Cora's predictions. She hadn't known Sebastian Amory and barely knew Isaac Roman. She had no connection to the murdered man except through Sidney. She had no reason to want him dead. The only links between them were the fact that she'd talked to the victim only hours before his death, and she'd found his body. That didn't guarantee she wouldn't be dragged into this nefarious affair, however.

"I don't know if that helps," Cora said as she scooped up the cards and wrapped them again in the square of silk.

Lizzie rubbed her temples, trying to make sense of the maddeningly brief amount of information her friend had revealed. "You've given me something to think about, Cora. I guess I'll have to let it sink in."

Chapter Six

"I want to be with those who know secret things." — *Rainer Maria Rilke*

After her meeting with Cora, Lizzie tried again to telephone Alan to tell him about Sebastian Amory's murder. He had a right to know what he was walking into before he arrived at this macabre scene—and to steer clear of it if he chose. But he didn't answer the phone at either his home or office. Her first thought was of his mother, who suffered from a heart condition and clung tenuously to life. Last month, Alan had introduced Lizzie to her, a frail, gentle woman with a sweet countenance, now confined to her bed in an elegant townhouse on Boston's prestigious Beacon Hill, not far from Alan's own Louisburg Square home. Had she taken a turn for the worse?

He may simply be busy, Lizzie told herself. *Unless I hear otherwise, I'm going to assume that we're still having supper together this evening and that he'll be here in three hours.*

Before going back to her bedroom to bathe and change clothes, Lizzie made a circuit of Roman's ballroom to be sure everything was ready for tonight's performance. At The Troubadours' events, she oversaw the staging, acoustics, lighting, and other particulars that would affect the group's presentation. This engagement was pretty simple and straightforward. No skits. No carefully choreographed dance numbers. All she and her colleagues had to do was play music. Jazz. The music that quickened her pulse and stirred her soul. The music that hummed in her mind day and night, that kept her sane in the midst of chaos and in the depths of sadness.

How many of Roman's staff know Sebastian Amory was murdered here in the wee hours of this morning? she wondered. By now, she suspected, the story would have traveled through the entire household. The help always knew what went on under their roof, and Lizzie wished she knew what they knew.

After checking the lighting and the microphone at the center of the ballroom's stage, making certain all was in order, she climbed the stairs to the mansion's second floor and knocked on Sidney's door. When he opened it, she heard Clarence Williams's Blue Five singing "Everybody Loves My Baby" on the radio.

"I'm just about to pour myself a drink-ski," he said, inviting her in. "Want one?"

"What do you think-ski?" she answered as she lowered herself into one of the room's Art Deco armchairs. "Did Sergeant Darcy question you about the murder?"

He handed her a tumbler with two fingers worth of Lagavulin in it and sat in the companion chair. "No. I suppose he hasn't made the connection yet."

"How are you doing? I mean, I realize it was a long time ago, but still, Amory was your lover once upon a time. This must be upsetting for you."

"I hadn't thought much about Sebastian in all these years. I pushed him and our affair out of my mind after he dumped me. For a woman, no less. Until last night when he showed up at the party. Then it all came rushing back." He took a sip of his scotch and crossed his left ankle over his right thigh. "Now he's dead. Murdered." He shook his head. "I still can't believe it."

Lizzie studied her friend's movie-star handsome face, now clouded with confusion. "I'm guessing this wasn't just a casual fling."

"Back then I was goofy about him. But he worried that being known as a three-letter man would hamper his career."

"Why would he think that? The art world's full of people of all persuasions," she said. "The music scene too."

"He had sky-high ambitions, even though I pointed out that most artists don't get recognized until after they're dead."

The irony of Sid's comment wasn't lost on her. Sebastian's murder might, indeed, catapult him into fame, though not the sort of recognition he'd sought.

Sidney took a cigarette from an engraved tin, tapped it a few times on the lid, and then fitted it into his silver holder. "He is—was—a talented artist, but he sold out."

"How so?"

"He worked as a copyist, reproducing paintings by famous artists for people who couldn't afford the real thing."

"Isn't that illegal?" Lizzie asked.

"Not if you don't pretend the picture's authentic." Sidney studied her with his dark, piercing eyes. "Enough about me. Are *you* all right, Bearcat? I mean, it's not every day you stumble upon a guy shot full of arrows. Even though you didn't know Sebastian, it must've been unnerving."

This was the third body she'd discovered in less than a year. It hadn't gotten any easier. "It doesn't seem real. More like something out of a nightmare."

"Are you okay to perform tonight?"

"Of course. Are you?"

He nodded. "What about Melody?"

"I told her what happened. Initially, she panicked but she's all right now. We visited the House of the Seven Gables today and she acted like every other tourist."

"How did Bert take the news?"

"Okay overall. He seemed confused, like the rest of us, about why people keep dropping dead wherever we play."

"You didn't tell him I knew Sebastian, did you?"

"No. Better he doesn't know that little detail—wouldn't want it to slip out accidentally." Lizzie took a sip of her scotch and contemplated the situation. "I guess it's up to us, Sid, to downplay things so they feel comfortable enough to finish this job. It's only for a few days. Roman's paid us a bundle to perform this weekend and he wants us to stay on. I don't like to seem mercenary, but

I'm not willing to sacrifice all that dough if the problem isn't my fault."

* * *

For her date with Alan, Lizzie had bought a lovely spring dress made of delicate layers of shell-pink silk that resembled feathers. But with the temperature dropping to near-freezing tonight, that one would have to wait. She substituted a warmer, rose-colored crepe frock with a low waist and long, tight sleeves. Still, it was seductive enough with a hemline that barely covered her knees and a V-neckline that revealed perhaps a bit too much of her cleavage.

Alan and Roman were sitting by the fireplace, engaged in conversation, when she entered the parlor. In contrast to his formal black evening suit, Alan's red hair blazed brighter than the hearth flames. Roman's white locks sloped like a hill of snow down to the shoulders of his white tuxedo. Both men stood, and Alan crossed the room to greet her.

"You're even more beautiful than the last time I saw you," he said, taking her hand and kissing it in an old-fashioned way she found charming.

The glowing sensation she always felt in his presence swept through her body, as if he'd flipped a switch and filled her with light. She still couldn't believe this rich, handsome man from one of Boston's most prestigious families, who could have any woman he wanted, actually cared about her, a showgirl from a poor immigrant family in the Bronx.

Trying to contain her excitement, she said, "Thank you, Alan. It's wonderful to see you again."

"Have a nice supper," Roman said. "Save room for dessert. I've ordered a hundred tiny cakes decorated to look like Fabergé eggs."

As they walked across the Common, Lizzie asked Alan, "How's your mother?"

"Her spirits are good, and she never complains, but each day, she grows a little weaker. She's slipping away from us inch by inch."

"I'm sorry to hear that. I enjoyed meeting her very much."

"She enjoyed meeting you too. She sends fond wishes."

He stopped walking and pulled Lizzie into an embrace that chased away the evening's chill. After a long, slow kiss, he said, "I've been wanting to do that for thirty-one days." He kissed her again. "Consider this a prelude."

She laughed. "I look forward to the entire opera."

The Hawthorne Hotel's graceful dining room welcomed them. A waiter showed the couple to a quiet corner table, away from the other guests. After they ordered, Alan said, "Roman told me about the murder."

"I tried to call you to let you know what happened."

He laid his hand over hers and stroked it gently with his thumb. "Discovering him like that must have been awful for you."

"It was quite a shock," she admitted. "I suppose Roman also told you about the Gallagher girl's show-stopping act."

"Yes. I'm sorry I missed it."

The waiter brought their first course, delicate filets of flounder in what Lizzie felt certain was a wine sauce with a touch of lemon and sprinkled with fresh tarragon.

"I didn't realize you knew Roman," Lizzie said.

"He helped me purchase a Van Gogh painting several years ago. I'd seen some of the artist's work in Amsterdam and Paris while I was traveling in Europe in 1911. His popularity was growing by then, and he made a big impression on me. After the war ended, a number of art enthusiasts in France and Germany had to sell off pieces from their private collections. I managed to acquire one of his paintings, with Roman acting as a go-between."

"I've never seen Van Gogh's pictures," Lizzie said. "I've only read about him."

"Then you must come to my home again soon, so I can show my painting to you."

She debated whether to tell him what she'd heard about Roman dealing in stolen art. But her host had joked easily with Lizzie about his controversial reputation, so apparently it was an open secret. Or completely untrue. After the waiter had served pink spring lamb, asparagus, and new potatoes in a cream and parsley sauce, she decided to mention it.

"I've heard that too." Alan cut a piece of lamb and chewed it while contemplating her misgivings. Finally, he said, "Honestly, I have no way of knowing if my painting was stolen. Europe was chaotic at the time. I have only the paperwork Roman provided—and his word—that the transaction was legit. The painting is spectacular nonetheless."

Chapter Seven

"You didn't take your clothes to parties; they took you."— Elizabeth von Arnim, The Enchanted April

"I have to change clothes for tonight's performance," Lizzie told Alan at the bottom of the staircase in Isaac Roman's foyer. "If you'd like a drink, the champagne fountain in the ballroom is probably flowing. But please don't get too captivated by the pretty young ladies who tend to throw themselves into it."

He laughed and strolled down the hallway to the ballroom as she hurried upstairs to her bedroom. After touching up her makeup and combing her hair, she pulled a daring black evening gown from the wardrobe. *I couldn't wear this anyplace else,* she thought, *and even here, it's sure to raise eyebrows.* She slipped into the dress and was studying herself in the cheval mirror when she heard a knock on the door.

"It's open," she called.

Melody entered, carrying her flute case in one hand and violin case in the other. When she saw Lizzie, her eyes grew wide with astonishment.

"You can't wear that, Lizzie!"

From a deep, jeweled, insinuating V at her hips, the silk skirt cascaded to the floor like a black waterfall. The bodice, however, appeared transparent. Only a strategically placed flower and a silver crescent moon offered the slightest covering.

Lizzie laughed at the shocked look on Melody's face—but she often shocked her more innocent friend. "Poor little bunny. It's an illusion. The top's made of skin-colored silk."

"You're going to fool everyone. They'll all think you're half naked."

"After that lady on the horse last night, I have to do something to get attention." She set an Egyptian-inspired headpiece studded with rhinestones on her head and glanced in the mirror one last time. "Okay, let's get a wiggle on."

* * *

"Holy moly, Bearcat," Sidney said as Lizzie stepped onto the ballroom's stage. "I think you left half your dress back in your bedroom."

"It just looks that way. Actually, I'm quite well covered," she assured him. "It's the idea that counts."

"Well, I can tell you what idea every man in this room is going to have as soon as he lays eyes on you."

"Ish kabibble." *I only care what one man thinks.*

Lizzie scanned the ostentatious ballroom with its garish furnishings, searching for Alan. Already at least fifty guests milled about in their glamorous evening attire, sipping champagne. She spotted him talking to Cora Delaney and her attorney friend Karl Blume, his hair shining like polished copper in the chandeliers' light. Lizzie still hadn't figured out the exact nature of Cora and Karl's relationship. Beyond a professional one, they claimed to share interests in canasta, gardening, and mystery novels. She suspected they had a more intimate connection, although they showed no signs of affection publicly.

Near the Three Graces fountain stood her host, Isaac Roman, splendid in his snow-white tuxedo. Beside him, a tall, reed-thin young man, shoulders hunched as if he wanted to make himself seem smaller, was engaged in an animated discussion with the art gallery owner, Hugh Franklin. He kept jabbing his finger at Franklin until Franklin finally swatted the young man's hand away and went to fill his glass from the fountain.

How many of these people knew Sebastian Amory? How many know he was murdered here last night? she wondered. Then, another thought came to her. Supposedly, a murderer always returns to the scene of the crime. *Did one of these guests kill him?* She couldn't possibly remember everyone who attended last night's gala, although she noticed both Joan Amory and Thea Gallagher had opted out of tonight's bash.

Sidney stepped away from the piano, where he'd been playing songs Lizzie knew he'd written, and spoke into the microphone. "Good evening, ladies and gentlemen. Happy Spring Equinox Eve, although it seems like spring took a wrong turn and got lost before she reached Salem. I'm Sidney Somerset and we're The Troubadours from New York City, here at the behest of our magnanimous host, Mr. Isaac Roman, to entertain you this evening. We'll be playing a mix of hot and cool jazz, along with some blues and Broadway hits. If you have a favorite song you'd like to hear, we'll try to accommodate you. No polkas or Irish jigs, though, please."

Some of the guests chuckled. All clapped their hands to welcome the quartet as Bert grabbed his saxophone and launched into Ben Bernie's "Sweet Georgia Brown." Sid returned to his piano bench and joined in as Lizzie moved to center stage and began to sing.

For the next hour, The Troubadours performed a variety of jazz numbers and popular show tunes, as Sidney had promised. When they eased into a medley of the Gershwins' songs, including "Somebody Loves Me" and "The Man I Love," Lizzie caught Alan's eye and saw him wink. *Does he know I'm singing these songs for him?*

By now, the group of revelers in Roman's ballroom had swelled to about seventy-five beautiful people dressed in fabulous clothes. A lot of them, she guessed, must have driven up from Boston—surely Salem didn't have this many socialites in its population. Some might even be fellow New Yorkers. Her host moved among them easily, welcoming everyone. Fetching young women in sequined gowns and feathered headdresses sidled up to him, drawn to the allure of money and power like hummingbirds to his heavy sugar.

At the far end of the ballroom, Lizzie spotted a man who didn't fit in with the rest of the glamorous crowd. He walked with a soldier's rigid stance rather than a dancer's grace, and his cheap, off-the-rack suit jarred like an errant note in a symphony of designer tuxedos. Sergeant Richard Darcy. The cop edged his way along the wall, trying not to attract attention, while he observed everyone and everything.

It didn't take long for Roman to approach the policeman. He extended his hand and the sergeant shook it. They chatted briefly, then Roman moved on to talk with other guests. *Darcy knows he can't bust Roman for the champagne, and Roman knows that too,* Lizzie realized. The Volstead Act only forbade selling, manufacturing, or transporting alcohol, not consuming it. Or serving it in one's home. *Roman probably pays off the cops too,* she figured.

Sidney stepped away from the piano. "We're going to take a short break," he told Roman's guests, "after which I understand our host will be welcoming in the holiday with a panoply of edible Fabergé eggs. Ladies and gents, you won't want to miss this unique and unparalleled treat, so stick around. We'll have a lot more music for you, too, as we celebrate the advent of spring."

Alan approached the stage and took Lizzie's hand. Unabashedly, his eyes scanned her provocative gown. "Can you skip the rest of your performance and come upstairs to your bedroom with me right now?"

"I'm committed to sing for three more hours." She stood on her tiptoes and kissed him. "That gives you three hours to fantasize about ways we might enjoy each other for the rest of the night."

He chuckled as he folded her hand into the bend of his elbow and led her to the Three Graces fountain. While he filled their glasses with champagne, she asked, "Will you wait for me?"

Quoting Shakespeare, he replied, "Forever and a day."

A gaggle of housemaids carrying platters of egg-shaped petit fours began moving through the crowded ballroom. Fanciful icing decorations on the tiny cakes imitated the jeweled treasures Peter Carl Fabergé designed for the Russian Czars Alexander III and Nicholas II.

Lizzie accepted one with red, blue, and green frosting "gems" encased in a golden net. "It's too pretty to eat," she said, admiring the effort that had gone into making it.

"But if you don't eat it, the baker's art will be for naught," Alan pointed out.

She bit into the confectionery and felt something decidedly un-cakelike on her tongue. As delicately as she could, she removed a slip of paper about an inch long from her mouth. She smoothed it out on her palm and read the single word written there: Illusion.

"Oh, it's like a Chinese fortune cookie." Delighted, she showed Alan the slip of paper.

He read it, then swept her torso with his eyes. "I think it refers to your gown. How do you suppose the baker knew what you'd wear tonight?"

Lizzie laughed. "Does yours contain a message too?"

He broke his petit four in half and extracted a paper strip. "Pleasure," he said with a smile. "Maybe there's something to this fortune-telling stuff after all."

Soon, the ballroom buzzed with delight as people discussed the "fortunes" they found in the beautifully decorated eggs. Cora and Karl Blume wended their way through the crowd toward Lizzie and Alan. As usual, Blume wore a boutonniere on his lapel—Lizzie called it his "pretty nametag" because his name meant flower in his native German. The card reader eyed Lizzie's dress but made no comment.

"What message did you get in your egg?" Lizzie asked Cora.

"Truth."

In a teasing tone of voice, Blume said, "Even a piece of cake can be an oracle."

Cora answered, "I'm reminded of what Ralph Waldo Emerson said: 'Truth is always present; it only needs to lift the iron lids of the mind's eye to read its oracles.'"

"Do you think it's a reference to Sebastian Amory's murder?" Lizzie asked.

"Possibly."

Lizzie recalled the tarot reading Cora had given her this afternoon. The cards showed a naïve young man, a financial backer, and a warning of deception. Maybe the word "truth" in Cora's egg meant the artist's killer would soon be revealed.

"What does yours say?" Alan asked Blume.

"'Don't offer advice unless the client pays you for your services.'"

Cora snatched the slip of paper from his hand and read it aloud. "Money."
Blume laughed. "Isn't that what I said?"

"Excuse me, but I have to go back to work," Lizzie told her friends. "I hope you enjoy the rest of the show."

Holding on to Alan's arm, she swung by the fountain and filled her glass one more time. "What do you make of all these predictions? Is it just childish fun, or do you think there's something to it?" she asked.

From his pocket Alan pulled the slip of paper he'd found in his egg. *Pleasure.* "I'm trusting this one," he said, as he glanced at his Patek Philippe watch. "And I predict it will come true in three hours."

At quarter to one, Sidney announced, "Last dance, ladies and gentlemen. Grab your best doll or sheik and cuddle, while we wind up the evening with Bix Beiderbecke's 'Davenport Blues.' I'd like to thank our illustrious host, Mr. Isaac Roman, for inviting us here to perform this weekend. You've been a swell audience, and we've had fun playing for you. I hope you enjoyed it as much as we did."

Cheers and clapping rang through the ballroom.

"We're The Troubadours from New York City. I'm Sidney Somerset," he continued and took a bow. "Melody Fitzgerald is our lovely flute and violin player. Our maestro of the horn is Bert Halley." Snickers from the guests made the young musician blush, and he grinned self-consciously. "And our beautiful chanteuse, whom I know you fellas have been ogling all night, is Lizzie Crane." She blew a kiss to admirers who whistled and applauded. "Next time you're in Manhattan, look us up. Or maybe we'll see you around these parts again someday. Happy spring, everyone."

As Sid played the first sultry notes of the instrumental piece and Bert joined in on his trumpet, Alan approached the stage. He held out his hand to Lizzie. "May I have this dance?"

He swept her into an embrace that promised something even sweeter lay ahead. When the song ended, he brushed a kiss on her lips. "I'm going to say goodnight to a few people while you finish up here."

Guests circled past the champagne fountain to fill their glasses before descending onto the streets of Salem, although Lizzie guessed many of them would continue to party *sans* music until dawn. Alan dipped his glass in the fountain, too. There, a gorgeous young woman sidled up to him and pressed her palm to his cheek with an air of familiarity. Before Lizzie could stop it, the green-eyed monster raised its ugly head, spewing venom into her chest. *Breathe, Lizzie, breathe,* she told herself. *He's mine tonight.*

She turned back to the stage, where her friends snapped their instruments into cases and congratulated one another on a job well done.

"Incredible show tonight, everybody," she said. "Hey, what messages did you get in your 'eggs'?"

"Family," Melody said.

"That makes sense. I know you miss them, but you'll be back home in a couple days. How about you, Bert?"

"Success."

"I'm not surprised. You've got gobs of talent. No doubt you'll have plenty of success in the future." She looked at Sidney, who still sat at the piano. The vacant expression on his face defied the cheery banter he'd exhibited during their performance. "What did your message say, Sid?"

He shook his head. "I didn't take one. I don't want to know what the future holds."

A voice behind Lizzie interrupted them. "Miss Crane. May I speak with you?"

She turned to face the tall, thin, stoop-shouldered man she'd seen arguing with the art gallery owner, Hugh Franklin, earlier in the evening. Thinking he wanted to compliment her on tonight's performance, she said, "Good evening, or more accurately, good morning, Mister...?"

"Edward Oliver." He shoved his hands in the pockets of his long-out-of-date evening suit. "I heard you discovered Sebastian Amory's body."

"I had that misfortune, yes. Did you know him?"

"We used to be friends until he stole my work."

"You should tell that to the police," Lizzie said.

Oliver blinked several times. "They won't take me seriously."

"Why not?"

"Because he didn't steal anything *physical.* He stole my ideas. That's infinitely worse."

She glanced around, searching for Sergeant Darcy. For once, she would have welcomed the policeman's presence so she could turn this awkward young man over to him. But apparently, the cop had left the party early.

"Look, Mr. Oliver, this isn't my business. Please give whatever information you have to the cops—it may help them find Amory's killer."

"If I tell them, they'll think I murdered him."

"Did you?"

He seemed taken aback by her blunt question. After a long, uncomfortable pause that might, indeed, have caused Sergeant Darcy to raise a suspicious eyebrow, Oliver muttered, "No, no, of course not."

Lizzie saw Alan striding toward her across the ballroom. "Goodnight, Mr. Oliver. It's late, and I have other matters to attend to."

* * *

Lizzie positioned half a dozen candles around her bedchamber and lit them, then snapped off the electric lamps. From her bed, Alan watched her slowly remove the racy black dress.

With a playful smile, she said, "Time to strip away illusions and seize pleasure."

Chapter Eight

"Seek, and ye shall find." — Matthew 7:7, King James Bible

Lizzie pulled on her Chinese silk robe with the dragon embroidered on the back and answered her bedroom door. A young housemaid wearing a tiny silver cross on a chain around her neck stood there, holding a tray with breakfast for two.

"Thanks, I'll take it," Lizzie said and handed the girl a coin.

If she's worked in Isaac Roman's household for any length of time, she's seen things more scandalous than a woman having breakfast in bed with her lover, Lizzie decided. She carried the tray to the bed, where Alan leaned against several pillows. Removing the linen towel that covered the tray, she said, "Yum, looks like we have waffles with blueberries and maple syrup for breakfast. I hope that's all right with you."

"This morning, all's right with the world," he said, accepting the coffee she poured for him. "I just wish I didn't have to go back to Boston so soon. I regret missing your performance tonight. Any chance you could stay and visit with me for a few days after you finish here? I'll have to work during the daytime, but we'd have the nights together. And I can show you my Van Gogh."

"How can I refuse an invitation like that?"

"Good, then it's settled. Please telephone in the morning and let me know which train you'll be on. I'll have my butler pick you up at North Station."

An hour later, Lizzie watched from her window on the second floor of

Isaac Roman's mansion as Alan drove away in his silver Bentley. Their Cinderella affair still seemed to be too good to be true. She kept waiting for reality to throw a stone at the rose-colored glass she looked through these days and shatter her dreams.

Lizzie had seen Alan in the company of women whose beauty outshone hers, whose wealth and pedigrees surpassed even his own. That he chose to spend time with her when he could have any of them continued to baffle her. Part of the intrigue might actually be due to the fact that she didn't come from the elite class to which he belonged. Highborn men, she realized, often dallied with women from the lower ranks and even fathered children with them. But marriage never entered the picture. And yet, she couldn't imagine being married herself, raising children, living in comfortable domesticity. Perhaps her independent nature and her unconventional lifestyle made her a mystery to a man like Alan. If so, she needed to maintain that mystery if she wanted to keep him in her thrall.

A knock on the bedroom door pulled her out of her ponderings. Lizzie opened the door to admit a chambermaid with a mask of freckles across her face.

"I've come to clean your room, ma'am, if it's convenient," the girl said.

"Please don't change the sheets," Lizzie told her.

* * *

Forty adults bundled up in winter garb welcomed a recalcitrant spring with a child's game that dated back to ancient pagan times. They scurried about Salem Common, where early this morning Roman's servants had stashed dyed hard-boiled eggs. Peaking under park benches, poking into holes in trees, they hoped to find one of the three special eggs that would garner the person who discovered it a prize. Although it was barely two o'clock, Lizzie thought some of them already seemed inebriated.

Before releasing his guests into the Common like a squad of schoolchildren, Roman had invited them into his ballroom for hot cider. There, dressed in one of what Lizzie called his gangster suits—a double-breasted number the color of claret with wide, pointy lapels and thick chalk stripes—he explained the significance of the holiday.

"On the spring equinox, our ancestors honored the Germanic goddess Ostara—we get our word for Easter from her name. After the long, hard winter in northern Europe, the equinox signaled a time of hope, rebirth, and fertility. Flowers bloomed, birds returned to nest, and baby animals were born. According to mythology, a rabbit painted beautiful eggs as a gift for the goddess. Ostara liked them so much that she told the rabbit to share them with everyone in the world. Of course, we connect rabbits and eggs with fertility. So, ladies, if you want to get in a family way, now's the time—and if you don't, well, I warned you."

Laughter rippled through the ballroom, as Roman continued. "Here are the rules of today's game. While you were sleeping off last night's indulgences, my hard-working staff hid one hundred eggs out there in the Common. You'll have one hour to hunt for them. Keep whatever you find. If you're lucky enough to discover an egg painted copper, you'll go home with a bottle of champagne. Whoever finds the silver egg will win a painting by an artist of my choosing. And the person who stumbles upon the golden egg will be treated to a once-in-a-lifetime event on Wednesday afternoon."

He consulted his wristwatch. "Okay, everyone, the game starts now!"

* * *

The young woman seated on a park bench in Salem's Common looked vaguely familiar, but it took Lizzie a minute to place her. She'd plaited her long, chestnut-colored hair into a loose braid that hung down to her waist and wrapped herself in a dark blue woolen coat that covered her almost to her ankles. A purple bruise stained her left cheek and her eye was swollen almost shut.

"At first, I didn't recognize you with your clothes on," Lizzie said.

With her good eye, Thea Gallagher stared hard at Lizzie, trying to recall who this woman was and how she knew her. "Oh yeah, you're that singer from Isaac's party."

Lizzie could barely contain her anger at the woman who'd upstaged her Friday night. At the time, she'd found Thea's Lady Godiva stunt amusing. But the result was disastrous—and more lives might be ruined in its wake.

"Right. And you're the silly girl who had the audacity to tromp on my scene. I could write it off as a childish prank, except a man lost his life because of you."

Thea shoved her hands in the pockets of her coat. "I didn't kill him."

"Whether you did or didn't, you were surely the catalyst. What are you doing here anyway? Shouldn't you be home or in church mourning your dead lover?"

"Don't try to pin this on me. I'm not responsible for his death."

Thea glared at her, but beneath the belligerence, Lizzie saw pain and fear in the young woman's face. *She can't be more than eighteen or twenty. Melody's age. Too young to lose a sweetheart—especially in such a hideous way.*

"Have the cops talked to you yet?" Lizzie asked, her tone softening a bit. She sat down on the bench beside Thea.

"Yeah. They think I murdered him." She pulled a cigarette case from her purse and lit a smoke, then offered one to Lizzie.

"No, thanks. Got to take care of my voice, you know."

Sliding the cigarette case back into her purse, Thea asked, "Why would I murder the man I loved? I never meant him any harm. I just got sick and tired of waiting for him to leave his shrew of a wife and marry me."

"So you decided to force the issue?"

Thea nodded and lifted her chin defiantly. "You saw Sebastian chose me over her in the end."

"Yes, and it may have cost him his life."

A chilly breeze blew loose wisps of Thea's hair across her bruised cheek. "You think Joan Amory killed him because he dumped her for me?"

"Do you?"

Thea blew out a stream of smoke. "She's on my list of suspects."

"Who else is on your list?" Lizzie asked.

A shout went up from the crowd of egg hunters as a man with a Douglas Fairbanks moustache held up a copper-colored egg. Several people clapped and cheered, before resuming their search.

"My father," Thea said.

Her admission surprised Lizzie. "Did your father give you that shiner?"

The younger woman puffed on her cigarette for a few moments before answering. "That wharf rat ordered me to stop seeing Sebastian. I refused, so he cuffed me. It's not the first time."

Lizzie recalled what Cora had said about Paul Gallagher, now an executive at the Pequot cotton mills across the river from Salem's wharves. *Does Thea know her ancestors were slave traders?* she wondered.

"Are you saying he would have killed Sebastian to keep him away from you? That seems pretty extreme."

Thea shrugged. "I wouldn't put it past my old man."

A shriek startled Lizzie. In the middle of the Common, a woman jumped up and down, waving the golden egg that would net her first prize in Roman's game.

"Want to see some of Sebastian's paintings?" Thea asked.

"Ab-so-lute-ly."

"C'mon, then." She took a last drag on her cigarette, then dropped the butt on the ground and crushed it with her shoe.

The two women walked down Hawthorne Boulevard to Congress Street, across the South River to an expanse of red-brick factory buildings that stretched like a small city along Salem's waterfront. At the end of one row of buildings, Thea unlocked a door and motioned Lizzie in.

"This whole place burned to the ground in 1914, but the Naumkeag folks rebuilt and modernized the plant. Now it's operated totally by electricity," Thea said. "My father's a big cheese with the Mills. I stole his keys and had copies made. Then I bribed a custodian to give Sebastian an unused room here for a studio."

She pressed a switch, and dingy yellow light illuminated a long hallway. Lizzie followed Thea up three flights of stairs. Their footsteps rang on the metal steps in the quiet Sunday afternoon when the mill hands had the day off and the machinery that made Pequot bed linens sat silent. *Did the sheets Alan and I slept on last night come from here?* she mused.

Thea unlocked another door that opened into a high-ceiling room about eighteen by thirty feet. The odor of oil paint and turpentine permeated the air. A makeshift kitchen took up part of one wall. At the other end of the room, a double bed had been shoved into a corner. A paint-splattered table occupied the central area; on it sat jars of paintbrushes and boxes overflowing with tubes of paint. *Is this where Sebastian wanted me to model for him?* Lizzie wondered.

Canvases of all sizes filled the rest of the room. Some perched on easels, others hung on the walls or rested on the floor, vying with one another for space. Slowly, Lizzie made her way around the studio, studying the paintings. Their styles and themes varied widely, as if they'd been painted by many different artists from a number of time periods. They ranged from the iconic images of the early Christian artists to the nightmarish scenarios of Hieronymus Bosch, to the sun-splashed gardens of Monet.

In one section of the room hung a collection of cityscapes. Among them, Lizzie recognized scenes of Salem's waterfront and Manhattan's Washington Square. Saturated with color and glowing with what seemed to be inner light, they radiated vitality. They invited the viewer to enter the pictures and participate in the artist's vision. To chat with the pedestrians on the sidewalks. To drive autos down one of the streets or buy flowers from a vendor's cart.

"Which ones did Sebastian paint?" Lizzie asked.

"All of them."

Chapter Nine

"There are all kinds of love in this world, but never the same love twice." — F. Scott Fitzgerald, The Great Gatsby

"Why did he paint in so many different styles?" Lizzie asked. She knew the answer, but wanted to hear what Thea had to say.

She confirmed what Sidney had already told Lizzie. "Isaac got him jobs duplicating other artists' pictures and sold them to people who couldn't afford the real thing."

"You mean Sebastian was a forger?" Lizzie asked, feigning naïveté.

Again, Thea echoed Sid's explanation. "No, he was a *copyist*. Forgers trick buyers into paying a bundle for what they think are genuine masterpieces. That's a crime. Sebastian admitted he just copied works by famous guys, and he sold them for peanuts. That's legal."

"He was really talented," Lizzie said, reaching to touch a picture of young men rowing sculls on Boston's Charles River. "And prolific."

"If only the rest of the world could've seen that. He desperately wanted to be appreciated for his own work, but he never got the chance." Thea pointed to the cityscapes Lizzie found so engaging. "Those are Sebastian's originals."

"They're the best of all."

"Yeah, I think so too."

As Lizzie continued her circuit of Sebastian's studio, Thea lit a cigarette and puffed on it as she reminisced. "He used to go to the Boston Museum of Fine Arts and the Isabella Stewart Gardner Museum to draw from the paintings there. You can't take photographs, but they let you sketch the works on display. He copied some of the pictures in Isaac's private gallery too. He's got quite a collection."

"Yes, I know. I've seen it."

"Really? He must've wanted to get in your bloomers then, because he doesn't allow many people into his inner sanctum." Thea blew out a lungful of smoke and laughed. "Did he succeed? Is that how you got the job singing at his parties?"

"It's none of your business," Lizzie replied coldly, "but the answer to both questions is no. He's always behaved quite the gentleman around me."

Lizzie paused before a copy of a Vermeer painting of a young woman writing at her desk. Something about it seemed oddly familiar—and not only because she'd seen the original at the Museum of Fine Arts during her last visit to Boston in February.

"The lady in this picture looks like you," she said to Thea, tapping the canvas with her fingertip.

Like a plaster wall crumbling during an earthquake, Thea Gallagher's tough-girl attitude shattered. Tears streamed down her face. She burst into a series of high-pitched wails, interspersed with harsh sobs as if she were gasping for breath. Flinging herself into a tattered easy chair, she howled like the Irish banshee, whom folklore says keens at the homes of the newly or soon-to-be dead.

Lizzie had never known grief like this. She'd never lost anyone she loved deeply and she hadn't a clue how to react. How to offer comfort to this abrasive young woman she barely knew and didn't like. Yet Thea's abject sorrow touched her. In the studio's paltry kitchen, she found a kettle, filled it with water, and set it on the stove. While it heated, she located a tin of tea, a canister of sugar, a teapot, and two cups.

With a brief nod, Thea accepted the tea Lizzie served her. She stopped sobbing and sipped the soothing beverage. When she finished, Lizzie refilled Thea's cup. She poured herself a cup, too, and sat drinking in silence while her companion grappled with the bitter reality of a future without the man she loved.

After a bit, Thea said, "I used to model for him."

Lizzie recalled the way she'd felt when Sebastian asked her to model for him. Objectified. Dehumanized. Creepy. But perhaps it was different for Thea who had an intimate relationship with the artist. *Does she know he sought other women as models? Perhaps as lovers, too, as Joan Amory intimated?* Lizzie asked herself. And then, *Does Thea know about Sebastian's affair with Sid?*

The afternoon sunlight began to fade, and the shadows in the studio deepened.

"I've got to leave now. I have a show to do tonight," Lizzie said as she stood and collected their teacups. "Will you be all right?"

Thea looked up at her, eyes red and puffy, bruised cheek purple and swollen. "I'll never be all right again."

* * *

Only after Lizzie arrived back at Roman's mansion and started dressing for the evening's performance did she realize what a stupid thing she'd done. She'd left her fingerprints all over the dead artist's studio, on the furniture, the kitchen counters, and dishes, even the paintings themselves. If Thea Gallagher wanted to implicate Lizzie, she now had dirt to offer Sergeant Darcy. Perhaps she'd try to swap Lizzie for her own freedom.

* * *

Even here on the mansion's second story, Lizzie could hear Roman's guests in the gaudy ballroom downstairs, laughing, drinking, and celebrating the start of spring. Many of those who'd participated in the egg hunt would probably stay on for The Troubadours' performance tonight.

As she rouged her cheeks, a feeling of sadness came over her. How could these people have fun, play silly children's games, when less than forty-eight hours ago, a man died here, slain in a violent, grotesque manner? Why weren't they mourning Sebastian's death? Observing funereal rites? After all, he was a husband, a son, a paramour. Isaac Roman's friend. Men and women loved him. Surely, that must count for something.

Lizzie brushed her bobbed coffee-colored hair, then fastened a jewel-encrusted comb into place. Even if Sebastian's death were still being investigated, even if the police refused to release the body for burial, the people who knew him could mark his passing in a respectful way, couldn't they? The casual behavior of Roman and his hangers-on, acting as if nothing had happened, made her feel slightly sick. *Ashes to ashes, dust to dust. Is that all we really are? Don't our lives have any greater meaning?* She thought about the paintings in Sebastian's studio, the work of a talented artist who, according to both his wife and his lover, longed to share his gift with the world.

As she slipped into her evening dress and rolled on her stockings, Lizzie regretted that Sebastian Amory wouldn't go down in history for his paintings. If he were remembered at all, it would be for his gruesome death.

* * *

Still dressed in her evening gown, Lizzie kicked off her shoes and sank into one of the Art Deco chairs in Sidney's bedroom. "Bye Bye Blackbird," performed by Sam Lanin's Dance Orchestra, played on the radio. Sid started to turn the volume down, but she stopped him.

"Good show tonight," she said. "Not our best, but I think everyone enjoyed it. How about a drink-ski?"

"I've got some I.W. Harper left. What do you think-ski?" he asked.

"Ah, just what the doctor ordered," she said, referring to the fact that the Kentucky distillery was one of only ten in the country allowed to continue producing "medicinal liquor" under Prohibition's laws.

Sidney poured amber liquid into two tumblers and handed one to her. Then he grabbed the other glass and sat in the matching gray suede armchair.

"Bearcat, I've got some bad news. I didn't say anything earlier because I didn't want to gum up our performance."

"How bad?"

"I don't know yet. That cop, Darcy, talked to me this evening, just before we went onstage."

"That was lousy timing. I bet he did it on purpose to try to rattle you."

Sidney nodded. "He had a photograph of Sebastian and me, taken at a men's club in the Village eight years ago." He leaned forward, resting his elbows on his knees, and cast his eyes down at the floor. "Let's just say it left no doubt about the nature of our relationship."

"Where did he get it?"

"From Joan Amory."

"Holy moly." Lizzie sipped her whiskey and contemplated what he'd said. "Why would she give a photo like that to the copper?"

"I think she might be trying to frame me or at least implicate me in his death. Love gone wrong, a long-standing grievance, that sort of thing. It's been the motive for many a murder."

"Your affair was eight years ago, for heavens' sake."

"My guess is Darcy figures she's the killer, and she's trying to send him off the trail in another direction." Sidney set his glass on the floor, took a cigarette from his engraved tin, and fit it into his silver holder. "Here's the rest. Darcy told me not to leave Salem until further notice. He's going to want to talk with you, too, maybe insist you stay in town as well."

"But why?"

"After all this time, Sebastian shows up here where we're playing, then has the misfortune to get himself murdered. And then you just happen to be the one to find the body. A coincidence?" He lit the cigarette and took a deep pull. "It doesn't look good, Bearcat."

"Looks like a bad story plot to me," she said. "He hasn't got any evidence, only suspicions."

"Just so you know, in case someone comes knocking on your door in the morning."

"If someone comes knocking on my door in the morning, it better be a housemaid bringing me breakfast."

She sipped her drink and studied Sid, trying to ascertain his feelings as he puffed on his cigarette. Her ordinarily cool, debonair friend nervously wiped the sides of his glass with his thumbs and tapped his feet on the floor as if he wanted to run away. In an attempt to sound calm and reassuring, she said, "It's only a photograph, and an old one at that. It's not like that cop has a dozen eyewitnesses swearing they saw you shoot the fella."

"People make decisions based on emotions rather than facts," he said. "I'm not guilty; the police don't have any evidence to blame Sebastian's murder on me. But I've already got three strikes against me, the three letters F-A-G."

He's right, Lizzie thought, remembering Salem's infamous Witch Trials at the end of the seventeenth century. Twenty innocent women and men were put to death with no more evidence than the fantastical accusations of two young girls.

"Should we tell Melody and Bert we might be hanging around Salem a while longer?" Sid asked. "How do you think they'll take this?"

"There's no reason to tell them. They're not involved." Lizzie said. "Frankly, I think we should send them home posthaste, before things get stickier. We've finished our engagement here. We've fulfilled our contract and Roman's paid us. Let's put them on the train to New York in the morning."

Sidney blew smoke rings at the ceiling. "Good idea."

Lizzie sipped her whiskey and tried, unsuccessfully, to quiet the disconcerting thoughts spinning in her mind. "Darcy can't hold us for long. A suggestive old photograph and my happenstance discovery don't weigh in heavy on the evidence scale. The fact that Joan Amory gave the photo to the cops increases her motive for killing Sebastian. Not only does her hubby take up with another woman, he's got a thing for fellas, too. How very embarrassing."

"Maybe Darcy will let you go home, too."

"Oh no, I'm not leaving you here alone," she insisted. "And I'm going to find out more about Mrs. Amory and that Gallagher girl. They've got secrets hiding in the shadows. I plan to bring them out into the light."

* * *

After saying goodnight to Sidney, Lizzie walked down the hall to her own bedroom. She took off her evening gown, hung it in the wardrobe, and pulled on her silk bathrobe. In the *en suite* bathroom, she washed off her face paint and brushed her teeth. Still too keyed up to sleep, she sat in a Queen Anne armchair upholstered in dark rose damask and thought about Sid.

They'd met eight years ago when she was eighteen at a fashionable nightspot in New York's Greenwich Village, where she'd just landed a job as a waitress. For three years before that she'd worked in dives, slinging hash, washing dishes—whatever she could find to help her parents feed and clothe her six younger siblings and pay the rent on their flat in the Bronx. The job at Marco's restaurant seemed a godsend.

Best of all was the dapper piano player, Sidney Somerset, who entertained diners on Friday and Saturday nights. Smitten by his panache, talent, and sleek good looks, Lizzie flirted with him shamelessly. But although he was friendly enough, he never encouraged her affection. It took her longer than it should have to figure out why.

Early one evening, before the supper crowd arrived, he began playing Charles Harrison's "I'm Always Chasing Rainbows." Lizzie sang along while she set tables.

"You've got a swell voice, Lizzie," he said. "Want to do a few songs with me tonight?"

She did. In between taking orders, pouring drinks, and serving plates of prime rib, lamb, or halibut, Lizzie belted out popular tunes accompanied by Sidney's virtuoso piano. Soon, Marco's customers dubbed her "the singing waitress" and tipped her a little extra. Her boss gave her a raise as her popularity grew. Never before had Lizzie considered a musical career. Now she did.

Then came the dark days of the Spanish flu. People stopped going out for fear of catching the deadly virus. Businesses were forced to shut down. Somehow, Marco's managed to remain open, but just barely, and Lizzie knew her position was as precarious as the establishment's own.

In 1920, the Volstead Act took effect. Without the profits from alcohol sales, Marco's couldn't hang on any longer. The teary-eyed owner wished them well as he handed Lizzie and Sidney their final pay envelopes.

The two musicians stepped outside, into the bitter New York night. Snow flurries spun around them, flakes already gathering on their heads and shoulders, as Sid hailed a taxicab.

"Lizzie, can you come to my apartment for a bit?" he asked. "I have an idea I'd like to discuss with you."

"Okay."

They rode to his apartment building near Washington Square and took the elevator to the penthouse. Over glasses of Irish whiskey, he laid out his plan. Prohibition didn't prevent citizens from drinking booze in their own residences or serving it to their guests. Only making, selling, and transporting the stuff was against the law.

"We'll perform in private homes. Holiday parties, special events like weddings and such," he said. "Now that most of the nightclubs have closed their doors, people are desperate for entertainment. We can provide that."

Lizzie kicked off her shoes and propped her tired feet up on Sid's coffee table. "Keep talking."

"We've made a lot of friends at Marco's. I think we can get some jobs through them." He paused to light a cigarette, then blew a series of smoke rings at the ceiling before continuing. "You may not know this, but my family is well off. My connections can help us get in with the right crowd."

As she slowly sipped her drink, Lizzie contemplated the possibilities. They had no guarantee that anyone would hire them. They might fall flat and disgrace themselves. The life of a musician was unstable, fraught with risks and uncertainties. For a woman, it was also tinged with social stigma—people assumed female singers were prostitutes. But just thinking about it made her heart beat faster, made her want to dance and sing until the sun came up.

"Well, what do you think?" he asked.

"Let's do it!"

Things hadn't been easy at first. They started out playing in living rooms around the city for audiences of a dozen or so, sometimes twenty. Occasionally a friend of Sid's who played clarinet joined them. Sidney hired a seamstress to make Lizzie a few evening gowns to wear at their performances. When work was scarce, he slipped her cash.

But Sid was right. People were hungry for entertainment. Slowly, their reputation grew; they began getting bigger and better-paying jobs. In the summer of 1923, they heard Melody playing violin at a wedding and hired her on the spot. It took a lot of arm-twisting, though, to convince her parents to let their seventeen-year-old only daughter indulge her passion for music. Jazz, no less. Next, they brought a gifted saxophonist named Henry Ives on board and took their show on the road. Sid started booking The Troubadours for longer, grander events outside New York. Events that introduced them to society's movers and shakers.

As well as some of its criminals, Lizzie rued. Seven months ago, Henry had been murdered at one of their engagements. Two months later, a guest at another of their stints became a victim. She and Sidney had gone through it all together. He wasn't merely her business partner; he was her best friend, her biggest fan, and the older brother she'd never had.

Now, they found themselves involved in yet another murder, one that hit harder and closer to home. When she counted the years, Lizzie realized that Sebastian might have been Sidney's lover when she first met him. Yet she'd never known about their affair until the artist's death. *We'll get through this, too,* she promised herself.

Chapter Ten

"All truths are easy to understand once they are discovered; the point is to discover them." — Galileo Galilei

Instead of a breakfast tray, the maid who knocked on Lizzie's bedroom door at 7:30 in the morning brought a message—an order, really—from Sergeant Richard Darcy to come to the police station at nine for questioning. Sid had warned her this might happen. Now it had.

"Drat," she muttered as she buttoned her modest green daytime frock, rolled on her stockings, and slid her feet into low-heeled pumps. She debated whether or not to paint her face—it might be advantageous to downplay her beauty and big-city sophistication—finally settling for a dusting of powder and just a hint of lipstick.

On her way downstairs to the kitchen to grab a cup of coffee, she stopped at the door to Sidney's bedroom and knocked. She knew he'd be annoyed that she'd wakened him at this too-early hour, under less-than-happy circumstances, but it couldn't be helped. After a few minutes, he answered. Dark half-moons hung under his eyes and his cheek was creased with the imprint of his pillow.

While tying his bathrobe over his pajamas, he quickly assessed her appearance. "They've come for you."

"Don't be so dramatic, Sid. Darcy just wants to ask me some questions; he's not going to lock me in a dungeon and throw away the key."

He motioned her inside and closed the door, then pulled a velvet cord near the doorway to summon a housemaid. After asking the girl to bring them bacon and eggs and a pot of coffee, Sidney slumped into one of the room's armchairs, lit a cigarette, and took a few puffs.

"I'll need you to drive me there," Lizzie said. "Unless you want to give me the keys to the breezer and save yourself the trouble. It's probably best if I talk to Darcy alone. He might not even let you sit in the same room with me anyway—can't have you kicking me under the table if I start to say something incriminating."

He ran a hand through his thinning dark hair and looked at her apologetically. "I'm sorry I dragged you into this, Bearcat."

"How could you have known?" she said. "It's not your fault, so let's dispense with the guilt stuff, okay?"

He nodded and leaned back in his chair, crossing his left ankle over his right knee. "When Sebastian was alive, I rarely thought about him. After we stopped seeing each other, I mean. But now that he's dead, I can't *stop* thinking about him. Does that seem strange?"

"I don't know what's strange anymore. It seems logical that his death, especially under the circumstances, would resurrect all sorts of memories of your time together. Things you missed out on, things you could have done differently," Lizzie said. "What do you know about his wife Joan?"

"Not much," Sidney admitted. "He met her only a month or so before he and I split up. I do know he wanted a more conventional, respectable life. She offered him that. She knew people who could help him move up in the art world."

"Like Roman, you mean?"

A knock on the door interrupted them. Sidney opened it and accepted a breakfast tray from the same housemaid who'd brought Darcy's summons to Lizzie less than half an hour earlier. Sid set it on a birch table between the two armchairs and told Lizzie, "Dig in."

For a while, they ate in silence, easing into the morning, drawing comfort from the plain, familiar food. Sunlight spilled through the bedroom window, promising a more spring-like day than the last few had been. Lizzie poured herself a second cup of coffee before telling Sid about her meetup with

Sebastian's paramour.

"Did you know Thea Gallagher?" she asked tentatively.

"The naked horsewoman?" He shook his head. "Nope, never met her."

"I ran into her yesterday afternoon on the Common during the egg hunt. She took me to Sebastian's studio and showed me some of his paintings."

"You saw Sebastian's paintings?" He seemed surprised and more than a little envious. "What did you think?"

"He's quite talented. *Was.* Thea confirmed what you said about him working as a copyist. She said Roman helped him sell his reproductions. Sort of an agent or intermediary, I guess you'd call it."

"Did you see any of his originals? His own stuff, not the fakes?"

"Yes, quite a few. I thought they were wonderful."

He lit a cigarette and puffed on it for a few moments before continuing. "What did you think of the girl?"

"I'm not sure what to make of her," Lizzie answered. "She had an air of defiance about her, kind of brash and contentious, like she felt a need to best me. She even asked if I'd slept with Roman."

Sidney laughed. "That probably means she has."

"Hmm. I hadn't thought of that. But jeepers creepers, he's what, sixty? And she can't be more than twenty."

"Money and power are heady aphrodisiacs. You saw all those dolls hanging on him at his parties," Sid reminded her. "Besides, Roman's good-looking for an old fella. And he's sure no fuddy-duddy."

"True." Lizzie offered the coffee carafe to Sid. When he shook his head, she poured the last of the steaming, dark brew into her cup. "While I was perusing Sebastian's paintings, she suddenly broke down in a fit of waterworks, and I don't mean just tears. Howling and gasping for breath, like she was on the Titanic when it was going down."

"What did you do?"

"Made tea for her. I couldn't think of anything else. I don't know what you're supposed to do in circumstances like that. I've never lost a loved one. After a while, she calmed down, and I left."

Sidney stubbed out his cigarette in a glass ashtray and lit another. "Do you think she was putting you on?"

"Pretending to be grief-stricken, you mean?"

The idea hadn't occurred to her before, but now that he'd raised the question, she considered it. After all, Lizzie was an actress herself. She'd used her talents more than a few times to get what she wanted or to extricate herself from difficult situations. She should have recognized a fellow thespian's act. Thea Gallagher was the last person known to have seen Sebastian Amory alive. That, in addition to her intimate relationship with him, made her a key suspect. If she'd killed Sebastian, it might behoove her to play the brokenhearted lover as a ploy to detract from her guilt.

But the question of motive remained. Why would she murder the man she loved just when she'd finally managed to steal him away from his wife?

* * *

"Thank you for agreeing to meet with me, Miss Crane," Sergeant Darcy said as he entered the bleak, windowless cubicle at Salem's police department. Painted an ugly slime-green, it contained only a table and four straight-backed chairs that could have come from any schoolroom. Lizzie sat in one of them.

"I didn't realize I had a choice," she said, trying to sound neither impertinent nor intimidated. From her previous dealings with police, she'd learned not to let them frighten or push her around, but not to be disrespectful either. Simple, direct answers delivered without emotion were usually the best responses to coppers' questions.

"Not one that would behoove you." Darcy took a seat across the table from her and set his coffee mug on the scarred wooden surface. He didn't offer her a cup.

"I've already told you all I know, which is nothing."

Darcy tapped his pencil on a writing tablet. "Are you sure of that, Miss Crane?"

"What do you mean?"

"It's come to my attention that your colleague, Mr. Somerset, and the deceased were friends. Very *close* friends."

Lizzie considered pretending she knew nothing of Sidney's affair with Sebastian Amory, but figured the lie would eventually come out and cause more trouble. "That was a long time ago, before I knew him."

"Did Mr. Somerset plan to meet up with his old pal while he was in Salem?"

"No, he was quite surprised to see Mr. Amory," she said.

Sergeant Darcy rubbed his jutting, squared-off jaw. "Miss Crane, I find it an odd coincidence that you happened to be the one who discovered the body of your colleague's *friend*. Why did you decide to go to Mr. Roman's greenhouse that morning?"

"I wanted peace and quiet. The greenhouse seemed like a good place to escape from the activity of Mr. Roman's busy household."

"Did Mr. Somerset have contact with his friend the night of his death?"

Lizzie shook her head. "Not that I know of. Amory bolted with the Gallagher girl on horseback. That's the last we saw of him."

"Until you found him the next morning, dead."

"Do you suspect me of Mr. Amory's murder, Sergeant? Or my colleague?"

"I'm a suspicious man, Miss Crane. Occupational hazard."

"Then perhaps you should look at Paul Gallagher. I understand he wasn't pleased about the affair between his daughter and Amory."

Lizzie thought she saw a spark in the cop's eyes, as if this hadn't occurred to him. But maybe it was just the effect of the poorly wired ceiling light that kept flickering overhead.

"What makes you think that?"

"Thea Gallagher suggested it. She also said her father hit her when she refused to break off her relationship with Amory."

Darcy made a few notes on his tablet. "You told me you didn't know Miss Gallagher."

"I only met her yesterday on Salem Common."

"Sounds like you two ladies had a lot to talk about."

"Mostly, we talked about Amory's artwork. He was a fine painter."

The sergeant drank some coffee, which Lizzie thought must be getting cold by now, and then jotted something on his notepad. "That will be all for now, Miss Crane. Thank you for your time."

"You're welcome," she said politely, trying to hide her nervousness. *He's just fishing,* she told herself, *he hasn't a thing on Sid or me.* "We all have the same objective, Sergeant Darcy. To find Mr. Amory's murderer and see justice prevail."

The policeman stood, squared his shoulders, and opened the door for Lizzie. "Oh, and Miss Crane. Let me remind you that I'd like you to stay in Salem for the time being. I may want to speak with you again."

Chapter Eleven

"Life is a series of natural and spontaneous changes. Don't resist them; that only creates sorrow." — Lao Tzu

Sidney answered her knock on his bedchamber door, wearing his professional demeanor like a well-tailored suit. But Lizzie sensed that underneath his cool façade he was a tangle of nerves.

She handed him the keys to the Buick. "Thanks for letting me use the breezer."

"How'd it go with the copper?" he asked as he motioned her in.

"Pretty much what I'd expected."

"Spill."

Lizzie sat in one of the Art Deco armchairs and filled him in on the details. "Darcy's stumbling around in the dark. He hasn't an inkling who bumped off your friend."

"What makes you so sure?"

"He seemed surprised when I told him Thea Gallagher's father wanted her to break off the affair with Sebastian. I suggested he should consider Papa Gallagher a suspect. A sharp cop would've already known about that and checked it out, don't you think?"

"Maybe he's got other fish to fry."

"Let's hope so, because I don't plan to be on the menu."

Sidney fitted a cigarette into his silver holder and lit it. "Did he tell you not to leave Salem?"

"He did. I doubt he can clamp the irons on us like that, though, without charging us with a crime. He doesn't even have any evidence against us, only suspicions. I'm going to talk to Cora's attorney friend, Karl Blume. Even though he generally handles wills, estates, and that sort of thing, he might know what we should do." Lizzie kicked off her shoes and tucked her feet underneath her, trying to find a reasonably comfortable position on the uncomfortable chair that was more art than furniture. "There's a train leaving for Boston at noon. I think we should put Melody and Bert on it. From there they can catch one to New York. There's no reason for them to stay on here."

"You're on the trolley there," he agreed. "Does that mean you and I are sticking around, as per Darcy's request?"

"Looks that way. How about I tell Melody, and you tell Bert?"

"Who's going to tell Roman?"

Lizzie flashed him a pretty smile. "I'll handle Roman."

* * *

"Call your parents and let them know you'll be home this evening on the train. There's a telephone downstairs in the foyer," Lizzie told Melody. "Sid will drive you and Bert to the station."

"What about you and Sid?" Melody had already packed her bags in preparation for leaving Salem today, along with the rest of The Troubadours. She hadn't expected to go home on the train.

"We have to hang around a little longer to help the police until things get resolved."

"Are you and Sid in trouble?"

"No, but this whole situation has gotten a bit sticky. I'd rather you and Bert stayed clear of it. You want to see your fiancé and your parents, don't you?"

They're going to be furious when they find out we've gotten Melody mixed up in another murder, Lizzie realized. *Even if she weren't getting married in three months, they'd probably forbid her from ever traveling with us again.*

66

Melody fingered the amethyst pendant at her throat that she considered a good luck talisman. "I do, ever so much."

"Well, then, it's settled. I'll call a maid to take your luggage down to Sid's auto." Lizzie pulled a velvet cord beside the bed to summon a servant. "Now get a wiggle on."

"Will you get to see Alan again while you're here?"

Good question, Lizzie thought. She hadn't told him about this latest wrinkle yet, nor had they discussed what her part in this murder investigation might entail. She'd been looking forward to spending some time with him in Boston, now that they'd completed their commitment to Roman. However, Sergeant Darcy's mandate had temporarily altered the fulfillment of her fantasies.

"I hope so."

A chambermaid carried Melody's luggage down to the granite-paved area behind Isaac Roman's mansion. Sidney leaned against the Buick smoking a cigarette as the maid slid the suitcases in the auto's trunk.

"Bert says he wants to stay as long as we're stuck here," he told Lizzie. "He's been seeing that girl he met when we were here in Salem during Christmas. Did you know?"

Lizzie shook her head. "No, but we've only been here a few days, and things have been hectic, to say the least. Outside of our performances, I've barely had a chance to talk to Bert."

Usually, Lizzie felt protective toward the shy horn player, whose gap-toothed grin and recalcitrant cowlick gave him a goofy, boyish charm that made him seem younger than his twenty-two years. Six months ago, she'd heard him playing his dead father's saxophone in Central Park. He'd lived there throughout the summer, sleeping in the shelter of a thicket of bushes and eating when he could collect enough change from passersby to pay for a meal. After listening to him play two songs, Lizzie impulsively invited him to join The Troubadours. Now, she felt an almost maternal concern for Bert, even though she was only four years his elder. *Maybe it's like that Chinese proverb says, if you save someone's life, you're responsible for him.*

Sidney tapped his fingers along the breezer's rag roof, as if he were toying with a keyboard. "If we stay on, and Roman wants us to keep playing, Bert's horn would be a plus."

"And how," she agreed. "Why don't I talk to Roman and see what's what, before we decide Bert's fate?"

Sidney nodded and slid behind the wheel of his Buick. Lizzie hugged Melody and wished her a safe trip. Tears filled her eyes. She struggled not to let them fall, trying to keep her friend from seeing her sadness. *This is the last time we'll play a stint like this together. The supremely talented member of my band. The smart, sweet, pretty lady who's been there for me in good times and bad. How will I get along without you, Mel?*

As if reading her mind, Melody said, "It's not like I'll never see you again." She pried herself free from Lizzie's embrace. "I'll still perform with you around town and at local parties. And you're going to sing at my wedding and be my maid of honor."

But Lizzie could hear the finality in her friend's voice, the knowledge that this was the end of a stage in their lives, both professionally and personally. When they got back to New York, she promised herself she'd arrange a party to commemorate their years together.

Sid cleared his throat. "We'd better get going if we want to catch your train, Melody."

"Call when you get home, so I know you've arrived safely." Lizzie kissed the blond flutist on her cheek. "Fare thee well, little sister."

* * *

Lizzie nearly bumped into Isaac Roman as she entered the foyer after seeing Melody off. Dressed in powder blue knickers, a diamond-patterned sporting vest, and a yellow cap atop his long, white hair, he appeared ready for a day on the links. Behind him stood the Boston art gallery owner, Hugh Franklin, also attired for the golf course, but more tamely so.

"Miss Crane, top o' the morning to you," her host said. "Looks like it's going to be a splendid day."

"Good morning, Mr. Roman. Please excuse me—"

He cut her off. "Have you come to say goodbye? Heading back to New York?"

"That's what I wanted to talk with you about." She glanced at Franklin, then back at Roman. "I don't want to interfere with your golf game."

"Nonsense. Hugh, you won't mind waiting a few minutes while this lovely lady and I have a few words, will you?"

"Not at all," Franklin said, but Lizzie thought he sounded perturbed, as if interferences such as this happened more often than he wished.

The gallery owner returned to the formal parlor while Roman motioned Lizzie upstairs to his office. She sat in one of the Wassily chairs as he seated himself behind the cluttered desk and removed his cap.

"So, Miss Crane. What's caused that worried look to cloud your pretty face?"

Lizzie rubbed the polished steel arms of the chair with her thumbs, trying to decide whether to tell Roman about Sidney's relationship with Amory. She chose not to say more than necessary at the moment. "Sergeant Darcy asked me to remain in Salem for the time being until he's sure I didn't kill Sebastian Amory."

"He told me the same thing," Roman said, "although I have no plans to go anywhere anyway."

"For some peculiar reason, he seems to think I may be guilty simply because I happened to be the one who found your friend's body."

"And he seems to think that because a man died in my home, I may be responsible. Between you and me, Miss Crane, I have doubts about Sergeant Darcy's ability at logic." Roman folded his hands on the desktop, and Lizzie couldn't help noticing the gold ring with its dime-sized red stone on his right index finger. "Under the circumstances, how would you feel about staying on here for a bit? It just so happens that I have a unique and unprecedented activity planned for Wednesday afternoon. It would be an added attraction if I could say you and your friends will perform that evening."

"Ab-so-lute-ly. I'm sure I speak for my colleagues when I say we'd be honored. Thank you ever so much." She recalled the prize he'd offered to the person who found the golden egg at yesterday's hunt on the Common. An invitation to a once-in-a-lifetime event on Wednesday. "What's the event?"

Roman laughed. "If I told you, it would spoil the surprise."

"I must confess that one of our group—Melody, the blond flutist and violin player—won't be with us. She's already taken the train back to her home in New Jersey to prepare for her wedding in June. I hope that won't be a problem."

"Her departure or her wedding?"

"I meant her departure," Lizzie said. "You contracted for four musicians, but now you've only got the three of us."

"I knew what you meant, Miss Crane. I apologize if I sounded sarcastic," Roman said, twisting the gold ring around his finger. "I've tried marriage three times—it never worked out. My fault, probably. I'm not an easy man to live with, as you might imagine. Anyway, I wish your friend all the best—she seems like a sweet girl. And I'm sure that even without her, you'll be the cat's meow."

* * *

After talking with Roman, Lizzie telephoned Alan to tell him about the change of plans.

"I doubt Sergeant Darcy can hold you on such a flimsy excuse," Alan said. "He doesn't even have any evidence of culpability on your part or a motive."

"True, but I worry about Sid. The cops may decide to implicate him simply because of the, um, unconventional nature of his relationship with Sebastian Amory. They could trump up something, even without evidence."

"Lizzie, are you okay?" he asked, his voice laced with concern.

"Yes, thank you. I only wish I could take the train to Boston this afternoon and meet you for supper the way we'd planned."

"Actually, this turn of events may be for the best. My firm has just taken on an important new client, and I'm going to have to work late the next few nights. I was worried that my work would interfere with our time together. But now that you'll be here longer than expected…" Alan paused to let her process the information, and to consider the demands his career—and hers—

would make of them. "Shall we plan on seeing each other this weekend instead? Maybe by then, the cops will solve the crime, and you'll be free to come and go as you like."

"I certainly hope so."

"Please call every day and let me know what's going on."

"Even if nothing's going on?"

"Yes indeed. If I don't hear from you, I'll fear you've been hauled off to jail or vanished into the wilderness without a trace."

Lizzie laughed. "My, my, Alan Peabody. You do have a fantastical imagination."

Only after she'd hung up the telephone's earpiece, fretting about how much the long-distance calls she'd made thus far would amount to, did she remember she hadn't told Alan about the surprise, once-in-a-lifetime event on Wednesday.

Chapter Twelve

"Secrets are generally terrible. Beauty is not hidden—only ugliness and deformity." — L.M. Montgomery, Emily Climbs

Lizzie bought a bouquet of tulips and irises from a vendor on Salem Common, then walked down Essex Street and veered onto the narrow side street where Sebastian Amory had lived. As Isaac Roman predicted, the afternoon turned out to be splendid. The damp chill of the previous few days had given way to glorious sunshine with the temperature inching toward fifty degrees. Snowdrops and crocuses blossomed here and there. Hyacinths and daffodils promised to follow soon. Pink buds sprouted on the branches of magnolia trees.

She knocked on the door of a two-story clapboard house, not as grand as many of its neighbors, but graceful in design and in good repair. Older, too, than most in this district. A plaque near the entrance read "Built 1740, moved to this location 1842 by twenty-four oxen." Lizzie tried to imagine oxen hauling a house through the streets of Salem, but she couldn't conceive of such an astounding feat of pre-automotive engineering and brute strength.

After a bit, Joan Amory opened the door. The blond woman Lizzie had met less than three days ago seemed to have aged ten years. Her eyes were red and swollen, her cheeks drained of color. She squinted at her visitor, perplexed, trying to recall how they knew each other and why this tall, dark-haired woman now stood on her doorstep.

"Good afternoon, Mrs. Amory," Lizzie said. "I'm Elizabeth Crane. We met at Isaac Roman's home Friday night. I've come to offer my condolences."

When Sebastian's widow still didn't appear to recognize her, Lizzie explained, "I'm the one who found your husband's body. May I come in?"

"Yes, I remember you now," Joan said, taking a step back to let the singer enter.

Lizzie handed her the bunch of spring flowers, and Joan glanced at them briefly. "Thank you. Let me put these in water."

While Joan disappeared down a wainscoted hallway, Lizzie wandered into the parlor. Like other parlors she'd seen in Salem, its furnishings echoed the tastes of the English gentry a century ago. The Amorys' chairs, cabinets, and tables, however, might have been made in the nearby town of Gardner, Massachusetts, not England.

An uncomfortable silence filled the house. It reminded her of a church sanctuary in which the congregation no longer met, where a slow decay had set in and would eventually cause the structure to crumble from the sheer weight of loneliness. No bustle of servants cleaning, cooking, putting everyday affairs in order. No patter of children's feet running on the pine floorboards overhead. *Why didn't the couple have children?* Lizzie wondered. If she didn't know about Sebastian's affair with Thea Gallagher, she might have assumed the artist wasn't attracted to women and had simply used Joan for her ability to advance his career.

Lizzie circled the pretty parlor with its floral wallpaper, gazing at the pictures hanging on the walls. She guessed Sebastian had painted them. Like those in his studio, they depicted a variety of styles and periods. One that reminded her of Edouard Manet's work caught her eye.

Footsteps behind her caused Lizzie to turn around. Joan Amory stood in the doorway, holding a vase with the flowers Lizzie had given her.

"Did your husband paint this?" Lizzie asked. "It makes me think of the pictures the French artist Manet did."

"You know something about art?" Joan said.

"Only a tiny bit. I go to New York's Metropolitan Museum whenever I can."

Joan set the vase on a table and crossed the parlor to stand beside Lizzie.

"Sebastian liked to paint what he thought famous artists would have painted if they'd lived longer. He tried to mimic their styles, their choice of subject matter. It was a game for him. Manet died in 1883 at the age of fifty-one from complications of syphilis. Sebastian imagined what he might have done had he lived today."

"Your husband was very talented."

"Yes, he was. I don't know why the art world didn't recognize that." Indignation crept into his widow's voice. "You'd think Hugh Franklin, at least, would've given my husband a one-man show at his gallery, after all Sebastian did for him. That could have been his big break." She shook her head. "I thought they were friends."

Now that Joan's mood had shifted from sadness to irritation, Lizzie decided to press on. "I met a rather odd man at Mr. Roman's party Saturday night who claimed your husband stole his ideas. A fella named Edward Oliver. Do you know him?"

"Ha! That little twerp. Manet said the same thing about Monet," Joan scoffed. "You don't *own* ideas. Artists have painted landscapes and vases of flowers and pretty women forever. How they interpret and render the subject is what matters. Besides, if Sebastian wanted to steal someone's ideas, it wouldn't have been poor, pathetic Eddie's."

Lizzie moved away and repositioned herself in front of another painting, one reminiscent of John Singer Sargent's lush, sensual portraits. The woman's face and chestnut hair looked familiar. *Had Thea Gallagher posed for this picture?* she wondered.

Questions rolled around in her mind like stones in a riverbed, stirred up and rearranged by the shifting currents. Did Sebastian Amory's wife know about the studio his lover had arranged for him at the mill where her father held the reins of power? How much did Joan know about her husband's affair with the young woman who'd publicly humiliated her?

Or about his relationship with Sid?

Finally, Lizzie asked the question she'd come here to ask. "Why did you give Sergeant Darcy the photo of your husband and my friend Sidney?"

Joan's body stiffened. She stood rubbing the skirt of her black gabardine frock for a few moments before answering. "I thought it might help his investigation."

"Sid didn't have anything to do with the murder. He hadn't even spoken to Sebastian in eight years."

"How do you know?"

"He told me so."

Joan laughed, but without mirth. "Men tell us all sorts of things that aren't true and neglect to tell us the things that are. Surely, you must know that, Miss Crane. But as Confucius said, 'Three things cannot long be hidden: the sun, the moon, and the truth.'"

* * *

It felt strange to have a whole day to herself, with no plans or responsibilities. The Troubadours weren't even scheduled for a performance tonight— apparently, even the indefatigable Isaac Roman needed a break now and again. Although Lizzie longed to take the train to Boston to see Alan, she knew he was busy with a new client, and she didn't want to interrupt his work. She had to be content with what time he could spare between the demands of his career and the needs of his ailing mother.

She considered visiting Cora, but then remembered the elderly gentleman she'd met during her last trip to Salem who owned an antique shop nearby. A friend of Roman's from whom Lizzie had purchased a delicately carved jade statue of Quan Yin, the Chinese goddess of shipwrecked sailors. His store held an eclectic mélange of art treasures and oddities from around the world. Perhaps he could offer insight into Sebastian Amory's life and death, or at least some good gossip.

Tibetan temple bells hanging on the door tinkled as she entered the shop. The white-haired, white-bearded proprietor, who reminded her of Old Saint Nick, looked up from his newspaper.

"Good day, dear lady," he said cheerfully. "Lovely to see you."

"Good day to you, too, sir."

"What brings you to our fair city again?"

"Your friend Mr. Roman hired my colleagues and me to play music for a few parties he threw to mark the spring equinox."

"Ah, yes. At long last, it appears Salem has welcomed spring." He stood slowly, pushing himself out of a turn-of-the-century schoolmaster's chair, and picked up a blue china mug. "May I offer you a cup of coffee?"

"Ab-so-lute-ly."

Lizzie noticed that he took his first steps stiffly and with apparent discomfort. But he straightened his spine and shuffled toward an oak file cabinet where a coffeepot sat percolating on top. He filled his cup and hers, then set them on a cherrywood dropleaf table, pulled up a chair, and motioned for her to join him.

"How is Quan Yin?" he asked, his pale blue eyes twinkling behind his spectacles.

"She's adapted well to life in New York City," Lizzie answered. "She even has a companion now, a cinnabar statue of the Buddha."

The old man chuckled. "And is Isaac well? I haven't seen him in a while."

"As colorful as ever and apparently in robust good health." Lizzie sipped the thin, bland coffee and thought *I must bring him a bag of good French roast the next time I come.* "Unfortunately, a friend of his was murdered Friday night. Perhaps you read about it in the papers?"

The shopkeeper nodded.

"Did you know Sebastian Amory? The artist who died?"

Again, the old man nodded. "I met him a time or two. Once he tried to sell me a painting he insisted was a sixteenth century El Greco. I knew instantly it was a fake and suspected Amory of having created it himself."

"How did you know?" Lizzie asked, her curiosity roused.

"It was a very cunning copy, I must admit, and handsomely rendered too. But one telltale feature gave it away." The shopkeeper sipped his coffee, eyeing Lizzie over the rim of his cup to make sure he had her full attention.

"What?"

"The signature. Apparently, Mr. Amory didn't realize that El Greco was the artist's nickname: The Greek. He signed his paintings with his real name." The antiquarian wrote the Greek letters on a piece of paper and handed it to

Lizzie: Δομήνικος Θεοτοκόπουλος."

Lizzie laughed. It could've been a case study for a book titled *How Crooks Get Caught.* Sebastian Amory devoted so much attention to duplicating an artist's style, yet failed to notice an obvious and incriminating practical detail.

"Sounds like he was forging artwork," Lizzie said. *Maybe Sebastian wasn't merely the copyist he pretended to be. Maybe he had more lucrative goals in mind.*

"It seemed that way to me at the time. When I pointed out his error, he grabbed the painting and dashed away with it. I never heard from him again."

Lizzie wondered if the painting hung in the studio she'd visited at Pequot Mills. She finished her coffee and stood. "May I browse around for a bit?"

"Of course, my dear. Ostensibly, that's the reason I own this store, so that people can enjoy viewing the merchandise and perhaps buy something." He pushed himself up, his knees cracking as he straightened his legs. "Truth be told, though, it's an excuse to acquire things I find appealing and to talk with people who interest me. Like you, Miss Crane."

She meandered through the shop that, despite its electric lighting, seemed shadowy and claustrophobic. Its musty smell reminded her of an old trunk that no one had opened in years. Yet everywhere she looked she saw something beguiling, elegant, or unusual that invited her to explore further.

In a vitrine near the back of the store, she spotted a collection of erotic Japanese netsuke. She'd seen the intricately carved, walnut-sized sculptures here before, but now they fascinated rather than shocked her. Even gazing at them caused a buzz to start running through her body. After examining the eight pieces on display, she decided to buy one that portrayed a sex act she'd never engaged in before becoming Alan's lover. *Will he think me too brazen if I give it to him?*

Trying to hide her embarrassment, she asked the white-bearded shopkeeper to unlock the case for her. She pointed to the miniature sculpture. He picked it up and held it on his outstretched leathery palm so she could study it more closely.

As if he'd read her mind, he asked, "Would you like me to gift wrap it for you?"

Chapter Thirteen

"From a little spark may burst a flame." — Dante Alighieri

Upon entering Salem Common, Lizzie spotted Sidney strolling on the footpath that circled it, apparently enjoying the pleasant afternoon. She cut across the grassy lawn to catch up with him. *I won't tell him I visited Joan Amory, at least not yet,* she decided as she approached her friend.

"Hail, Sidney," she called to him.

"Greetings, Bearcat. What have you been up to today?"

She fell in beside him and matched her stride to his. "I went to see the old man at the antiquarian shop where I bought my Quan Yin statue."

"Don't tell me you bought another Chinese goddess."

"No, she's one of a kind," Lizzie said, avoiding the subject of the netsuke figurine. "Say, what would you think of taking a trip to the Salem Willows amusement park? It's only a few miles away, and from what I've read it's pretty famous. Duke Ellington played there. It has balloon rides and a roller-skating rink and an open-air theater."

Sidney laughed and tousled her bobbed hair. "You sound like a little kid. Does it have a rollercoaster, too?"

"I don't know, but there's a carousel."

"You're on. We've still got a couple hours 'til sunset."

"Should we invite Bert to come with us?"

Sidney frowned. "Haven't seen our man Bert today. Frankly, I'm concerned about this affair he's got himself into."

Lizzie remembered the girl in whom Bert had taken an interest during their last visit to Salem. A shy, soft-spoken Irish lass with sandy hair and a face full of freckles, she worked as a housemaid at the home of The Troubadours' previous employer. Barely seventeen, she still carried some of her baby fat. Although few people would describe her as pretty, she had a sweet smile and a gentle demeanor that made Lizzie like her immediately.

"If he knocks up the girl and decides to marry her, The Troubadours are in big trouble," Sid continued. "We can't afford to lose him and Melody both."

"I've read him the riot act before, but I'm not his Mother Superior," Lizzie said, hooking her arm around Sid's. Considering her relationship with Alan, she could hardly play the morality card. Still, she shared Sid's concerns. Although she wanted Bert to be happy, she desperately hoped their young colleague would be careful. "Maybe you should have a chat with him."

"Why would he listen to me? I'm not exactly the voice of experience when it comes to preventing girls from getting in a family way."

"Then I guess we'll just have to trust him."

"Hmph. I just hope he's got a whole slew of French letters," Sid grumbled.

* * *

Behind Roman's mansion, they climbed into Sidney's dark green Buick and then motored out of town toward the tip of Salem's peninsula. While he drove, Lizzie read from her tourist guidebook.

"It says here, 'The Salem Willows Park was named for the European white willow trees planted here in 1801 to provide shade for convalescing smallpox patients from the nearby hospital who wanted to take the air. In 1875, a British painter named Daniel Gardner purchased the thirty-five-acre plot of land and began developing it. Two years later, the Naumkeag Street Railway Company started running horse-drawn trolleys from town to bring tourists here, and in 1880, the park officially opened for business. Up to 10,000 people came here in a single summer day.' That's a quarter of Salem's population. Can you imagine it?"

"Okay, I'm impressed," Sidney admitted. "It's not as big a deal as Coney Island, but big for these hinterlands."

At the end of Fort Avenue, he turned into a parking area and switched off the Buick's engine. Only two other motorcars and an old truck occupied the lot.

"Looks like the hordes have found other ways to amuse themselves this afternoon, Bearcat. We've got the place to ourselves."

Disappointed, Lizzie said, "I suppose it's too early. Summer hasn't started yet."

"It was snowing the day before yesterday," he reminded her.

"Can we go inside anyway and see what's what?"

"Sure, why not? We've come this far; we might as well give it a look-see."

White willow trees, more than a hundred years old and seventy feet tall, greeted them. Thousands of pale green buds sprouted from gnarled branches, promising hope and renewal. Instead of a carnival's raucous festivity, the seaside park off-season exuded a sense of calm—perhaps the very quality patients had sought when they came here years ago to recover from the ravishes of smallpox.

"It feels like a ghost town," Sidney said as they passed the shuttered concession stands, the empty theater, the silenced sideshow games, and rides.

"It's not dead," she said. "Only sleeping. Resting up for the busy season ahead."

When they reached the carousel, Lizzie stopped to marvel at the fanciful horses—more than fifty in all—decked out in colorful saddles and flowered bridles, with manes and tails made of real hair. Not only horses stood on the merry-go-round's stage, though. Camels, buffalo, lions, dogs, and even fanciful sea creatures accompanied them in rows three deep. Curious, she approached the platform and reached to touch a white steed with an emerald green mane.

"Closed 'til June," a man's voice behind her said.

She turned to see a portly, florid-faced man seated on a park bench and eating a sandwich. "I won't be here in June," she told him. "I'm from New

York City, just visiting this week. I'd so hoped to see Salem's famous flying horses."

"Sorry, miss, but those horses aren't gonna fly today." He licked mustard off his fingers. "They're not really 'flying' horses anyway; they're mostly jumpers and standers."

"What's the difference?" Lizzie asked.

"Early flying horses hung on chains. When the carousel turned, the motion made them swing out sideways, like they might break loose and take to the sky. These beasts are all firmly attached."

"You seem to know a lot about carousels."

"I should. Been operating this one for near on twenty years."

"If you're the operator, you can make it run, can't you?"

The man finished his sandwich and wiped his hands on his trousers. "Too much trouble to fire up the steam engine unless the carousel's going to be in use the whole day."

Time for some theatrics, Lizzie decided. She climbed onto the platform and wove between the painted ponies, patting each as she went. Occasionally, she stopped to hug a horse's neck or twist its mane in her fingers. She mounted a chocolate-brown mare with a golden tail and sat sidesaddle, wishing she'd worn trousers so she could straddle its wooden back more comfortably. Lying down along the horse's neck, she stroked it and pretended to talk to it, as if it were a living creature, all the while keeping her eyes fixed on the carousel's operator.

"Pretty pony, I really wanted to ride you today. I've read so much about you and the Salem Willows. About Mr. Brown who carved you, and Mr. Savage who found a way to make you gallop up and down, like a real horse…"

The heavy-set man, whose jaw sported a dab of mustard, rose from his park bench. "Okay, okay. I'll see if my horse can turn the contraption. That's how we did it in the old days. But don't expect any calliope music and no brass ring either."

Lizzie glanced at Sidney, who'd been standing beside the merry-go-round, watching her performance. He rolled his eyes, then grinned and gave her a thumbs-up. She motioned for him to join her, but he shook his head and lit a cigarette.

The carousel operator led a big, broad-chested bay with a black mane and tail to the carousel and introduced him to Lizzie. "This here's Atlas. I ride him around the park most every day, weather permitting, to check on things." The man hooked a thick leather strap to the horse's saddle, and then fastened it to a pole that protruded from the carousel. "You ready?" he called to Lizzie.

"Ready."

The man slapped the horse on the rump, and it marched forward, jerking its head up and down as if annoyed at having been disturbed from its leisure to perform this demeaning task. Slowly, the merry-go-round began to turn in a counterclockwise direction. The wooden steed with its golden tail on which she sat gently loped along at a pace even a toddler could handle. Lizzie held the brass pole that affixed the horse to the carousel and imagined what it might be like to ride it at full speed on a hot August night, accompanied by lively music and bright lights, and children's laughter. Sidney was right. Salem Willows didn't compete with Coney Island, but it would be a delightful place to come for a summer outing nonetheless.

She'd never ridden a real horse, not even a pony, when she was a child— her parents didn't have the money for frivolous merriments like pony rides. As she tried to imagine the sense of freedom a person might feel galloping across an open prairie as cowboys in the Western movies, the memory of Thea Gallagher trotting around Isaac Roman's ballroom flashed in her mind. Mounted on her dappled gray steed, perched high above the rest of the guests, the young woman must have felt supremely confident of her own power, of her ability to command the situation and seize what she wanted. Where had she taken Sebastian when they left the party? And why had he come back to meet his gruesome death in Roman's greenhouse? Did Thea return with him, intending to murder her lover, or had the artist come alone?

After a dozen turns, the carousel's operator halted his horse and the ride slowed to a stop. Lizzie slid off her wooden mount, patting it on the neck one last time. Then she stepped down from the platform and stroked the neck of the bay named Atlas, wishing she had a sugar cube to give him.

"Thank you ever so much," she said as she handed the man fifty cents—five times the price of an ordinary ride.

He tipped his cap and pocketed the money. "You're surely welcome, miss."

Sidney stood up from the park bench and crushed his cigarette butt with his shoe. "Having fun-ski?"

"I've just begun-ski," she said. "Let's see what else we can find."

"While you poke around, I'm going to try to scare up something to eat. I should've asked that carousel fella where he got his sandwich."

"An ice cream cone would be darb."

"And how," he agreed. "Okay, I'll give it a try."

Lizzie passed the theater, the casino, and the rollercoaster, all locked down until summer. When she reached the arcade, however, she noticed a door standing open. Inside, two men rolled dice while a woman with waist-length chestnut-colored hair fired a rifle at a row of tin animals that moved against a background painted to look like a forest. Each time she hit one, the creature toppled over, and a light flashed to register her "kill." Lizzie recognized her immediately: Thea Gallagher. The men glanced up briefly at the newcomer, whose attire marked her as a tourist, then returned to their game. The woman's attention, however, remained fixed on her targets. Lizzie jumped as rifle blasts took down a deer, then a fox, a bear, and finally, what looked like a gopher.

After she'd finished her round, Thea turned and did a double-take when she saw Lizzie. "Are you following me?" she demanded.

Startled by the animosity in her voice, Lizzie said, "This is a public place."

"It's closed to the public until summer. Park employees and friends only. You don't fit into either category and have no business here."

"Why would I bother following you?"

"That's what I'd like to know," Thea said, resting her rifle on her shoulder in a way that seemed simultaneously casual and menacing.

"You're a good shot. Can you shoot a bow and arrow, too?"

Thea tossed her head, making her long hair ripple like snakes winding down her back. "Why don't you ask Joan Amory that question? She grew up in England riding to the hounds and hunting real foxes, not just tin cut-outs in a tacky arcade."

"Thanks, I will."

As Lizzie turned to go, Thea called out to the two men playing craps. "Hey, guys. Come over here and meet Isaac's pretty new whore."

The insult stunned Lizzie, like an unexpected slap. What had she ever done to warrant Thea's ire? *I should be the one who's cross at her for causing so much trouble for Sid and me,* Lizzie thought angrily.

The men looked up from their crap game and grinned, eager to witness a more intriguing sport.

Lizzie spun around to face her antagonist, unable to contain her annoyance. "You act like a dog who's been thrown out of the house at night into the snow. Now, all you can do is howl at the moon."

Thea laughed, but only with her mouth. Her eyes remained as cold and lifeless as stones. She slid her rifle down to her side and held it against her leg, then licked her finger and made a mark in the air. "Score one for the showgirl."

Breathe, Lizzie, breathe, she told herself. She straightened her shoulders, held her head high, and strode out of the arcade into the late afternoon sunshine. Behind her, she could hear the two men guffawing.

"There you are," Sidney called to her. "I've been looking everywhere for you. Sorry, I couldn't find any ice cream. This place is emptier than Old Mother Hubbard's cupboard."

"Never mind," Lizzie said, uncertain whether to tell Sid about her run-in with Thea Gallagher. "Let's get out of here. We can find a restaurant in town. I've seen all I need to see here today."

Chapter Fourteen

"If I maintain my silence about my secret it is my prisoner...if I let it slip from my tongue, I am its prisoner." — *Arthur Schopenhauer*

"I have to tell you something, Bearcat," Sidney said.

He finished his supper of fish and chips at one of Salem's waterfront eateries and pushed his plate to the edge of the table. Lizzie laid down her fork and stared at him anxiously, dreading the worst.

"Oh? What now?"

"Sebastian wrote to me, two weeks ago. Roman must have told him we'd be performing here. He said he wanted to reconnect with me. I agreed."

Anger crept into her voice as she realized he'd lied to her. "So you weren't surprised to see him on Friday night after all."

Joan Amory's words echoed in her ears. "Men tell us all sorts of things that aren't true and neglect to tell us the things that are."

He pulled a cigarette from his decorative tin and went through the ritual of tapping it on the lid a few times, before fitting it into his silver holder and lighting it. "After all this time, I was curious to see if I still had feelings for him, or if he still felt anything for me. As soon as I saw him talking to you in Roman's ballroom, all those emotions came rushing back, like a flash flood."

"Jeepers creepers, Sid. Did you 'reconnect'?"

He shook his head. "We didn't get the chance."

Lizzie picked up her coffee cup and took a sip while she contemplated the significance of his words. "Do you still have the letter?"

"Yes."

"Get rid of it. Burn it as soon as we get back to Roman's house. That's incriminating evidence. You don't want it to fall into Sergeant Darcy's hands, do you?"

"But—"

"No buts," she said, as if speaking to a petulant child. "You're a suspect in a murder investigation. Anything and everything can—and will—be used against you."

He blew a lungful of smoke at the ceiling and nodded. "I know."

Exasperated, Lizzie asked, "How can I help you if you don't come clean? Why do you keep blindsiding me like this? That letter proves you planned to meet up with Sebastian, which a good prosecutor could twist to indicate premeditation."

Suddenly, she wanted to wash her hands of the whole sordid mess, jump on the next train to Boston, and take refuge in Alan's home. Get away from this fiasco while she still could. Let Sidney fend for himself.

"I'm sorry, Bearcat."

As she studied his forlorn face, a horrible thought popped into her mind. *Maybe Sid really did kill him.* "Is there anything else you haven't told me?"

"I think I'm still in love with him."

* * *

"Pour me a drink," Lizzie said as she dropped into one of the chairs in Sidney's bedroom.

"What's your pleasure?"

"Some of that Lagavulin, if you've got any left."

Sid pulled a half-full bottle from the wardrobe and splashed a healthy amount of the peaty scotch into two glasses. He handed one to her, then sipped his own while pacing uneasily back and forth across the room.

"Give me the letter." She held out her hand, wiggling her fingers.

He sighed melodramatically, then from the inside pocket of his jacket—the pocket that lay against his heart—he withdrew a folded piece of stationery.

"Is this really necessary?"

"Ab-so-lute-ly," she said. "Aren't you scared? If you're not, you certainly should be."

"A little," he admitted.

"I'm sorry, Sid. I wish you could keep a memento of your friend, but you don't want to go to the electric chair, do you?"

"I didn't kill him. Why would I murder the man I loved?"

Thea Gallagher had asked Lizzie the same thing. Yet men and women killed the people they loved with dreadful frequency. And they rarely considered themselves capable of doing such a heinous thing until it happened.

"Try convincing a judge and jury of that. Joan Amory's already put the cops on your trail to get them off her back. The god-fearing citizens of Salem will surely look more favorably on a respectable widow from a good family than a three-letter man from the sinful city of New York." She tossed back her scotch and set down the empty glass. "Your lighter, please?"

He gave it to her and, as she took it, she squeezed his hand. "C'mon, let's see this through."

Together, they entered the *en suite* bathroom. Lizzie lifted the toilet lid and held the incriminating letter over the bowl. She flicked the lighter, lit the corner of the folded piece of paper, and watched the flames take hold. The paper began curling into black ash, eating away at Sidney's secret. When the fire threatened to singe her fingers, she dropped what remained of the paper into the basin. It sizzled briefly, then went out. For a moment, they both stared at the charred remnants floating in the toilet water, until Lizzie pulled the chain and flushed the evidence away.

She hugged Sid hard, laying her cheek on his shoulder. "When we get back to New York, let's see about having a ceremony of some sort for him. What do you say-ski?"

"Okay-ski."

In Sidney's bedroom, Lizzie turned on the radio, searching through the channels until she found a jazz station. When Louis Armstrong's "Big Butter and Egg Man" came on, she grabbed Sid's hand. "C'mon, let's dance. It'll make us both feel better."

She pulled him into an easy Charleston, then a faster one when the disc jockey followed up with the lively Dixieland favorite "Cake Walking Babies."

"You're right. I do feel better," Sidney said when the song ended. He refilled their glasses, then sat down in his armchair again.

Lizzie took her seat across from him and shifted the conversation away from Sebastian Amory. "We've talked about making a record in the not-too-distant future, but I think we should also consider performing live on the radio. Radio is transforming popular music. Who knows, you could be the next Clarence Williams, and Bert could be the next Louis Armstrong. What's your take on it?"

"I think it's a swell idea. When we get back to the City, I'll see if I can set something up."

* * *

Lizzie hadn't set foot in the solarium where Sebastian Amory died since the morning she found his body. The memory of him perforated with arrows still gave her chills. But after her conversation with Sidney, she felt a need to revisit the scene of the crime, hoping it might reveal something she'd missed before. Maybe the serene sanctuary would soothe her jangled thoughts. The possibility that Sid might have killed his former lover made her feel sick, as if she were riding a rollercoaster and had entirely lost her sense of equilibrium. *How much do we really know about the people closest to us, the secrets they hide, what they're capable of?* she asked herself.

Birds chirped as she meandered along the pathway that led through the lush indoor garden. Amid the many scents, she recognized the sweet aroma of jasmine and looked around for the subtropical shrub with its shiny, dark green leaves and delicate white blossoms. The Victorians, she'd read, associated jasmine with love, romance, and seduction. Each flower had a unique meaning that allowed a suitor to send secret messages to his lover in the guise of a bouquet.

As she passed the white wicker settee and chairs, where she'd sat while Sergeant Darcy questioned her about Sebastian's murder, she spotted Isaac

Roman. He stood with his back to her, gazing at the tree to which the artist had been tied. Not wanting to interrupt him, she paused, thinking *I should go back and leave Roman alone with his grief.* But before she could retrace her steps, he turned around to face her.

"Good evening, Miss Crane."

"My apologies, Mr. Roman. I didn't mean to disturb you."

He waved his hand, brushing aside her concern. "You didn't. I was just trying to imagine who might have killed Sebastian, and why. As I suppose everyone who knew him is doing these days."

He wore a midnight blue evening suit, a dove-gray vest, and a flashy red bow tie patterned with chevrons and diamonds. She supposed he was headed out for the evening, perhaps to Boston to enjoy supper and the theater, or to go to a celebrity-packed party in the city's fashionable Back Bay. Did Roman attend parties at other people's homes, or only invite them to come to his? Who else could compete with his galas? His long white hair sparkled like a slope of pristine snow. Lizzie felt a sudden urge to run her hand down that frosty slope to lay her head on his shoulder. To let him sort out all the discombobulated bits and pieces of the puzzle and fit them into some sort of order she could understand.

"Have you arrived at any conclusions?" she asked.

"I have my theories, naturally—who doesn't? But they're unsubstantiated."

Lizzie edged closer to her host and gazed up at him, her smoky eyes bright with curiosity. "Who do you suspect?"

"Well, Joan's the obvious one. After all, her husband jilted her and rubbed her nose in it. But somehow, I can't see her actually doing the deed."

"Why not?"

"She hasn't the stomach for it. A few years ago, Hugh Franklin and I went fox hunting with her at the Myopia Hunt Club in Hamilton, just north of here. Have you heard of it?"

"Yes, I've been there," she said, recalling her visit with Sidney five months ago.

Roman raised an eyebrow, apparently surprised that a New York showgirl was familiar with the prestigious and rather stuffy Massachusetts club. "Well," he continued, "when it came time to shoot the fox, Joan balked. She couldn't pull the trigger."

"What about Thea Gallagher?" Lizzie asked, remembering how competently the young woman picked off tin animals at the Salem Willows shooting gallery. Did Thea have the stomach to kill real animals—or perhaps a human being?

"Possibly…"

Lizzie waited for him to elaborate. When he didn't, she prompted, "Thea thinks her father might have killed Sebastian to keep him away from her."

"You know Thea?"

"We've met."

Roman fingered the pearl buttons on his vest. "I wouldn't put anything past Paul Gallagher."

"She said her father slugged her because she refused to stop seeing Sebastian," Lizzie said. "I understand Papa Gallagher wanted his daughter to marry a man named Timothy Whiting, his protégé at the Mills. Do you think Whiting could have killed Sebastian to eliminate the competition?"

"Miss Crane, if you weren't so beautiful, you might have made a good detective."

A blur of white fur dashed between them, then scooted up the tree.

Startled, Lizzie asked, "What was that?"

"My cat, Zanzibar. He enjoys stalking around here, watching the birds. So far as I know, he's never caught one, but he hasn't given up hope. He's quite intrepid." Roman stepped toward the tree to which Sebastian had been tied and ran his hand along its bark. "I've thought about having this tree cut down, so I don't have to look at it and be reminded of what happened here."

"It's not the tree's fault. Why should it die?" she asked. "Besides, you'd deprive the intrepid Zanzibar of his perch." *And maybe destroy incriminating evidence the cops haven't discovered yet.*

He looked up at the cat clinging to one of the branches and watching them from his lofty perspective. "You're right," he agreed.

"Mr. Roman, I wanted to talk to you about tomorrow," Lizzie said, bringing the conversation back to business. "I'm planning to go to Boston in the morning, and I need to know what you have in mind for us on Wednesday. It all seems so very secretive."

A yellow parakeet swooped down from the tree and landed on Roman's shoulder. He reached into his pocket, pulled out a small bag of birdseed, and handfed some to the bird.

"Have you ever wanted to fly like a bird, Miss Crane?"

"I suppose everyone has imagined it, at least."

"Then show up Wednesday afternoon at 2:00, at the corner of Flint Street and Mason, just across the North River." The parakeet twittered, and Roman fed it some more seed. "I'd like your troupe to start playing for my guests in the ballroom at eight and continue until midnight or so. Can you do that?"

"Of course. Your wish is our command."

He glanced at his watch. "Well, then. I must excuse myself. I have another engagement. Good evening, Miss Crane."

"A pleasant evening to you too, Mr. Roman."

* * *

Lizzie had tried to reach Alan by telephone twice earlier in the day, without success. The first time, his secretary told her Mr. Peabody was having lunch with a client. When she called later, the woman said he was in a meeting and couldn't be disturbed. At 7:30, she dialed his home number, hoping she didn't appear too insistent. *But he asked me to phone every day, so he knows I'm okay,* she reminded herself.

A housemaid answered. "He's been expecting your call, Miss Crane. One minute, please."

It took nearly three minutes before Alan came on the line. "Sorry I couldn't talk when you telephoned earlier," he apologized. "How's everything?"

"Too much to tell over the phone."

"Maybe I should drive up to Salem right now and fetch you back here."

"What about your work?"

"Yes, there's that. I still have a pile of paperwork to take care of tonight for an eight o'clock meeting in the morning," he said. "Would you consider taking the train to Boston tomorrow? My butler will pick you up at North Station; just let me know what time. If you think you can amuse yourself in my fair city for the day, I promise to leave the office no later than 5:30."

"That sounds swell." She already knew the train schedule by heart, and the idea of seeing Alan sent a lovely resonance coursing through her body, as if she were a harp and he were strumming her strings. "There's a train that gets in at 10:20 tomorrow morning."

"Perfect. Then I'll bid you a fond goodnight and try to keep my mind on my work until I see you again, though I daresay that will be a monumental task."

"Goodnight, Alan, and sweet dreams," she said, hoping he'd dream of her.

She climbed the stairs to Roman's second-story guest quarters to tell Sidney her plans. The idea of seeing Alan thrilled her, but she also longed to see the Isabella Stewart Gardner Museum and the Boston Museum of Fine Arts. Maybe she'd even visit Hugh Franklin's gallery. By the time she knocked on Sid's bedroom door, she felt like a little girl in a candy store.

Chapter Fifteen

Alan's butler met her in the bustling lobby of North Station, holding a black umbrella the size of a pup tent in his hand.

"Good morning, Norman," Lizzie said to the very proper gentleman she'd met when she visited Alan at his Boston home last month.

He reached to take her suitcase. "Good morning to you too, Miss Crane. I wish the weather were better so you could enjoy seeing the city."

"The rain won't be a problem. I've planned to spend the day viewing art at Boston's museums anyway."

"Very well. Shall I drive you to one of them then? Or would you rather I take you to Mr. Peabody's townhouse first?"

"If you don't mind, I like to go straight to the Gardner Museum. Would you be kind enough to see to my bag?"

"Of course, miss." He held the umbrella over her as they crossed the street beneath the el to Alan's silver Bentley. "I'll pick you up when you've finished."

"Thanks, but that won't be necessary. I can get a taxicab."

The butler frowned as he opened the elegant auto's door for her. "Mr. Peabody might not approve of that."

"Applesauce," Lizzie replied. "Truth be told, I don't know what else I might feel like doing today. I'd rather not take up your whole afternoon ferrying me about."

"Begging your pardon, miss, but that is part of my job."

Norman started the Bentley's engine and slid smoothly into the late morning traffic. The windshield wipers slashed at the rain. The auto's tires whooshed through the puddles on the street, sending fans of gray water spraying behind them. Lizzie wiped a clear circle on the window so she could see a bit of the city as he drove. Norman motored past Boston Common, then along Huntington Avenue to the Back Bay Fens, one of the parks in what was known as landscape architect Frederick Law Olmstead's Emerald Necklace.

After a few miles, they pulled up in front of the museum. Inspired by fifteenth-century Venetian palaces, it had been home to the noted art collector—and a center for artists of all stripes—until her death two years ago. In her will, Mrs. Gardner stated that her residence and its collections remain open to the public forever.

Norman reached behind the driver's seat and came up with another, neatly folded umbrella. He handed it to Lizzie. "I expect you might need this, miss," he said. Then he hurried around to open the door for her, holding the tent-like umbrella overhead to shield her from the pelting rain.

Inside the museum's foyer, he paid her entrance fee. "Mr. Peabody has given me a certain allowance to cover your expenses while you're sightseeing today, Miss Crane," he explained. "If you insist on taking taxicabs—"

"Thank you, Norman. Mr. Peabody is most generous, but I can handle a few cab fares myself."

The butler frowned again. Lizzie thought *he's altogether too serious.* She wondered if her independent attitude confused him, or if Alan's other lady friends expected him to foot all their bills.

Norman cleared his throat. "Well, then, Miss Crane. I'll leave you to enjoy the museum. When you've finished your day's amusements, will you please telephone me and allow me to collect you? I fear Mr. Peabody would consider me quite remiss if you weren't comfortably ensconced in his home when he returns from his office this evening."

Suppressing a smile, Lizzie said, "Of course. Thank you, Norman. I look forward to being 'comfortably ensconced.'" *And to many other things as well.*

* * *

On this rainy morning, the atrium garden in the center of the Gardner Museum offered a welcome sanctuary. Orchids, narcissus, cyclamen, and calla lilies bloomed among lush ferns and palm trees. Water trickled from a marble fountain at the end of a courtyard paved with first-century Roman mosaic tiles. A weak, gray light filtered through the skylit roof four stories above and fell on the shoulders of the ancient statues that populated the garden. Thick stone walls blocked the sounds of the city, enclosing Lizzie in a world where time stood still and only beauty mattered. Where murder was a subject for paintings, not real life.

Meandering through the rambling mansion, she tried to take in the overwhelming array of paintings, sculptures, furniture, ceramics, textiles, and oddities Mrs. Gardner had amassed from around the world. She imagined Sebastian Amory with his sketchbook, copying the works of the great masters displayed here. Botticelli's *The Story of Lucretia*. Rembrandt's *Self-Portrait* and Vermeer's *The Concert*. Titian's *The Rape of Europa*.

Mrs. Gardner, Lizzie knew, had been the patron of the artist John Singer Sargent, so she wasn't surprised to come upon a painting he'd done of his benefactor. As she stood admiring it, however, Lizzie couldn't help comparing the rather staid image to the artist's more evocative and sensual *Portrait of Madame X* of the American expatriate, Mrs. Gautreau, that she'd seen at New York's Metropolitan Museum of Art. Her thoughts circled back to Sebastian Amory's request that Lizzie model for him. *If I ever pose for a portrait, I want it to be one like Madame X.*

On the third floor, she stepped out onto one of the small open balconies that overlooked the courtyard below. She rested her palms on its cool stone railing, admiring the richness all around her. During the hour she'd been here, she'd seen only a few other people. Now footsteps nearby caused her to turn around.

A tall, thin, stoop-shouldered man whom she'd met at Roman's party Saturday night stood an arm's length behind her. The indignant artist Edward Oliver. Former friend of Sebastian Amory. As he loomed toward

95

her, Lizzie noticed the razor burn on his jaw and the scar beneath his left eye that resembled a teardrop.

Instinctively, she pulled away. She backed against the baluster and felt it bite into her spine. Trapped on this narrow overhang, she had no place to go. She held up her hands to push him if he came closer. After several uncomfortable moments, Oliver stepped aside, and Lizzie scooted around him into the gallery.

"You startled me," she said, not attempting to hide the annoyance in her voice.

He shoved his hands into the pockets of his too-short, badly pressed trousers. "Sorry. I saw you and thought I'd say hello."

"What are you doing here?"

"I work here. I'm a guard. Usually I'm on the night shift, though. I'm filling in for another fella today."

Lizzie relaxed. *He doesn't mean any harm, he just lacks good manners.* "This must be a nice place for an artist to work. Lots of inspiration."

"I suppose. Can't make a living painting," he grumbled.

She decided to tease him. "Have you considered a life of crime, like Vincenzo Peruggia?" When Oliver frowned, Lizzie explained, "Surely, you've heard of him. He was a guard at the Louvre who filched the *Mona Lisa* in 1911. One of the most famous art heists ever. Peruggia considered himself a patriot—he believed Napoleon had stolen da Vinci's masterpiece from Italy and he wanted to bring it home again."

As she spoke, Lizzie noticed that Oliver began rapidly tapping his right thigh with his fingers. His face seemed to pale, but it could have been caused by the shifting light from the atrium's skylight.

"Miss Crane, I have to get back to work now. I hope you enjoy the rest of your afternoon."

"Thank you, Mr. Oliver. I plan to."

* * *

If the weather had been better, Lizzie would have walked the few blocks to the Museum of Fine Arts. But when she left the Gardner Museum, rain was hammering the streets relentlessly, as if determined to scrub the city clean of every scrap of dirt and detritus. She hailed a taxi, whose driver seemed put out at the short-distance fare. She tipped him more than she should have, considering his surly manner, then dashed through the rain holding the umbrella Norman had given her to the Beaux-Arts style building with its handsome ionic columns.

After two hours of looking at artifacts from ancient Egypt, Greece, and Rome, treasures brought from the Orient on clipper ships in the mid-nineteenth century, and paintings by European and American artists, Lizzie needed a break. She found a cafeteria on the ground floor, where she ate a slice of Boston cream pie and drank coffee at a corner table. Twice, she noticed a tall, thin man who resembled Edward Oliver standing near the doorway. *It can't be him,* she told herself; *he's working at the Gardner.*

She'd seen enough art for one day, but she couldn't quell her curiosity about the gallery Roman's friend Hugh Franklin owned. The gallery that refused to show Sebastian Amory's paintings. And she still had more than two hours to kill before Alan finished work.

Lizzie climbed into a taxicab outside the museum and gave the driver the address of the Franklin Gallery. The rain had slacked off a little, though clouds as dark and dense as Brillo steel wool pads still covered the sky. The driver motored down Massachusetts Avenue and turned onto Newbury. The seven-block-long street, which began at the Public Garden, appealed to art lovers as well as upscale shoppers and was becoming a fashionable locale for those with sophisticated tastes.

Once a marshy tidal flat, Boston's Back Bay had been filled in over a period of more than forty years and was only completed in 1900. Now its elegant Victorian brick and brownstone townhouses were home to many of Boston's elite—particularly those with new money—as well as the Christian Science Church and the Boston Public Library. Even Isabella Stewart Gardner once lived here.

Lizzie paid the cabbie and entered Hugh Franklin's gallery. Located on the ground floor of a Bullfinch-designed brownstone, the gallery's interior sparkled with electric lighting. Gleaming maple floors, large expanses of glass, and Art Deco borders running along the tops of the walls marked the showroom as a place for the most modern forms of expression.

Two young men carefully hung canvases on the gallery's smoke-colored walls. Lizzie stopped to study the paintings already in place. One she recognized as the work of Edward Hopper, a picture of a rambling three-story house in the nearby town of Gloucester. Sunlight and shadows danced along its clapboards, making it seem alive.

"Good afternoon, Miss Crane."

"Mr. Franklin," she said, holding out her hand to the man whose gray afternoon suit nearly blended into the gallery's walls.

"I see you're admiring Edward Hopper's painting."

"Yes, I find his work most enchanting. I had the good fortune of meeting him at a dinner party during the Christmas holidays. He told me his 'favorite thing is painting sunlight on the side of a house.' His fondness shows in this picture, don't you think?"

Franklin raised an eyebrow, apparently impressed that a showgirl had socialized with the up-and-coming artist and could appreciate his work. "It's for sale. A good investment. I'll give you a discount if you purchase it before the show opens this weekend."

"I'd love to own it, of course, but I haven't the means to buy art of this caliber," she said, wondering if Alan might be as captivated by the painting as she was. "Maybe one day…"

"The show is titled 'Light and Shadow.' It asks us to consider the light and shadows that abide in each of us," Franklin explained. "I hope you'll come to the reception on Friday evening. We'll open at seven o'clock. Several of the artists will be here. Not Hopper, though, alas."

Franklin's two employees finished positioning a painting the size of a door that portrayed a young woman huddled at the entrance to a cave. Most of the picture was hauntingly dark and gloomy, but pale golden light crept across the sand at the bottom of the canvas toward the cave's entrance, entreating the crouching figure to come outside. The painting made Lizzie think of the Swiss psychiatrist Carl Jung's theories about how dark, repressed memories stuffed away in the unconscious inhibited our efforts to emerge into the light of self-awareness.

"You're familiar with Dr. Jung's ideas, I see," Lizzie said.

Again, Franklin seemed surprised by her comment. "You are correct, Miss Crane. I hope those who view the exhibit will make that connection too."

The two young picture-hangers repositioned their ladder and prepared to nail up another canvas. The shorter of the two, who wore his dark hair tied in a ponytail at the nape of his neck so that he looked like a Colonial-era patriot, hoisted a painting up to the other man who stood on the ladder. Then, he stepped back to assess the picture's placement.

"Up a tad on the left," he said. "No, too much. Go back."

Lizzie decided to broach a subject with Franklin that she'd been mulling over since her meeting yesterday with Joan Amory. "Why didn't you ever show Sebastian Amory's work here?"

"Did you know Sebastian?" the gallery owner asked.

"I only met him briefly at Mr. Roman's party, on the night he died. According to his widow, you and he were friends. It seems logical that you would have encouraged his career."

"Have you seen his work?"

"Yes. I don't claim to be an expert, but he seemed to be a good painter. Even Isaac Roman has one of Mr. Amory's pictures hanging in his home."

Franklin chuckled, as if enjoying a private joke. "Miss Crane, as you admit you are not an expert. I represent artists who have more than skill. Men and women on the cutting edge of the art world, whose vision extends beyond the present and into a distant realm. The avatars of art's future."

The picture-hanger on the ladder let out a sharp yelp. He scrambled to grab hold of the painting that had gotten away from him, snagging it just before it hit the floor. In the process, he slipped and nearly fell. His colleague rushed to his aid, receiving a blow on the shoulder from the toppling ladder for his efforts.

"Excuse me, Miss Crane," Franklin said as he hurried toward his workers to avert any more possible disasters. "I hope to see you here Friday evening."

Chapter Sixteen

"He looked at her the way all women want to be looked at by a man."
— *F. Scott Fitzgerald, The Great Gatsby*

After Alan's butler fetched her from the Franklin Gallery, Lizzie bathed and washed her hair, applied her makeup, and donned an apricot-colored dress of silk layered to look like a hibiscus flower opening its petals to reveal its inner beauty. She clipped on a topaz necklace and gold earrings studded with pearls. She dabbed perfume on her throat. Then she went downstairs to allow Norman to "ensconce" her while she waited for her lover.

"Would you like me to light a fire, miss?" the butler asked.

"Thank you, Norman, that would be lovely."

With a few deft motions, he sparked a flame that gave the spacious parlor a romantic ambiance, even though the townhouse's modern heating system already kept the room comfortably warm.

"May I serve you a libation?" he asked.

"Yes, please. Would you be kind enough to bring me a splash of scotch on the rocks?"

"Of course, miss."

As he left to fulfill her request, Lizzie thought *I could get used to this.* She'd spent a few days here in February, but very little of it in the formal rooms of Alan's four-story brick townhouse in Beacon Hill's elite Louisburg Square. Now, she studied the elegant parlor's furnishings and adornments with an appreciative eye: the Isfahan carpet, the striped silk wallcovering, the handsome Chippendale furniture that was both graceful and distinctly masculine. *Like Alan himself.*

On one wall, above a mahogany sideboard, hung the Van Gogh. A field of red, orange, and yellow flowers stretched beneath a bright blue sky, their brilliant hues blazing in the sunshine. No people appeared in the picture, however a path invited observers to enter and stroll amid all that color. The artist's bold brushstrokes filled the canvas with movement—it looked as though the flowers were dancing. She stepped closer, mesmerized by the painting's vitality. *How lovely it would be to look at this picture whenever I wanted to, especially on dreary days like this.*

Lizzie reached out to touch its surface, tracing Van Gogh's strong, fluid brushstrokes with her fingertip. Alan had told her that Isaac Roman helped procure this painting for him. Had it been stolen from a private collection in post-war Europe? Was it a fake? Did it matter if simply viewing its exuberant beauty gave one pleasure?

"Here you are, miss," Norman said. "Mr. Peabody just telephoned and asked me to let you know he'll be here in fifteen minutes."

Lizzie sat on the leather Chesterfield sofa facing the hearth and accepted the crystal glass he presented to her on a silver tray. "Thank you, Norman. I believe you may be spoiling me."

A hint of a smile played at the corners of the butler's mouth. If she hadn't been paying attention, she would've missed the fleeting expression that softened his otherwise serious countenance.

"It's my job to spoil Mr. Peabody's guests, miss."

* * *

Lizzie looked up to see Alan standing in the doorway to the parlor. Dressed in a beautifully cut midnight blue suit, his red hair blazed like a comet against a dark sky. She stood and took two proper, dignified steps toward him, then dispensed with decorum and ran across the room to throw herself into his arms. He swept her up, spun her around a few times, then kissed her until she felt dizzy with desire.

"I've been thinking about you all day," he said. "I should've given up trying to work and come home—I accomplished next to nothing."

"I never meant to distract you from your job."

"Too late now." He kissed her again. "What did you do on this rainy day in my fair city?"

"I went to the Isabella Stewart Gardner Museum, the Boston Museum of Fine Arts, and the Franklin Gallery."

Alan laughed. "After viewing all that art, you must be completely exhausted."

"I hadn't expected it to be so, well, demanding," she admitted.

He laughed again, then held her at arm's length and swept her figure with his gold-flecked brown eyes. "I apologize for not telling you straight away how beautiful you are." He kissed the hollow at the base of her neck, then trailed a line of kisses along her collarbone. "Where would you like to go for supper?"

By now, Lizzie was having trouble focusing on supper or art or anything else except the exquisite tingling running through her. "Would you be terribly disappointed if we stayed here?" she asked. "The weather's dreadful."

"It is indeed. I'd rather not forge out in it again, either. I'll have the kitchen staff prepare supper for us. Is there something special you'd like?"

Lizzie shook her head, realizing suddenly how hungry she was. The Boston cream pie she'd eaten in the museum was all she'd had since breakfast.

"Let's go see what we can scare up, shall we?" Alan said, taking her hand.

At the end of a long hallway, they turned into a spacious kitchen with walls covered in blue-and-white Delft tiles. Cherrywood cabinets fitted with polished brass hardware ran down both sides of the high-ceilinged room. Gleaming copper pots and pans hung from iron racks. As they entered, four kitchen maids jumped to attention.

"Is Mrs. Babcock here?" he asked a young woman who had the round, rosy cheeks and tilted nose of Boston's Irish immigrants.

The woman curtsied. "I'll go fetch her for you, sir."

A few moments later, the Irish maid returned in the company of a more-than-plump, broad-shouldered woman with a pockmarked face and gray-streaked hair peeking out from under her crisp white cap. Lizzie caught a whiff of smoke on the cook's clothing and suspected she'd been outside enjoying a cigarette when they interrupted her.

"Good evening, Mr. Peabody. How may I be of service?"

"Good evening, Mrs. Babcock. Miss Crane and I are in search of supper. It's last minute, I know, but I have infinite faith in your ability to turn out a feast worthy of a king even so. What do you suggest?"

The cook blushed at his compliment and wiped her hands on her apron. "Got some lovely spring lamb chops, just bought today, and some fresh green peas and new potatoes." She nodded at the Irish kitchen maid. "Mary, here, baked a rhubarb pie this afternoon. Would that suit you and your lady, sir?"

"What do you think?" he asked Lizzie.

"I think that sounds delicious."

"Then I leave it in your capable hands, Mrs. Babcock."

"Certainly, sir."

Next, Alan led Lizzie down a flight of stairs behind the kitchen to his wine cellar. He unlocked the heavy oak door and switched on an overhead light. Floor-to-ceiling shelves full of bottles lined both sides of the cool, dank room.

"Watch your step," he warned as he made his way along the uneven brick floor sheened with moisture. He paused in front of a bay of French reds, pulled a bottle from the shelf, studied the label, then put it back. Three more times he did this, before deciding on a Bordeaux that had been bottled before the war began. "What do you think about this one?" he asked, holding it up for her to see.

"I defer to your greater knowledge and experience. A man who keeps a cellar like this understands wine better than I ever will."

"Perhaps you'll allow me to teach you."

"I'd like that."

He tucked the bottle under his arm, turned off the light, locked the door, and followed her upstairs, where he handed the wine to his butler. "Would you please open this now, Norman, and set it on the dining table to breathe?

And bring Miss Crane and me a bit of scotch on the rocks while we await supper?"

"Of course, sir."

While the kitchen staff prepared their meal, Lizzie and Alan sat side-by-side on the sofa. He pressed his thigh lightly against hers. His fingertips found reasons to brush her hand, her arm, her cheek.

"What did you see today at the museums?" he asked.

"More than I could possibly absorb."

"You'd need weeks to take it all in." He sipped his scotch before continuing. "Why did you choose to go to the Franklin Gallery?"

"Isaac Roman and the owner, Hugh Franklin, are friends. I met Franklin at Roman's party the night Sebastian Amory was murdered. Sebastian knew him too—he did work for him, repairs, copies, and such. According to Joan Amory, Franklin refused to show her husband's paintings in his gallery. She seemed quite bitter about the slight."

"And you wanted to check it out."

Lizzie nodded. "The gallery's on Newbury Street, only a few blocks from the Public Garden. Have you been there?"

"No, but that's high-end real estate."

"It's very modern. They were just starting to hang pictures for a show that opens Friday evening, so I didn't get to see much. One painting by Edward Hopper caught my eye. Did I tell you I met him the last time The Troubadours performed in Salem?"

"I don't think so. What's he like?"

"Very tall, nearly a head taller even than you. Quiet, introspective. I guess you could call him solemn or maybe brooding. The painting is quite whimsical, though, full of sunlight and playfulness. It's of a house in Gloucester, which sounds rather dull, I know, but it's enchanting, really. Just looking at it made me happy."

"Would you like to have it?"

"Of course, but I'm sure it's beyond my means. I didn't even look at the price tag."

"Then you must let me buy it for you."

Stunned, Lizzie stared at him, uncertain how to react. "I didn't mean to suggest any such thing, Alan. I hope you don't think I set you up for that—"

"Nonsense. It would be my pleasure to give it to you." He brushed his lips against hers and squeezed her hand. "I'll have my secretary telephone Mr. Franklin in the morning and make the arrangements. If you can extend your visit here, we'll go to the opening Friday night."

Before she could reply, a man's voice behind them said, "Excuse me, Mr. Peabody. May I serve supper to you and Miss Crane in the dining room?"

Alan stood and held out his hand to Lizzie. "Thank you, Norman," he said. "We'd be delighted."

* * *

Alan leaned against a pile of pillows on his four-poster bed and stretched out his long legs. Lizzie handed him the box that contained the ivory netsuke. He opened it and gently lifted the miniature erotic sculpture from its nest of paper.

"Where did you find this little beauty?" he asked, holding it in the light of the electric lamp on the nightstand so he could see it more clearly.

"At the antiquarian shop where I purchased my Quan Yin statue. It's more than a hundred years old."

Alan chuckled. "I can only imagine what the proprietor thought when he wrapped this up."

"I admit, it was a bit embarrassing. But I get the impression he's seen quite a lot in his time."

Tracing the netsuke's delicate features with his fingertip, Alan asked, "Is this an invitation?"

"Ab-so-lute-ly." Lizzie sat on the bed beside him, letting her Chinese silk robe fall open to expose her leg from ankle to mid-thigh.

He untied the robe's sash. "Remind me to show you my collection of Persian miniatures."

Chapter Seventeen

"It is the greatest shot of adrenaline to be doing what you have wanted to do so badly. You almost feel like you could fly without the plane." — Charles Lindbergh

Lizzie unpacked the suitcase that held her best frocks and hung them back in the walnut wardrobe in her temporary bedroom at Isaac Roman's home. She still didn't know how long she'd end up staying here, so she left most of her clothing stashed in her luggage, including the silky undergarments she'd purchased in hopes of pleasing Alan.

Opening her heart to him made her feel vulnerable. She had no idea what he did on the nights when they were apart—and she never asked—but she doubted he spent them alone. With his money, pedigree, and good looks, Alan ranked high on the list of Boston's most eligible bachelors. Rich, powerful men held all the high cards in life and in love. Lizzie's only currency was her erotic appeal, and at twenty-six, she couldn't count on that much longer.

She wished her friend Melody were here so they could talk about her feelings for this man whose affection both thrilled and frightened her. For more than two years, the women had worked and lived side-by-side as artists, coworkers, and friends. They'd even faced death together. Although they came from vastly different backgrounds, their mutual love of music erased the barriers that might otherwise have stood between them. Melody seemed more like a sister to Lizzie than any of her own blood kin. Of course, she realized she could telephone Mel, but she couldn't discuss anything private on the phone in Isaac Roman's parlor with housemaids listening to every word. And intimate things were what she most wanted to talk about now.

A knock on the bedroom door pulled her out of her thoughts. "Miss Crane, a policeman is here asking for you," a woman's voice said.

Lizzie opened the door to see Roman's housekeeper standing in the hallway. "Good morning, Mrs. Nutley. What's this about?"

"I have no idea, miss. Only that a Sergeant Richard Darcy with the Salem Police Department insists on talking to you. Would you come downstairs with me, please?"

Lizzie followed the housekeeper down the sweeping staircase to the mansion's first floor, questions spinning in her mind. *Has Darcy discovered that Sidney planned to meet Sebastian the night he was murdered? Has he talked with Sid already?*

"Does Mr. Roman know the sergeant is here?" she asked Mrs. Nutley. "I think I should talk to him first, considering I'm in his employ, and this is his home."

"Mr. Roman is out for the day," the housekeeper answered.

She led Lizzie into a small sitting room at the back of the mansion, furnished less lavishly than the formal parlor at the front of the house. It seemed like a cozy place where family members might play a board game or put a jigsaw puzzle together. But Lizzie had yet to meet any of Roman's family, nor had he talked about them. She hadn't even seen pictures of his relatives anywhere in the house.

The hatchet-faced policeman stood when Lizzie entered. He straightened the already straight creases in his uniform's dark blue trousers, squared his shoulders, and then speared her with his steely eyes, as if he were an entomologist pinning an insect in a specimen case.

"Thank you for agreeing to meet with me, Miss Crane," he said.

"Do I have a choice? If so, we can end this meeting right now and save us both some time and trouble."

"Your cooperation is preferred," he answered.

Lizzie sat in a chair as far from Darcy as possible. "Sergeant, without Mr. Roman's permission and the benefit of legal counsel, I have very little to say to you."

The policeman remained standing. "Mr. Roman has given his permission. I spoke with him before coming here. If you insist on legal representation, I'll insist you come to the station with your attorney to discuss this matter more formally. However, I'd hoped we could talk casually this morning, Miss Crane, in order to shed some light on this unfortunate situation."

Lizzie sat as still as she could. She folded her hands in her lap and kept her face blank. "What is it you want from me, Sergeant?"

"Any information you have that might help me solve this crime."

"I've told you all I know."

Darcy raised an eyebrow. "Really? I don't recall you telling me that you paid a visit to Joan Amory on Monday. May I remind you that Mrs. Amory is a person of interest in this case?"

"I wanted to offer my condolences to a grieving widow. It seemed the polite thing to do."

"Nor do I recall you telling me about your meeting with Thea Gallagher that same day at Salem Willows. Another person of interest in Mr. Amory's murder."

"That 'meeting,' as you call it, was completely accidental."

"And yesterday, you went to the Franklin Gallery in Boston—a business establishment for which Mr. Amory did occasional work—after I'd asked you to remain in Salem while we investigated this crime." Darcy held out his hands, palms up in a gesture of frustration and futility. "Miss Crane, it would appear you have *not* told me all you know. Not by a long shot."

* * *

How does that copper know so much about my activities lately? Lizzie wondered. *Did he put a tail on me?*

If it weren't for Sidney, she would have gone back to Manhattan already—or at least to Alan's home in Boston—regardless of Sergeant Darcy's orders.

But Sid's affair with Sebastian made her longtime friend and business partner a suspect in the artist's murder. She couldn't abandon him now.

Lizzie glanced at the clock on her nightstand: half past twelve. Roman had told her to meet him on the other side of the North River at 2:00. She still didn't know what sort of adventure her host had planned.

She walked down the hallway and knocked on the door of Sidney's bedchamber. When he didn't answer, she went downstairs to the ballroom, where she found him playing the piano. She didn't recognize the song and thought it might be one he'd composed himself. For the past year, he'd been writing an opera. So far, she'd only heard bits and pieces of it. After he finished playing, she waited for him to look up from the keyboard and notice her before approaching him.

"Bearcat, you're back. How was your stay in Boston?"

"Everything a girl could ask for and then some."

Although Sidney liked Alan and believed he really cared for Lizzie, he still didn't trust Alan's long-term intentions toward her. Beautiful and talented as she may be, Lizzie was a showgirl, a high-school dropout, and the daughter of poor Irish immigrants. Alan Peabody came from one of Boston's most prestigious families and could have any woman he wanted. The fact that at thirty-four he'd never married suggested he enjoyed his freedom. And yet, stranger matches had happened. So in between fearing that Alan would break Lizzie's heart, Sid worried she might marry him, quit the band, and leave The Troubadours in the lurch. Melody's June wedding and her imminent departure only increased his apprehension.

Lizzie leaned against the Steinway grand, her body fitting smoothly into the piano's curve. "Say, did that cop Darcy talk to you today? He just finished reminding me he's the boss in this murder investigation. Actually, it was kinda creepy. He knows where I've gone and who I've talked to these past few days, although I can't imagine how unless he's got some elf following me around day and night. I'm just curious if he found out about, you know, the letter..."

Sidney shook his head and lit a cigarette. "I've managed to avoid our man in blue so far today, quite by accident. I walked into town to see if I could find a copy of *The New York Times* and just missed him. What did he ask you?"

"Mostly he berated me for not keeping a log of my comings and goings, and not reporting to him at every turn. I'm not talking to him again without a lawyer present."

"Good idea." His fingers meandered along the keyboard, picking out a refrain or a chorus here and there. "What's this big deal our illustrious host has in store for us this afternoon?"

"Haven't the foggiest, but I intend to find out. I love surprises, well, happy ones anyway." She let the insinuation sink in before asking, "Are you coming with me?"

"Wouldn't miss it."

"What about Bert?"

"He borrowed a bicycle this morning from one of the lads here and rode off after breakfast. I didn't get a chance to remind him about this afternoon's event." Sidney tapped his temple. "Bert doesn't seem to have his head on straight these days."

"I guess that depends on which head you're referring to." Lizzie rapped her knuckles on the piano's side. "Let's meet at the breezer in an hour and drive over to the site-ski."

"All right-ski."

"And if you run into Bert in the meantime, try to rein him in. I don't think he'll want to miss this event, whatever it is."

* * *

A crowd of perhaps fifty people had already amassed on the stretch of open land between North and Flint Streets, just beyond the river. Among them, Lizzie spotted Thea Gallagher, her long hair blowing like a banner in the wind, and Joan Amory, dressed in her widow's weeds, standing at opposite ends of the field. She noticed Cora Delaney and Karl Blume, too, and waved to them. On this relatively warm, sunny afternoon, the gathering had taken on a festive air as friends and neighbors eagerly awaited Isaac Roman's surprise.

"C'mon," Lizzie said, hooking her arm around Sidney's and pulling him toward Cora and Blume.

She found Sid's afternoon "sporting" attire—tan woolen knickers, an argyle sweater vest, tweed jacket, and cap—amusing, considering he'd probably never swung a golf club or baseball bat in his life. As they navigated their way across the broad strip of ground, still muddy from yesterday's rain, Lizzie heard a rumbling overhead, faint at first, then louder. She looked up as an airplane burst out of the clouds.

The aircraft circled above the field like a mechanical dragonfly. The pilot dipped its wings in greeting while spectators whooped and waved. Parents lifted children onto their shoulders. People held their hands above their eyes, shielding them from the sun as they cast their sights skyward. Suddenly, the biplane angled sharply to one side. The crowd gasped. Just when it seemed the craft would plummet into the North River, it righted itself. Then it somersaulted 360 degrees. A cheer rose from those on the ground as the pilot looped around the field again.

"It's Daredevil Lindbergh!" a man standing near Lizzie shouted.

Now the plane dove sharply toward the ground. It swooped so low, so fast, it seemed it would surely rip out its belly when it hit the dirt or crash in a fury of flames. But at the last moment, the pilot throttled his craft away from danger and soared up into the sky. Again, the crowd erupted in cheers. After another showy side roll, the pilot eased back the plane's engine and coasted to Earth.

A tall, handsome young man stepped down from the plane. He pushed his thick goggles up to the top of his leather-helmeted head and waved.

Spectators rushed him, hollering, "Lindy! Lindy!"

"Is that really Charles Lindbergh?" Sidney asked.

"Sure looks like him," Lizzie answered. "I've heard he does barn-storming events to make extra money. His job delivering mail for the post office probably doesn't pay much."

From the north side of the open stretch of land, away from the cluster of jubilant fans, a formidable figure with shoulder-length white hair emerged from his custom-made Isotta-Fraschini. He strolled toward the grinning aviator, careful not to splash mud on his white linen trousers, and extended his hand.

"Welcome to Salem, Mr. Lindbergh," Isaac Roman said as he shook hands with the pilot. "That was some pretty fancy flying you did there,"

The crowd applauded enthusiastically.

"For those of you who aren't familiar with Mr. Charles Lindbergh's illustrious career," Roman called to them, "you're standing in the presence of a great man, an avatar, whom I wager will transform our relationship with the skies and the field of aviation forever. Today, you'll witness even more of his skills in the art of flying. With his talent, courage, and vision, Mr. Lindbergh is about to take the world by storm. I have no doubt that due to his influence, humanity will be freed from the chains of earth, and one day soon, we'll soar like eagles into the heavens."

Again, Roman shook hands with the smiling aviator. Again, the gathering of gawkers shouted and whistled. Flashbulbs flared as newspaper photographers snapped their pictures. Lindbergh thanked Roman and tried to respond to the avalanche of questions directed at him. But after a couple minutes, Roman interrupted.

"Mr. Lindbergh has graciously agreed to give six people rides in his airplane. As his host, I'll decide which of you lucky folks will get to enjoy a tour of the skies today." He cast his gaze about until he spotted Lizzie in the crowd. "Miss Crane, are you ready to fly like a bird?"

"Ab-so-lute-ly," she said.

As she made her way toward the pilot and his biplane, envious onlookers parted to let her pass. Her whole body rippled with excitement. Her stomach was already doing flip-flops, even though she hadn't yet left the ground. Up close the aircraft looked like a wooden toy, so small and fragile it seemed impossible that it could soar a thousand feet in the air and travel hundreds of miles through all sorts of weather. Lindbergh, she knew, had already survived a few crashes, earning him the moniker "Lucky Lindy."

A newspaper reporter Lizzie recognized from her last visit to Salem aimed his camera at her. He took several more pictures of her with Roman and

Lindbergh, standing beside the plane as the aviator slid goggles over her eyes and put a protective helmet on her head.

"Wave, Miss Crane," the reporter called over the noise of the engine. "Smile for the camera."

Lindbergh took Lizzie's arm and helped her onto the plane's lower wing. As she swung her leg into the cockpit, a gust of wind blew her skirt up around her hips. Laughter and several catcalls rippled through the crowd of spectators. *Damn it,* Lizzie thought, *I bet that photographer got it all on film. My bloomers will be on the front page of tomorrow's paper. No wonder Amelia Earhart wears trousers.*

Lindberg buckled her into the passenger seat. With a broad grin, he waved to his fans, then climbed into his seat and revved the plane.

"Don't be afraid, Miss Crane," he said.

"I'm not."

"Good, because you're not just a passenger, you're going to be a pilot today. After we're airborne, I'm going to hand over control to you, while I climb out on the wing."

"You mean I'm going to fly this plane?"

"Unless you don't want to."

"Oh, I do. I do!" she insisted enthusiastically.

"Okay, you're on."

He waved to the onlookers, then rolled down the grassy runway and lifted off. Wind whipped around her. The engine's rumble made her entire body buzz. As the airplane climbed into the bright blue afternoon sky and the city beneath her grew smaller and smaller, Lizzie felt her worries fall away. From this perspective, her earthly concerns seemed distant and insignificant. For several minutes they circled the three-hundred-year-old city whose men once sailed the seven seas, but never dreamed of conquering the skies.

After the third circle, Lindberg descended to an elevation he considered satisfactory for his stunt. He tapped her on the arm. He leaned close, only a few inches from her ear, and said, "Take the yoke. All you have to do is hold it steady. Don't touch anything else."

Lizzie nodded, and the famous aviator unsnapped his seatbelt. Inch by inch, he crawled out onto the airplane's lower wing. When he'd judged the air currents and the plane's trajectory acceptable, he planted his feet, stood, and gave Lizzie a thumbs-up. A wide grin split his handsome face. He threw back his head and let out a howl that was somewhere between a battle cry and a shriek of pure delight.

Lizzie laughed and gripped the yoke tighter. Never before had she felt such a sense of freedom. *What would happen if I just kept going? Past Salem, past Boston, as far as this tank of gas can take us?*

Lindbergh waved his arms overhead, daring fate. Other than the tenuous contact between the soles of his shoes and the plane's wing, he stood untethered a hundred feet in the air, completely at the mercy of the elements, and the woman at the wheel who hadn't come within a mile of a plane before today. One flick of her wrist would send him tumbling to his death.

Amid the shouts and whistles from the fans below, Lindbergh knelt and crawled back along the wing to the cockpit. He eased himself into his seat and patted Lizzie on the shoulder.

"Well done," he said as they flew a final loop above the city. "If you ever think you might want to become a pilot, let me know."

"I will. Thank you, Mr. Lindbergh. This was one of the most thrilling things I've ever done."

They landed and bumped to a stop. Roman helped her down from the plane to a hearty round of applause. Tingling with excitement, Lizzie hurried through the crowd toward Sidney.

"That's nothing," one of the spectators said as she passed him. "Last year, I saw Ivan Unger and Gladys Roy play a game of tennis atop the wings of their biplane."

Sid hugged her like a long-lost sister he thought he'd never see again. "Bearcat, I was so worried about you. You could've been killed."

"But wasn't I the bee's knees?"

"Except when you showed your bloomers to the whole town."

"Don't remind me."

He studied her face, still flushed from the wind and exhilaration. "Weren't you scared?"

"Not a bit. It was exciting. A million times better than the roller coaster at Coney Island."

Shouts burst anew from the crowd as a middle-aged man wearing a minister's collar climbed into the airplane. Lindbergh rolled down the makeshift runway and lifted off. When they reached the desired elevation, the aviator again handed over control of the biplane to his passenger and left the cockpit. This time, he hung from a harness fastened to the axle between the plane's wheels, swinging back and forth as if he were on a playground.

Lindbergh ferried three more passengers into the sky, including the woman who'd won first prize in Roman's spring equinox egg hunt and a boy still in short pants. By now, the field was crowded with spectators who'd come to watch the wing walker's display of bravado. When it came time to choose the last person to soar above Salem, Roman pointed to Thea Gallagher.

The young woman tossed her head and strode toward the aircraft. When Roman tried to help her into the cockpit, she shook him off and climbed up by herself. Lindbergh maneuvered the plane into a series of somersaults, circled the area one last time, then landed with a series of bumps. The crowd whooped, whistled, cheered, and applauded as if they'd never seen anything finer. Most of them probably never had.

Thea Gallagher slid down from the plane and almost fell. Lizzie thought she looked a bit bilious. But she pulled off the leather helmet, shook out her beautiful hair, and waved both arms overhead. Her glory lasted only a moment before a man about Roman's age, dressed in a dark brown suit and a fedora, rushed toward the plane and roughly grabbed her arm. He yanked the helmet from her hand and tossed it at Lindbergh. In the man's grip, Thea suddenly grew submissive, like a wind-up toy that had run down. Without so much as a shrug, she allowed him to rudely escort her from the scene.

Is that her father? Lizzie wondered as the man pushed Thea into a parked automobile.

Sidney interrupted her thoughts. "Had enough fun for one day, Bearcat? We need to practice before we perform tonight. This is the first time we've played without Melody."

"You're right," she agreed, taking his arm. For the umpteenth time, Lizzie wondered, *How am I going to get along without her?*

* * *

Still buzzing with the excitement of flying a plane with Charles Lindbergh, Lizzie took longer than she should have to notice the hangdog expression on Bert's face when he showed up in Roman's ballroom for practice. Even under the most favorable circumstances, the awkward young saxophonist was shy, reticent, and self-effacing. Only when playing his horn did he appear confident enough to express himself—and when he did, he radiated such exuberance he swept listeners off their feet. Now, he stood at the back of the stage, hugging his sax like a child holding a beloved toy that he feared would be taken away from him if he eased his grip.

Lizzie stepped closer to him. "Bert, is something wrong?"

He shifted his weight from one foot to the other several times before answering, "My girl dumped me."

"Oh, Bert, I'm so sorry." Lizzie laid a hand on his arm. "Why? What happened?"

"She said she needs a relationship that's more stable than what a musician can offer. Someone who's home at night, on weekends and holidays and all that." He cracked the knuckles on one hand as he spoke. "Me living in New York and her being here doesn't help either."

Bert's girlfriend's concerns echoed those Lizzie struggled with in her relationship with Alan. How long would he put up with her independent, bohemian lifestyle? Her home in New York's Greenwich Village? Her extended out-of-town absences when The Troubadours performed for society's elite? Bookings that interfered with the holidays, vacations, and family gatherings that were part of his clan's social schedule?

"I know how hard it is."

"She's been seeing another guy all this time I've been courting her," Bert said, his anger at her betrayal starting to surface. "Fella that works at the Mills. Has a steady job, a family here in town." He shook his head sadly. "I can't compete with that."

Lizzie tousled his unruly brown hair, thinking that although he was only four years her junior, he seemed so much younger. "If you don't feel like playing, it's okay to skip tonight."

"Not a chance. Music's the only thing that makes all the rest of it bearable."

She recalled the words of Albert Schweitzer, who said, "There are two means of refuge from the misery of life: music and cats." Although she didn't have a cat, she agreed with the noted philosopher-scientist and Bert. Music not only soothed the savage beast, it eased the pain of everyday existence and gave meaning to her life.

"We musicians are an odd lot, Bert. All artists are. Our lives aren't stable and secure. We're not governed by the rules that guide other folks. We can't promise the people we love that we'll always be there, or that we'll fit into their expectations, their rituals and routines, even if we may want to. What's that saying, we march to a different drummer?"

"What are my odds of finding a girl who'll take me as I am?"

"I'm no statistician," Lizzie said, trying to sound optimistic, "but it seems that Melody has found a husband she's happy with and who's goofy about her."

Bert snorted. "Yeah, and she gave up her music for him."

Lizzie recalled Hans Christian Andersen's fairy tale "The Little Mermaid" that her mother had read to her when she was a child. In it, the mermaid sacrifices her beautiful voice and her ocean home in order to win the love of a human prince, who ultimately ends up leaving her for someone else. In hindsight, it seemed like an awful story to tell a young girl.

"What about you and Alan?" Bert asked. "Would you stop singing to marry him?"

She'd asked herself the same question many times. "I doubt I'll ever have to make that decision."

Chapter Eighteen

"Art is not what you see, but what you make others see." — *Edgar Degas*

Lizzie wrote a note to Roman, thanking him for giving her the chance to fly with Charles Lindbergh this afternoon. On her way to slip it under his office door, she spotted a painting of a handsome young man holding a gray glove, hanging on the wall near the staircase that led down to the mansion's foyer. For some reason, she hadn't noticed it before. Now it captivated her.

Moving closer, she studied the portrait, which had an Old-World air about it. Against a stark black background, the man's face glowed with appealing warmth. Yet his wistful expression, his eyes focused on something or someone off in the distance, made her feel as if she were observing a private moment of longing and loss. *Why does he seem so familiar?* she wondered. As she turned away to deliver her letter, the answer came to her. *He looks like Sidney did when I first met him eight years ago.*

The sound of a door opening jarred her out of her contemplation. Twenty feet away, Isaac Roman emerged from his office next to the private gallery that housed his precious art collection. The gallery hid behind a heavy double-locked door. Iron bars covered its windows. Metal plates positioned under its floorboards and in its ceiling deterred thieves. Inside, it held dozens of valuable paintings including a Vermeer and a Rembrandt, treasures from the Orient, plus Renaissance sculptures and even an ancient Greek statue of the winged goddess Nike.

"Oh, hello, Mr. Roman. I was just on my way to bring a letter to you. A thank-you note, really, for today."

He stepped toward her and held out his hand to accept the letter. "I take it you enjoyed the event."

"Enjoyed it? I still feel like I'm flying! It's the most exciting thing I've ever done. And I'm ever so grateful to you for the opportunity."

"Miss Crane, you are most welcome. It was quite a treat for me, too."

"Why didn't you go up in the airplane with Mr. Lindbergh?"

He leaned closer to her and whispered, even though no one else was in the hallway, "Can you keep a secret?"

Lizzie ran her fingers along her lips, as if zipping them.

"I'm scared of heights." He turned his attention to the painting she'd been staring at. "You appear interested in this picture. Are you familiar with it?"

She shook her head. "No, but it looks like it might have been done during the Renaissance."

"Good guess. It's a copy of Titian's 'Man with a Glove,' painted in 1520."

"A copy. That's why it's hanging out here, rather than in your vault."

"Right. The real one's in the Louvre." Roman tapped the picture's ornate gilt frame. "Can you guess who painted it?"

"Sebastian Amory?"

"Right again. It's quite a good facsimile. I'll show you a photograph of the original in one of my art books, if you like, so you can compare the two." He motioned her toward his office.

Unlike the other rooms in his home, which could have graced the pages of *Architectural Digest* magazine, Roman's office resembled a professor's study. Manila folders, binders, lined tablets, and piles of paperwork covered most of the top of a heavy oak desk of Jacobean design. A bookcase jam-packed with books stretched along one wall. More books were stacked on a refectory table and lay on the floor beside a leather armchair.

Roman crossed the cluttered room and plucked a book from a shelf. He flipped through it until he found what he was looking for, then offered the book to Lizzie. "Here," he said, pointing to a photo of Titian's masterpiece.

"What do you think?"

"The resemblance is amazing," she said. "But the man's face…may I take this out into the hallway?"

"Of course."

Standing in front of Sebastian Amory's copy, she studied the two images. Everything—the man's knuckles, the ring on his index finger, his lace collar and cuffs—was identical. Except his face. The handsome young man in Titian's original didn't look like Sidney, yet the one in Sebastian's version was a perfect likeness.

Lizzie handed the book back to Roman. "You're a collector. When you're paying a bundle for a piece of artwork, you must know how to determine if the painting is authentic."

"I like to think so, but even knowledgeable collectors get hoodwinked sometimes."

"What do you look for?"

"Ah, Miss Crane. This discussion should be carried on in a more comfortable setting than this hallway. May I interest you in a glass of sherry in the parlor downstairs?"

"Ab-so-lute-ly."

Roman crooked his arm. She slid hers through his, and together they descended the sweeping stairway to the mansion's entrance hall. He called for his butler, told him what to serve, then guided Lizzie into the beautifully appointed room that epitomized Federal Period elegance. After seating her on a sofa upholstered in sea-green silk, he settled into an armchair and crossed his long legs. Lizzie noticed the trousers of his white linen suit had escaped without a trace of mud from the damp, makeshift airfield.

The butler brought the bottle of sherry and two crystal goblets on a silver tray. After showing the label to his employer, he served Lizzie first, then Roman.

"Leave the bottle, please," Roman told him. "Is there anything else you'd like at the moment, Miss Crane?"

"No thanks. Everything's quite copacetic."

As she'd expected, the sherry was exceptionally good. *How delightful it would be to drink such wine whenever you pleased, even if it's not a special occasion.* But then she reminded herself *this is a special occasion. I just flew in an airplane with Daredevil Lindbergh!*

"Will Mr. Lindbergh attend our performance tonight?" Lizzie asked.

"No, unfortunately," Roman said. "He's on his way back to Chicago. The postal system needs him."

"I'm awfully lucky to have met him. I'll remember this day for the rest of my life."

The white Persian cat, Zanzibar, that Lizzie had seen in the solarium two days ago slipped silently into the parlor. He glided under Roman's chair, then jumped up onto its back and perched there, swishing his plume of a tail while observing Lizzie with golden eyes. Roman reached up and stroked the cat's silky fur.

"I'm glad you had a good time," he said.

Lizzie took another sip of her sherry before returning to the subject of art. "If a painting is already hanging in a museum, like Titian's 'Man with a Glove,' wouldn't an educated collector know that and realize a reproduction was a fake?"

"Maybe," Roman said. "Usually, though, forgers don't duplicate actual paintings, for that very reason. Instead, they create a piece a famous artist *might* have done and pass it off as a newly discovered work of art. Even the great Michelangelo pulled that trick. He carved a marble sculpture called 'Sleeping Eros,' beat it up to make it look old, then buried it on his dealer's property. The two partners-in-crime just *happened* to dig it up one day and claimed it dated back to ancient Rome."

"Which made it more valuable."

"Yes. It's a lucrative game if you can get away with it."

Lizzie considered the rumors she'd heard about Roman trafficking in stolen art—rumors he did nothing to discourage. She remembered what Alan had told her about the Van Gogh painting Roman helped him acquire. "I have only the paperwork Roman provided—and his word—that the transaction was legit." Did her host also broker forgeries?

"To answer your question about what collectors look for when buying a period painting," Roman continued, "we first assess the materials—the canvas, paper, or panel it's painted on, the content of the pigment—to make sure they're what would have been used at the time. Next, we examine the artist's technique. Every painter's brushstrokes are unique—smooth, choppy, flowing, assertive. Like handwriting. It's especially difficult for a right-handed artist to imitate the brushstrokes of a left-handed one, and vice versa."

Holding the image of the "Man with a Glove" in her mind, Lizzie asked, "A copyist, like Sebastian, has to replicate this, right?"

"Not necessarily. A copyist only has to produce a picture that closely resembles the original. But a forger…now that's a different story altogether. Have you ever heard of an Italian painter named Federico Joni?"

Lizzie shook her head.

"He specializes in recreating Renaissance Italian art. His 'Old Masters' have fooled some of the top collectors as well as the critics, including the noted art historian Bernard Berenson and the American collector Philip Lehman. Although to be fair, I can't say whether Joni intended to pass off his paintings as authentic *Quattrocento* originals or if he has simply embraced the period so fully that even the best authorities can't tell the difference."

"How does he do it?"

Roman refilled Lizzie's glass and his own. "I visited Joni in his studio not long ago, and he explained the process. He blends a little extra glue into his pigments, then bakes the painting in an oven to dry out the paint and make it crack in a way that looks realistic. Next, he carefully distresses the piece, as would happen naturally over time. By the way, I own one of his pictures—remind me to show it to you."

"He's still alive?"

"As far as I know. Unlike our friend Sebastian." Roman tapped his fingers on the arm of his chair. "I've often wondered if Sebastian knew the technique Joni used. He could've read about it in a book titled *The Craftsman's Handbook* that the fifteenth-century painter Cennino Cennini wrote, originally titled *Il Libro dell'Arte*."

Lizzie wondered, too, remembering the oven she'd seen at Sebastian's studio in Salem's Pequot Mills. She considered telling Roman that Sebastian had tried to sell a fake El Greco to the elderly proprietor of the antiquities shop, but decided to keep that information to herself. At least for now. Roman knew the shopkeeper, she realized, so perhaps he'd already heard the story anyway.

Roman uncrossed his legs and stood up. "Well, Miss Crane, I'm afraid I must excuse myself. I have a number of things to tend to before tonight's party. If there's anything else you'd like, please ask my butler or one of the housemaids to bring it to you."

"Thank you for the sherry," Lizzie said, raising her glass to salute her host. "And thank you again for a wonderful afternoon, Mr. Roman."

Chapter Nineteen

"Truth is always present; it only needs to lift the iron lids of the mind's eye to read its oracles." — *Ralph Waldo Emerson*

*T*his is *our last performance here,* Lizzie thought as she cast her gaze around Isaac Roman's garish ballroom, *and our first performance without Melody.* On this Wednesday night only about forty people milled about, chatting, dipping glasses into the champagne fountain, and eyeing themselves in the gilt-framed mirrors that hung on every wall.

Among the partygoers, she noticed Joan Amory, dressed in a floor-length black gown with long sleeves and a high neck, befitting her status as a new widow. But the flashy jeweled comb in her blond hair reminded Lizzie of a flamenco dancer's. She couldn't help wondering why a woman in mourning would show up at one of Roman's notoriously raucous parties, or why Joan had appeared this afternoon at Charles Lindbergh's exhibition. Especially considering the angry conversation between her and Roman that Lizzie had overheard, in which Sebastian's widow blamed the art collector for her husband's death. *Perhaps she's lonely and seeks a distraction,* she decided. Still, Joan's presence here tonight seemed, well, indiscreet in light of her husband's recent and violent death on the premises. Of course, Lizzie reminded herself, Sebastian Amory's behavior blatantly mocked the sanctity of marriage, so why should his scorned wife be held to a higher standard?

Sergeant Richard Darcy prowled around the ballroom's fringes, like a cat stalking its prey. Roman's guests paid little attention to him. By now, she supposed, they'd gotten used to seeing the badly dressed cop with his chiseled face and rigid demeanor nosing around and simply took him in stride.

Sidney launched into an upbeat rendition of George Gershwin's "Somebody Loves Me" while Lizzie tap-danced on the stage. Ordinarily, she and Melody did this routine together; she felt odd doing it alone. When the song ended, Sid eased into "Tea for Two" without waiting for the applause to end. Sticking to popular show tunes, keeping the mood light, he focused on the keyboard instead of interacting with the audience as he generally did. More than usual, he deferred to Bert, letting the young horn player take the lead. No one else would have noticed, but Lizzie heard each unspoken word in the notes Sidney played. The sadness behind the fun, the shadows that hid the light.

Sebastian's funeral was tomorrow. The police had finally completed their forensics and released the body. While The Troubadours sang and danced and entertained Isaac Roman's guests, gravediggers shoveled dirt from the hole where the slain artist's body would lie for eternity.

After an hour, Sidney pushed away from the piano and told the audience, "We're going to take a short break, but we'll be back soon with more great music, so stick around."

He headed toward the French doors that opened onto the porch overlooking Roman's backyard. But before he could step outside for a smoke, Joan Amory approached him and grabbed his arm. Curious, Lizzie hurried toward them.

"You planned to meet my husband that night, didn't you?" Joan hissed at Sid.

"I don't know what you're talking about," Sidney said.

Joan held up a small, black box. "This."

"What's up?" Lizzie interceded, trying to appear casual as she slid her arm around Sid's waist. From the corner of her eye, she saw Sergeant Darcy edging toward them.

Joan opened the box, revealing a gold lapel pin in the shape of a treble clef. She withdrew a piece of paper from the box, unfolded it, and read aloud, "From S to S."

Lizzie felt Sidney tense, although he shook his head and said, "Means nothing to me."

"Well, how about this?" Joan pulled another slip of paper from the box and held it up, so they could all see it was a receipt from the Daniel Low jewelry store. "A sales slip, dated Thursday, March 18. The day before Sebastian was murdered."

Sergeant Darcy stepped forward and held out his hand. "I'll take that, Mrs. Amory. Evidence, you know."

Joan snapped the lid shut and closed her fingers around the box, clutching it to her chest.

"Are you insinuating that your husband intended to meet with Mr. Somerset on the night of the murder?" Lizzie asked.

"Intended to and *did*," Joan spat back.

"But your husband rode off on a horse with Thea Gallagher," Lizzie pointed out. "At least seventy-five people witnessed it. She was the last person to be seen with him." She looked at Darcy for verification, but his stony expression conveyed nothing. "Besides, we performed here in this very ballroom until after one o'clock that night."

Lizzie spotted her host, Isaac Roman, weaving through the crowd toward them. Beside her, Sidney stiffened. She gave him a quick squeeze and tried to send him a telepathic message, *Don't say a word.* If he opened his mouth, she planned to pinch him, hard.

"After Sebastian left her, he could easily have come back here for a tryst. One that led to his death," Joan said bitterly as she turned to Darcy. "We don't know exactly what time my husband was murdered, do we, Sergeant?"

Sidney started to say something, but Roman spoke first. "Joan, this isn't the place to discuss this. You're upset, understandably. Why don't you let me have someone drive you home?"

"Are you tossing me out?"

As Roman reached to take her arm, Joan pulled away and threw the jeweler's box at Sidney. It bounced off his shoulder and fell to the floor.

Lizzie grabbed the box before Darcy could and shook her head. "Not without a warrant, Sergeant."

"Miss Crane, if you think you and your colleague can outwit me, you are mistaken."

* * *

Trying to keep her rising anger from creeping into her voice, Lizzie held out the black jeweler's box and asked, "Do you know about this, Sid?"

She'd begun to question how much she really knew about the man who'd been her friend and business partner all these years. Was this yet another secret he'd kept from her? How much danger had his secrets already put her in? She felt as if she were wandering through a dense forest, where the trees' leafy branches obscured the sun's light and cast shifting shadows across her path.

Standing on Roman's back porch, Sidney exhaled a lungful of smoke into the chilly night air and shook his head. "No. I didn't meet with him either. I bet Joan Amory bought that pin herself to frame me."

"But why you instead of Thea Gallagher?"

"Maybe she has other plans for getting revenge on Thea. My guess is she wants to punish us all for Sebastian's infidelity." He flicked ashes into the backyard. "My money's still on that black widow as his killer."

A door opened behind them, and Bert stepped out onto the porch. "What's going on?" he asked. "Are you all right, Sid?"

"Poor Bert, I'm sorry we've kept you in the dark. I didn't want to worry you and drag you into this mess," Lizzie said. She patted his head affectionately, as if he were a little boy, and tried to tuck his cowlick into place. "There's so much to tell. I don't know where to begin."

Sidney took a last drag from his cigarette and crushed the butt under his shoe. "Let's all meet in my bedroom after the show. It's time we filled you in, Bert."

* * *

As the three musicians took their positions onstage again, a middle-aged man with a bulbous nose, big ears, and hard lines etched into his ruddy skin strode toward them. He had the muscular body of a boxer, and although well-dressed, he looked more like a gangster than an executive with one of Salem's biggest companies. Try as she might, Lizzie couldn't imagine him seated in Pequot Mills' boardroom discussing the price of bed linens.

"What's your interest in my daughter?" he asked Lizzie. It was a demand, not a question.

She'd recognized him immediately, but didn't want to give him the satisfaction of knowing that. "Excuse me, but who are you? Who's your daughter?"

"Paul Gallagher. You've been hanging around my girl, Thea. I want to know why."

"Oh, yes," she said, trying not to let his rudeness rattle her. "Your daughter and I got to fly in Mr. Charles Lindbergh's plane this afternoon. Were you there? It was quite a spectacular event."

Paul Gallagher's belligerent attitude suggested he knew there was more to Lizzie's acquaintance with his daughter than enjoying Lindbergh's aerial stunts. However, Lizzie had no intention of adding fuel to his ire and chose not to mention her visit to Sebastian Amory's studio at the Mills where Gallagher worked—maybe he didn't even know about it. Nor did she bring up her encounter with Thea at the Salem Willows amusement park. Or his naked daughter's equestrian romp through Isaac Roman's ballroom the night of Amory's murder.

"Unless you want that pretty nose of yours rearranged on your face, keep it out of my family's affairs," Gallagher warned, jabbing his finger at her.

Lizzie remembered Thea's swollen eye, the bruise on her cheek, and the way the man had roughly dragged his daughter away from Lindbergh's demonstration. What was it Roman said? *I wouldn't put anything past Paul Gallagher.*

"It sounds like you're threatening me."

"Damn right, I am."

Lizzie motioned to the intrepid cop, who stood unobtrusively at the back of the ballroom, watching them. "Let me acquaint you with Sergeant Richard

Darcy of the Salem Police Department. You men may have some things to discuss."

As Darcy approached Gallagher, Lizzie smiled at the detective, for once glad of the policeman's presence. "Sergeant Darcy, may I introduce Mr. Paul Gallagher? He's a big wig at the Pequot Mills, and he's also Thea Gallagher's father. He just threatened to punch me in the nose. Perhaps you could remind him that's no way to treat a lady and that physical assault is a crime."

"I'm acquainted with Mr. Gallagher," Darcy said, his tone as sharp as his features, and Lizzie wondered if Gallagher might have had a run-in with the cops in the past.

Gallagher glared at Lizzie, his big hands clenched in fists at his side. "Brazen hussy," he growled, then turned and made his way toward the champagne fountain.

"Thank you, Sergeant," Lizzie said. "Do you know he beats his daughter? She told me he hit her because she refused to stop seeing Sebastian Amory."

"Do you want to make a complaint against him, Miss Crane? You'll have to come down to the station and fill out some paperwork."

"No, I just wanted to let Gallagher know he's out of line and that you're aware of his intimidation tactics. I assume you've got him in your sights as Sebastian's possible killer—he's high up on my list of suspects."

"I can't reveal that information, but I can assure you that the Salem Police Department is investigating this case thoroughly and that all persons of interest are under our careful watch."

"That's good to know. Thank you again, Sergeant, for your vigilance," Lizzie said. "And now, if you'll excuse me, I have a show to do. I hope you'll enjoy the rest of it."

Lizzie took her place on the ballroom's stage. She signaled Bert to start playing while she took several slow, deep breaths, willing herself to remain calm. Sidney raised his eyebrows, questioning the exchange between Lizzie, Gallagher, and Darcy, as he joined in on the piano behind Bert's sax. She let her friends run through a stanza twice, giving herself time to regain her poise before launching into "Everybody Loves My Baby." Although she tried to focus on the music, she couldn't help wondering what Sergeant Darcy knew about Thea's father and whether Paul Gallagher would make good on his threat.

Darcy resumed his observation post, stoically watching everyone and everything. Gallagher stuck around for two more songs, then exited through the French doors at the rear of the ballroom. Roman's guests continued to dance, drink, laugh, banter, and flirt as if nothing out of the ordinary had transpired. At the end of the hour, The Troubadours took another break.

Sidney touched Lizzie's hand, concern shadowing his face. Bert, too, seemed apprehensive; his crooked smile looked like a grimace. As they strolled across the ballroom together and out onto the back porch so Sid could smoke a cigarette, Lizzie said, "Enemies are crawling out of the woodwork, like cockroaches."

"I've got big feet. Maybe I can squish them," Bert said, stamping the floor of the porch in an attempt to lighten the mood.

"I wish it were that simple," she said.

"It's a good thing we're leaving tomorrow," Sidney said. "I'll be glad to put this grummy scene behind us."

"What about Darcy?" she asked.

"He hasn't charged us with anything. He can't hold us here on speculation."

"True."

Sid flicked his silver lighter and held the flame to the tip of his cigarette. "I've already settled up with Roman. We can head for home right after Sebastian's funeral."

"I'm planning to spend the weekend in Boston with Alan," Lizzie reminded him. "We're going to an art opening at Hugh Franklin's gallery Friday night. I'll take the train back to New York next week."

Sidney tapped his temple. "Oh, that's right. Gotta collect your painting. Odd duck, that Hopper chap."

"A swell painter, though."

"Bert, pack your bags, and we'll load them in the breezer in the morning. You too, Lizzie, whatever you want me to take back to the City for you. I plan to make a quick getaway tomorrow, before Darcy or anyone else can throw up any obstacles."

∗ ∗ ∗

Over tumblers of smoky Highland scotch, Sidney told Bert about his relationship with Sebastian Amory, which had led Sergeant Darcy to suspect him as the artist's murderer.

"But why would you kill someone you loved?" Bert asked. "Especially if you were getting back together now?"

Although that question kept coming up again and again, Lizzie still couldn't answer it. Too often, people killed people they loved. Joan or Thea might be among them. When determining a killer's guilt, investigators and prosecutors assessed three factors: means, motive, and opportunity. However, Sid's possible motive for murdering a long-ago lover seemed unclear at best.

"It makes no sense at all," Sidney agreed. "His wife's the logical choice."

"The lady who threw the box at you?" Bert said.

"Right. She's the one with the strongest motive."

Not the only one, though, Lizzie thought. *There's that awful Paul Gallagher and the disgruntled Edward Oliver, who believes Sebastian stole his ideas. Thea, too, if she thought Sebastian was going to dump her for Sidney. Even that fella Timothy Whiting, whom Gallagher wanted his daughter to marry to keep her from fooling around with Sebastian.*

"Maybe that cop's using you to flush out the real killer," Bert suggested.

"Could be." Sidney took a cigarette from his engraved tin and lit it. "Well, he's done surveilling me. His jurisdiction ends at Salem's city line. Tomorrow, right after Sebastian's funeral, I'm leaving him in my dust."

"What time's the funeral?"

"Ten o'clock," Sid said. "Shouldn't last more than an hour. Then we're homeward bound. You okay with that, Bert?"

Bert nodded, and Lizzie noticed a shadow of sadness cross his face. "Yeah. I'm ready to get back to the City. There's nothing here for me anymore."

Lizzie had been quietly sipping her scotch, listening to her friends discuss the situation. Now she asked, "Do you think Sebastian had other enemies we don't know about?"

"It's possible. We'd been out of contact for eight years, until this past week." Sidney took a drag on his cigarette, then blew smoke rings at the ceiling. "I don't want to think about that now. I just want to go home."

Bert stood, cracked his knuckles, and stretched his arms overhead. "I'm gonna go pack up my stuff."

"Good man," Sid said. "Lizzie, would you stick around for a minute?"

She nodded, then rose and gave Bert a quick hug. "See you in the morning."

After their young colleague had gone off to pack his belongings, Lizzie asked, "What's up?"

"I never looked at the place where Sebastian died. I didn't think I could bear it. Would you come with me to see it now?"

"Of course."

The grandfather clock in the foyer struck half past one as they descended the gracefully curving staircase to the first floor of Isaac Roman's mansion. The low rumble of conversations, broken by the occasional spike of laughter, drifted from the ballroom where guests continued to mingle, but the disembodied sounds, unaccompanied by music, were distant and indistinct.

Lizzie and Sid passed through the empty kitchen and made their way down the back hallway into the solarium. Here and there, electric lights shone behind foliage, illuminating the space with a magical glow and casting feathery shadows on the walls and floor. At this time of night, the songbirds slept. The glassed-in garden rested in silence.

Lizzie grasped Sidney's arm and led him along a brick sidewalk to the tree where Sebastian Amory had been tied and shot full of arrows. Pointing, she said, "That's it."

For a minute or so, he stared at the tree as if waiting for it to reveal its secrets. Then he stepped toward it and began circling the tree slowly, but without touching it. He'd gone halfway around when Roman's pet cat, Zanzibar, dashed between his feet, almost tripping him. The cat poked his paw beneath a fern frond, swishing his fluffy white tail enthusiastically as he hunted real or imagined prey hidden there.

"What have you got, Zan?" Lizzie asked.

Intensely focused on his task, the cat batted at something underneath the fern. With the agility only cats can master, he flipped a small black disk about the size of his eye onto the walkway. Sidney knelt and reached for it.

"Don't touch it," Lizzie ordered.

She bent beside him to get a closer look at what Zanzibar had revealed. From Sidney's jacket pocket, she pulled a silk handkerchief and picked up the disk, then held it to the light. Engraved on its surface, she saw a six-pointed star. The white cat glared at her, annoyed that she'd stolen his catch.

"A button," she said. "Jet, maybe onyx."

"What do you make of it?"

"I don't know. Anyone could have dropped it here. A housemaid, a gardener. Maybe one of Roman's guests."

Sidney studied the button. "It's too fine for a housemaid's dress or a gardener's jacket. Do you think it might have come off Sebastian's clothing, or his killer's?"

"Possibly," Lizzie answered. "But it could've been lying here for ages."

"Do you think we should give it to Sergeant Darcy?"

"Probably." She folded the handkerchief around the button. "I wonder why Darcy didn't find it. He searched all around here."

"It was pretty well hidden in the grass," Sidney said.

"I guess you'd have to have a cat's superior vision to see it," Lizzie said. She reached out to pat Zan, but he scooted away in a huff after having been robbed of his treasure. "Do you want to stay here longer, Sid? It's late and I need to pack."

"No, I guess not. I've seen what I needed to see. It wasn't as hard as I'd expected. Thanks for coming with me, Lizzie."

She nodded and gave him a quick hug. "I'm going to hold on to this button for the time being, okay-ski?"

"Whatever you say-ski."

Chapter Twenty

"Yea, though I walk through the valley of the shadow of death, I will fear no evil." — Psalm 23: 4, King James Version

After loading their belongings into Sidney's Buick, the three friends drove several blocks to the Unitarian Church on Essex Street, where Sebastian's funeral would be held. To Lizzie, the Gothic-style structure built of gray granite looked more like a fortress than a house of worship.

For some reason, she couldn't fathom—unless the widow saw an opportunity for free professional entertainment—Joan Amory had asked Lizzie to sing "Amazing Grace" at the funeral. A cappella. Initially, she'd refused. The woman had tried to frame Sidney for her husband's murder, after all. But Sid had persuaded Lizzie to do it.

"I'd appreciate it if you'd help to give Sebastian a proper send-off. Who knows, maybe the angels will hear you singing and whisk him up to heaven."

"I didn't think you believed in heaven," she said.

He shrugged. "It's better than the alternative."

The minister, a short, slender man with a kind face and an unexpectedly loud voice, greeted the three musicians. They followed him down the carpeted center aisle toward the front of the church, where they took their seats in the fourth row of the sanctuary.

Slowly, two or three at a time, people began entering the church. They spoke in hushed voices, glancing around to see who else had opted to attend the funeral of a man who'd been murdered in such a macabre way. A man who'd cheated on his wife—a wife who belonged to this very church. A man who, according to gossip, once loved another man. Lizzie wondered if they'd come out of sympathy, respect for his widow, or, more likely, simple curiosity. Scandal always attracted gawkers.

At ten past ten, with half the church filled, the minister approached the podium to begin the service. Lizzie spotted Cora Delaney and Karl Blume among the mourners. Other than Isaac Roman and the elderly proprietor of the antiquarian shop, she didn't recognize anyone else. Except Sergeant Richard Darcy, who stood at the back of the sanctuary wearing his uniform rather than a black suit like the other men, studying the people gathered this morning for Sebastian Amory's final send-off. *In mystery novels, the killer usually shows up at the victim's funeral,* she recalled. *Does Darcy hope to catch his prey here?*

As she bowed her head in prayer, Lizzie couldn't help thinking that this was the third funeral she'd attended for a murder victim in seven months. All three victims had died during parties at which The Troubadours performed. She'd been the unfortunate person to discover each body. *What are the odds?* she asked herself. *Am I jinxed?*

Joan Amory, dressed in a simple black suit and hat with a veil, sat in the front pew beside an older couple, whom Lizzie guessed were relatives. The minister offered an inspirational message, and the choir sang a couple hymns. One of the widow's brothers gave a lackluster eulogy. Another brother and two friends shared a few reminiscences.

"Didn't Sebastian have any family?" Lizzie whispered to Sidney.

"Both his parents died of the Spanish flu. He and Joan didn't have children, but you already know that. His only sister married a Swiss banker after the war and moved to Geneva. I guess she thought it was too far to come for the funeral."

"No friends?"

Sidney glanced around the half-empty sanctuary. "Doesn't look like it. Not here in Salem, anyway. He wasn't a very sociable fella."

"What about Thea Gallagher? I'm surprised she's not here."

"Maybe she doesn't want everyone gossiping and gawking at her."

"I doubt that," Lizzie said, remembering the first time she saw Thea, riding naked on her horse through Roman's ballroom. "Thea's not a shrinking violet, nor does she seem to care what people think of her. Frankly, I expected her to show up with bells on and dare the good people of Salem to chastise her today."

Then, another thought rose in her mind. *Maybe Paul Gallagher wouldn't let his daughter attend her lover's funeral.*

Next, Cora took her place at the podium. Against her stylish, two-piece black ensemble, her single strand of pearls glowed like a year's worth of full moons in a midnight sky. She unfolded a piece of paper and began reading a poem that Henry Scott Holland, a priest at St. Paul's Cathedral in London, first delivered sixteen years ago for England's King Edward VII.

"Death is nothing at all.

"It does not count.

"I have only slipped away into the next room..."

Lizzie grasped Sidney's hand and squeezed it, hoping the poem's account of life beyond the grave would give her friend some comfort. He smiled weakly. His dark eyes glistened, but no tears fell.

Finally, it was her turn. Lizzie pushed herself up from the pew and walked in what she hoped was a dignified manner to the front of the church. In her youth, she'd sung in the choir at her neighborhood church in the Bronx. But after leaving her parents' home, she'd stopped going to church except to attend weddings, christenings, and recently funerals. She took a few deep breaths to calm her nerves. Although she'd performed for audiences of all kinds, at toney upscale celebrations and in dingy taverns, this was the first time she'd sung at a funeral. Her eyes locked on Joan Amory's as she began:

"Amazing grace! How sweet the sound

"That saved a wretch like me!

"I once was lost, but now am found

"Was blind, but now I see..."

Her strong soprano carried easily through the church. She looked to Sidney for his opinion; he gave her a subtle thumbs-up. Bert threw her a lopsided grin, then quickly stifled it, as if he thought it improper to grin at a funeral. When she finished, Sidney smiled, and Lizzie was glad she'd agreed to sing. Although she would have welcomed Sid's backup on the pipe organ, she had to admit the song seemed even more poignant without accompaniment.

She returned to her seat beside her friend as the minister stepped up to the podium again to end the service. After a final prayer, Joan's brothers and four other men hoisted the casket to their shoulders. They solemnly carried it down the church's aisle and outside to a waiting hearse.

Sidney, Lizzie, and Bert joined the procession of automobiles, headlights turned on, winding through the streets of Salem to the cemetery.

"How are you holding up?" she asked Sid.

"Better than I'd expected," he answered. "Thanks for singing, Bearcat."

Mourners dressed in black gathered around the open grave, like a flock of crows. *A murder of crows,* Lizzie corrected herself, struck by the irony of the term. She realized this was the first time she'd seen Isaac Roman wearing black. The contrast with his long, snowy hair was striking. Behind him stood Sergeant Darcy. The minister led the group in reciting the Twenty-third Psalm, then read a few other pieces of scripture. When he finished, the pallbearers slowly lowered the casket into the gaping hole.

Joan Amory, supported by a brother on either side, approached the open grave. One of them handed her a shovel. As she scooped up dirt from the waiting mound and let it fall on Sebastian's casket, a dappled-gray horse cantered across the cemetery. On its back, a woman wearing a long black dress and mantilla rode sidesaddle.

"Thea Gallagher," Lizzie whispered to Sidney.

Mourners parted to let the horse through. Thea reined in her mount at the edge of the grave and threw a single red rose down on the casket. Lizzie noticed Joan's thin body stiffen, but she couldn't see the woman's face hidden by her veil.

Before her brothers could stop her, Joan raised the shovel and stepped toward the horsewoman. She took an awkward swing, but Thea kicked the shovel out of her hands. Joan grabbed for Thea's ankle, as if trying to pull her from her mount. Thea kicked her again, hitting the widow's shoulder with her foot and knocking Joan off balance. She stumbled, caught her heel in the soft dirt, and fell. As her legs slid into the grave, Joan shrieked, but one of her brothers grabbed her arm and pulled her back to safety.

Sergeant Darcy pushed through the mourners and hurried toward the scuffle. Thea turned her horse around, blew a kiss, and galloped away.

Behind her, Joan shouted, "You'll pay for this, Thea Gallagher!"

Lizzie nudged Sidney. "This looks like a good time for you to scram for New York."

"And how. C'mon, Bert."

"Safe travels. See you next week," Lizzie said and gave them both quick hugs.

Sergeant Darcy knelt beside Joan, who sat on the ground sobbing loudly. The widow's brothers stood behind her protectively, scanning the area for any more possible interruptions. Curious mourners pushed closer to get a better look.

Sid and Bert slipped away unnoticed.

Chapter Twenty-One

"Man is not what he thinks he is, he is what he hides." — André Malraux

Still reeling from the morning's events, Lizzie sought solace in a place she'd often retreated to in her youth: the public library. Housed in a handsome red brick mansion that once belonged to a noted Salem merchant, the quiet library seemed to wrap its comforting arms around her. Many of the books that peered at her from the oak shelves described times of hardship: *War and Peace, Les Misérables, Wuthering Heights.* Like understanding friends, they offered silent assurances: Yes, we know it's difficult, but all things pass, and time heals.

Instead of pulling one of those books down, though, Lizzie chose to read the morning edition of the *Boston Globe.* In it, she found an article about Charles Lindbergh's aerial exhibition yesterday, complete with a number of photos, including one of her standing beside the famous flyer. Thankfully, none showed her bloomers. *Great publicity,* she thought and made a mental note to buy a copy of the newspaper for her scrapbook. Next, she flipped to the Arts & Entertainment section and found an article about the art opening she planned to attend tomorrow evening with Alan. Halfway through the piece, she read:

"Although the Franklin Gallery is now known for showcasing contemporary painting and sculpture, it has only been a few years since it gave Boston art-goers a taste of something more ancient and exotic," the reviewer wrote.

"After archaeologists discovered King Tutankhamun's tomb in 1922, gallery owner Hugh Franklin put on a stunning exhibit of ancient Egyptian art. The following year, after Picasso's exhibit of African-inspired art at New York's Whitney Museum, Franklin hosted a show of native masks, sculptures, jewelry, and artifacts from the Dark Continent. Even when delving into the past, the Franklin Gallery has always been at the forefront of artistic and esthetic trends…"

A black-and-white photograph showed Hugh Franklin holding an African shield and a spear. Despite his upper-class European lineage, he appeared quite relaxed, posing with weapons that most proper Bostonians would have considered strange at best.

Lizzie replaced the newspaper on the rack where she'd found it, then approached the library's front desk. A woman with gray hair, a beaked nose, and long, thin arms who reminded her of a heron asked, "May I help you?"

"I'm trying to find articles about art exhibits a man named Hugh Franklin held at his Boston gallery a few years ago. Do you know if you have any magazines that might have covered those shows?"

Ten minutes later, the librarian returned with a stack of magazines and handed them to Lizzie. "You might find something in one of these."

Lizzie thanked her and carried them to a table near a window that looked out onto Essex Street, where the afternoon light spilled in and let her see clearly. After thumbing through several magazines, she came across a full-page piece about the Egyptian exhibit mentioned in the *Boston Globe*. It commented on Franklin's Dutch ancestry—his family name was Franke— and how his studies in Amsterdam as a young man had influenced his choice of a career. Another magazine featured a shorter article that discussed his interest in American Indian art, especially that of the Navajo and Hopi. According to the author, Franklin had traveled to the American Southwest, where he'd acquired an extensive collection of tribal art and crafts. He'd exhibited his collection at his gallery in 1924.

Lizzie stared at a photograph that accompanied the article. The non-descript, middle-aged man she'd only seen wearing conservative suits had donned a deerskin outfit resplendent with colorful beadwork for the occasion. He held a feathered bow in his right hand; a leather quiver full of arrows was slung over his left shoulder. As in the *Globe* photo, Franklin looked oddly comfortable and content wearing the garb of a culture totally unlike his own.

For several moments, Lizzie gazed at the picture. One by one, pieces began falling into place, like tumblers in a lock that opened a safe. She considered tucking the magazines under her jacket and smuggling them out of the library. Instead, she wrote down on a slip of paper the names, dates, and page numbers of the publications in which the articles appeared, then returned the magazines to the circulation desk. From a pay phone in the library's lobby, she dialed Sergeant Darcy's number.

*** * ***

An hour later, Lizzie met the policeman on the front steps of the library. Neither of them mentioned the fiasco at the cemetery this morning.

After telephoning Darcy, she'd walked back to Roman's mansion to collect the jet button her host's cat found in the greenhouse. She handed it, still wrapped in Sidney's silk handkerchief, to the policeman. The stony-faced cop opened the handkerchief carefully and looked down at the button.

"Why are you showing this to me, Miss Crane?" he asked.

"I think it may figure into Sebastian Amory's death." She explained how she'd come upon it in Roman's conservatory last night. "Maybe it got torn off the murderer's clothing in a scuffle with the victim."

Holding the button by the handkerchief, Darcy studied the star engraved on its surface. "You say a *cat* discovered this?"

"Cats are very clever creatures. They often see things we miss."

"Hmph," Darcy snorted, and Lizzie thought maybe he felt a bit embarrassed at having been upstaged by an animal. "May I keep this?"

"I'd like a receipt, please," Lizzie answered, remembering her insistence on a warrant before she relinquished the lapel pin Joan Amory claimed her husband had purchased as a gift for Sidney.

Darcy nodded. "You'll have to come to the station so we can log it in as evidence."

"Very well."

"Is this all, Miss Crane?"

"No, I'd like to show you some magazine articles and photographs that I think might interest you. Would you please come inside, Sergeant?"

At the circulation desk, Lizzie pointed to the stack of magazines she'd perused earlier, still lying on a cart behind the desk, waiting to be refiled. "May we look at the two on top?" she asked the bird-like librarian.

The woman studied the policeman's uniform. "What's this about?" she asked nervously.

"We're doing some research," Darcy said. "I'd appreciate it if you'd give us the materials we've requested, ma'am."

The woman seemed to contemplate their request, perhaps worrying if she could be held accountable for getting involved with the law, even in this minimal way, or be blamed for attracting unwanted publicity to the library. After apparently deciding there was nothing out of the ordinary about someone asking to see a couple outdated magazines—even if that someone was a police officer—she handed them over.

"In here," Darcy said to Lizzie.

He waved her into a room walled by floor-to-ceiling bookcases and furnished with only an oak table and four chairs. They sat across from each other at the table, cocooned in the library's silence. Lizzie pointed out the articles about Hugh Franklin, then sat back and waited while Darcy read them. When he finished, he tapped his index finger on the photograph of Franklin dressed in Navajo deerskins.

"Help me understand where you're going with this, Miss Crane," he said.

"I think Hugh Franklin may have killed Sebastian Amory."

"Because Franklin had an interest in Indian culture and dressed up with a bow and arrows to promote an exhibit at his gallery? That's a bit of a stretch, don't you think?"

When he put it that way, it did sound tenuous, Lizzie realized. Still, she sensed she'd uncovered something significant and she didn't intend to let it drop.

"Sebastian did restoration work for Franklin's customers who had old portraits of their ancestors that they wanted cleaned up. I expect you know that already. You also know Sebastian was a skilled copyist, who could duplicate pretty much any artist's style."

The librarian poked her head into the room where Lizzie and Darcy sat, leaning across the table toward one another. She shushed them, "Would you please keep your voices down?"

"Sorry," Darcy said, waving her away.

"According to Joan Amory," Lizzie continued in a whisper, "Sebastian was angry that Hugh Franklin refused to give him a show at his Newbury Street gallery. He felt that after all the years he'd worked for Franklin, he deserved appreciation for his own artwork. A show would have given his career a big boost. Maybe even freed him from having to work as a copyist."

Darcy drummed his fingers on the tabletop. "That gives us a motive, albeit weak, for Amory wanting to kill Franklin. But why would Franklin, who benefitted from Amory's skill, want to kill his cash cow?"

"My guess is, Sebastian was doing more than repairing old paintings for Franklin's customers."

She combed her fingers through her dark hair as she tried to fit the pieces of the puzzle together for the policeman. She thought about the elderly shopkeeper who claimed Sebastian tried to sell him a fake El Greco. She recalled the kitchen in Sebastian's studio at Salem's Pequot Mills and the stove on which she'd made tea for a distraught Thea Gallagher. A stove in which the artist could have baked canvases to simulate the passage of time. She remembered the angry confrontation she overheard between Joan Amory and Isaac Roman the afternoon after Sebastian's death. "All he ever wanted was to be recognized for his own work as an artist," his widow had insisted.

"I think Sebastian decided to put pressure on Franklin."

Darcy shook his head. "I'm still not following your reasoning, Miss Crane."

"My guess is, Sebastian was forging paintings, and Franklin was selling them to unsuspecting clients."

"That's a pretty serious accusation. Do you have any proof?"

"I'm just speculating, Sergeant. Trying to be helpful," Lizzie said. "Isn't finding proof what policemen do?"

Sergeant Darcy stood, pushed his chair neatly under the table, and picked up the magazines. "Come with me to the station, Miss Crane, so I can enter this button as evidence—and give you a receipt."

* * *

On Lizzie's last night in Salem, Isaac Roman invited her to have supper with him, just the two of them. They sat in his formal dining room at a mahogany Chippendale table that could seat twenty-four diners while his butler served a meal of roast beef, new potatoes, and fresh spring vegetables on gold-edged china plates. Wine sparkled like rubies in their crystal goblets.

"Miss Crane, it's been a great pleasure having you here this week. I know my guests have enjoyed hearing your music as much as I have."

"Thank you, Mr. Roman. My friends and I have enjoyed performing for you and your guests as well."

Roman cut a bite of rosy-pink beef and chewed it pensively while he studied Lizzie's face. Before speaking, he dabbed at his mouth with a starched linen napkin embroidered with the letter R. "I realize this has been a difficult time for you, what with Sebastian's murder and all the hubbub surrounding it. For your piano player, especially. I understand they were friends when Sebastian lived in New York."

"Yes, it was hard for Sidney."

"I must admit to some guilt regarding what transpired."

She lifted a forkful of tiny green peas to her lips. *What's he admitting to?* she wondered

Since discovering the photographs this afternoon of Roman's gallery-owner friend, Hugh Franklin, she kept thinking her host might have a finger in the pie. Before accepting this job, she'd been warned of his reputation for trafficking in stolen artwork—unverified, but still scandalous—and he did nothing to discourage the gossip. If her suspicions about Franklin were correct, Roman could be an accomplice in passing off forged paintings as

144

legit. Perhaps more.

He interrupted her thoughts. "Mr. Somerset didn't know when he accepted this job that he'd get tangled up in a crime, never mind the emotional dynamics surrounding it. I regret that I didn't get to say goodbye to him properly. Please convey my apologies to him, will you?"

"I will, thank you. But of course, you couldn't have known when you hired us that Mr. Amory would get murdered, or that he and Sidney knew each other."

Unless this was all a set-up. Unless Roman hired us precisely so he could frame Sid. The idea sent chills running up and down Lizzie's spine as she considered the possibility that the charming man who sat across the table from her might have killed Sebastian.

"Did your friends make it back to New York safe and sound?" Roman asked.

"I don't know. I haven't heard from them yet."

He refilled their wine glasses. "Quite a bit of excitement at the cemetery today, eh?"

"Thea Gallagher certainly has a flair for the dramatic. She should consider moving to the Big Apple and trying her luck in the theater," Lizzie said as she cut a baked redskin potato in half and dribbled it with melted butter. "How did she and Sebastian get together?"

"Guilty again," Roman said. "I introduced them. Did you know that Thea and I were lovers once upon a time?"

Lizzie shrugged. "It crossed my mind."

"Sebastian was here, discussing a project for a client of mine, when Thea slid down the banister into my foyer, wearing only a thin silk chemise." He chuckled, remembering the scenario. "I thought Sebastian's eyes would pop out of his head."

"Sebastian was hardly an innocent," she pointed out. "He'd been part of the Village art scene when he lived in New York and a three-letter man as well. A little bare skin shouldn't have surprised him."

"Thea's not a great beauty like you, Miss Crane," Roman said, letting his gaze sweep Lizzie's lovely face and torso unabashedly. "But her audacity and her brazen behavior have a certain kind of feral appeal, particularly for men who feel cramped by society's rules. Like Sebastian. The poor fella was smitten."

Lizzie remembered Sidney's explanation for why Sebastian married Joan Amory. He longed to fit in and leave his bohemian life behind. His unconventional ways hindered his chances for success, or so he believed. Had Thea awakened the part of him that he'd tried to squelch?

"Why hasn't Thea left her abusive father?"

"Good question," Roman answered. "Sigmund Freud might have something to say about that."

After they finished supper's main course, Roman's butler cleared away the dishes. He soon reappeared with dessert plates of pineapple upside-down cake. In Salem, Lizzie knew, pineapples symbolized hospitality. During the first half of the nineteenth century, when Salem held pride of place as a prosperous port, merchants and ships' captains displayed images of pineapples outside their homes, inviting neighbors to celebrate the safe return of their clipper ships from the Orient. To this day, carved wooden likenesses of pineapples hung above doors and perched on fence posts throughout the city.

Roman poked his cake with his fork. "Miss Crane, I hope you've had some good times during your stay here. It hasn't all been grief and turmoil, has it?"

"Certainly not. Overall, it's been the bee's knees. Mr. Lindberg's demonstration most of all. I can't thank you enough for letting me fly with him. Plus, I appreciate the opportunity to perform here in this swanky place—nothing makes me happier than playing music, especially for an appreciative audience. This has been a wonderful opportunity for us, Mr. Roman. You've been a gracious host and made us very comfortable in your beautiful home."

Roman nodded. He tasted his cake and decided he liked it well enough to take another, bigger bite. Lizzie had already determined it was one of the most delicious things she'd ever eaten. The butler appeared bearing a silver coffeepot and poured fragrant, dark coffee into delicate porcelain cups.

"I understand you've purchased a painting from Hugh Franklin's new show," Roman said.

"One of Edward Hopper's pieces. Actually, Alan Peabody purchased it," she corrected him. "We're going to the Franklin Gallery's opening Friday night. Will you be there?"

Roman shook his head. "No, but I'm sure it will be interesting."

Lizzie considered pressing him for information regarding the earlier shows at the gallery that she'd read about this afternoon, but decided to keep quiet for the time being. If Roman were involved in an illicit business, she didn't want to let him know she was onto him. Or that she suspected his friend, Hugh Franklin, of Sebastian's murder.

"Smart investment, a Hopper picture."

"Surely you'd know," she said. "Did I tell you I met Mr. Hopper and his wife during the Christmas holidays?"

"I don't think so. He's a little odd, but what artist isn't?" Roman said as he stirred sugar into his coffee. "I should buy one of his pictures myself. Mark my word, the man's going to be important in the art world."

Chapter Twenty-Two

"Three things cannot long be hidden: the sun, the moon, and the truth." — Confucius

Friday morning, Alan's butler met Lizzie's train at North Station and drove her to the Isabella Stewart Gardner Museum. He opened the door of the silver Bentley and held out his gloved hand to help her to the curb. "What time shall I collect you, miss?" he asked.

"Thanks, Norman, but really, you needn't bother. I can get a taxicab back to Mr. Peabody's home when I'm finished," she said.

"It's no bother. I am at your disposal during your stay here."

His very proper manner amused her. *Does he ever loosen up and have fun?* she wondered. "Well, then, would you be kind enough to see to my bags?"

"Of course, miss."

"And if I do need a ride, I'll telephone you. Okay?"

"All right," he agreed. "Shall I see you in then?"

"It's not necessary. I've been here before. I can find my way, thanks."

Norman frowned ever-so-slightly, as if baffled by her independent manner, and doffed his hat. "Very well. I hope you have a pleasant day, Miss Crane."

"You too, Norman."

Inside the Italian Renaissance-inspired mansion turned museum, everything looked the same as it had during her last visit. *Was it truly only three days ago?* Lizzie marveled at the disparity between the reality of time and her perception of it. So much had transpired, it seemed a month should have been necessary to accommodate it all.

The atrium still blossomed with narcissus, orchids, and calla lilies. Water still trickled from a marble fountain at the end of the stately courtyard. Sunlight still filtered through the glass ceiling and spilled onto the tile floor below. Only her reason for coming here today had changed.

She purchased an illustrated visitor's guide at the gift shop and climbed a flight of stairs to the second floor, to a section of the museum she'd bypassed before. If her suspicions were correct, she might find confirmation here. She entered the Dutch Room through a carved wooden doorframe into an elegant, dimly lit space. Walls covered in patterned green damask displayed somber paintings in ornate gilt frames. Next to the entrance hung Rembrandt's *Self-Portrait*, one of the museum's most prized pictures in this cornucopia of precious works. Beside it was a much smaller, older, and less well-known painting: Albrecht Dürer's portrait of "A Man in a Fur Coat."

For several minutes, she stood staring at the picture. The man's hat and coat appeared just as the master painted them four hundred years ago. Even the age-crackled surface seemed authentic. Her guidebook explained that the subject of the portrait, rendered in oil on an oak panel, was unknown. But Lizzie recognized the man's face immediately. And it didn't match the one shown in the guidebook.

How many art lovers have looked at this famous panel without noticing the alteration? Lizzie wondered.

Familiarity makes us blind. Day after day, we look at the world around us and see only what we're prepared to see, what we *want* to see. That's what makes the artist different from other people. Whatever he sees appears fresh and wondrous each time he looks at it.

She took a few deep breaths to calm her nerves, then walked toward the museum's atrium, barely noticing the artwork all around her. Stepping out onto one of several small open balconies, she gazed down at the courtyard below. The bits of information she'd gleaned tumbled like stones polished in a lapidary, as she tried to make sense of the perplexing situation she'd stumbled into. She could understand why Sebastian had engaged in what was probably a lucrative business, more profitable than the copy work he usually did. But why had he substituted the faces of his associates for the people in the original works? Was he playing a game? Interjecting his creativity into what he considered tedious tasks? Or did he plan to blackmail his cohorts if they ever tried to cheat or betray him?

Unsure what to do with the evidence she'd found, Lizzie turned around—and nearly bumped into Edward Oliver. In his rubber-soled shoes, the tall, thin, gawky young man had managed to approach her without being heard.

Stifling a gasp of surprise, she asked, "What are you doing here? Don't you work the night shift?"

"I noticed you staring at Dürer's portrait," he said, ignoring her questions.

"Staring at paintings is what people do in museums."

"What did you make of it?"

She could dodge him with some nondescript reply, like "It's swell," or she could press Oliver for answers. Lizzie chose the latter. "I found it peculiar that the picture on the wall doesn't match the one shown in this guidebook." She tapped the page. "See here, the man's face is different."

Oliver's hands clenched and unclenched at his sides. His left eye twitched, making the teardrop-shaped scar beneath it jump. Instead of looking at the photograph she pointed to, he glanced about nervously as if he feared someone might see or overhear them. But this section of the gallery was empty of visitors.

"Why did Sebastian do it?" Lizzie asked.

Oliver shrugged. "He wanted recognition for his work. And he enjoyed knowing he'd pulled one over on the people who set themselves up as authorities. What good is duping the experts if you can't rub their noses in it? Take the snobs down a notch, eh? Sebastian was so proud of his 'caper'—it was a game to him, not a serious crime that could put us all behind bars."

"You smuggled the real Dürer out of here and replaced it with Sebastian's forgery, didn't you?"

He paused a moment, then nodded. "It wasn't difficult. At night, I'm the watchdog here. It's a small painting, after all, easy enough to hide under my overcoat."

Lizzie thought Oliver seemed proud of his own part in the scam, of having "pulled one over" on the "snobs."

"What happened to the original?"

"I handed it over to Hugh Franklin. After that, I have no idea. It's probably in a vault somewhere. The people who buy these things do it as an investment, not because they love art."

Oliver stepped closer to Lizzie. Instinctively, she backed away. Her heart pounded like a snare drum, so loud she thought surely he could hear it. Having revealed his secret, would he try to eliminate the person who could incriminate him and his partners in crime, too? She glanced furtively down the corridor, but saw no one. Now that she thought about it, she realized she hadn't encountered another person on the entire second floor. Except Oliver.

"Once any reasonably clever individual notices the disparity, he can follow the money trail," Lizzie said, trying to sound confident and keep her voice steady. Stalling for time. "It won't be hard to figure out who's involved and expose them."

She'd been watching her adversary's eyes the way martial arts practitioners did. But Oliver's steady gaze didn't change as he lunged at Lizzie, slamming her back against the stone railing of the balcony. She gasped with pain. Tears sprang into her eyes. The impact stunned her momentarily, long enough for Oliver to clench his hands around her neck and force her shoulders back. The upper half of her body arched precariously over the rail. She clawed at her assailant's fingers, trying to loosen Oliver's grip. But he held on tight, digging his nails into her skin.

Choking, unable to scream, Lizzie kicked frantically at Oliver's legs—a mistake that threw her off balance and allowed him to push her partway over the railing. The museum guard knocked her other foot out from under her. Larger and stronger than her, he leaned down heavily on her chest. Dizzy with fear, Lizzie saw the courtyard floor twenty feet below as a white-and-green blur that kept swaying from side to side, like a landscape viewed from a swing.

In every life-and-death struggle, there comes a point when the conscious mind relinquishes its command and the instincts take over. No longer aware of her actions, Lizzie quit trying to dislodge Oliver's hands from her throat and grasped the railing instead. She stopped straining against the pressure he exerted on her and let herself go limp.

Now that her body provided no resistance, his weight and thrust worked against him. Before her assailant could compensate and adjust his balance, Lizzie brought her knee up between his legs and pulled back as hard as she could.

Oliver pitched forward, his arms flailing as if he were a fledgling bird on its first flight. In her crisis-distorted frame of mind, he almost appeared to be floating as he slipped toward the courtyard below. For a moment, Lizzie believed he might simply drift down gently as a feather and land unhurt among the lush greenery.

A shriek, then a dull thud, snapped her back to reality. As she slumped onto the floor of the balcony, she heard cries of alarm below. Running feet clattered on mosaic tiles. She leaned her cheek against a cool stone baluster, gasping for breath. Unaware of the blood dripping onto her collar, she gazed down at the commotion below.

A crumpled figure lay face down on a white stone background.

Museum personnel and visitors gathered around. A man knelt, touched the figure's neck tentatively, then drew back his hand and shook his head. As if that were their cue, the other people in the courtyard turned their faces upward and stared at the spot from which Oliver had fallen. A woman pointed at Lizzie.

Moments later, Lizzie heard someone speak softly to her, but the whirring in her ears made it hard to understand the words. A pair of strong arms lifted her to her feet She was vaguely aware of being led through the museum and down the stairs to a cluttered office on the ground floor, where someone placed a cold, damp cloth on her burning neck. A young woman brought Lizzie a glass of water.

* * *

A uniformed officer bent over the contorted body of Edward Oliver while a man with a camera snapped several photographs, before the policeman directed a staff member to cover it with a tarp. Two museum employees, the young woman who'd brought Lizzie water and a balding man with wire-rimmed spectacles, showed another cop who identified himself as Detective McKinnon and the photographer into the office where Lizzie waited.

"Do you want me to call an ambulance?" the man with the spectacles asked her.

"No, I don't need to go to the hospital. I'll be okay," she insisted.

"We'll need to take a few photographs of your injuries, Miss Crane. For our investigation," McKinnon said in a voice surprisingly soft for such a big man. "Will you give us permission to do that?"

Lizzie nodded. She removed the damp cloth from her neck, trying to keep her hands from shaking, and closed her eyes to block out the camera's flash.

"I understand the deceased was a guard here at the museum," the detective said. "Do you have any idea why he might have assaulted you?"

She dug into her purse and withdrew Sergeant Darcy's card. "Please contact him."

McKinnon raised an eyebrow. "Miss Crane, are you involved with the Salem Police Department in some fashion?"

Lizzie smiled wryly. "I guess you could say that. Not in an official capacity, though."

The Boston policeman excused himself to make a telephone call. After several minutes, he returned and handed the card back to Lizzie. "Sergeant Darcy is on his way here. We'd both like to talk with you further, if you feel up to it."

"I'll wait for Sergeant Darcy," Lizzie agreed. "But I'm feeling pretty rattled right now, as you might imagine. And my back hurts—I'd really like to lie down for a bit."

McKinnon shot a questioning look at the man with the spectacles, whom Lizzie guessed might be the museum's director. He fiddled with his tie nervously and chewed on his lower lip, obviously rattled himself. *He's probably worried more about the impact this incident will have on the museum's well-being than he is on mine,* she surmised.

"There's a couch in the employees' lounge," offered the young woman who'd brought Lizzie water. Her badge identified her as a docent. "You could rest there until your Sergeant Darcy arrives."

"Thank you," Lizzie said and followed the docent down a hallway to a windowless room that smelled of coffee.

"Don't you think you should see a doctor?"

Lizzie sat on the couch and leaned against its cushioned back. "No, but I'd love a cup of coffee."

· The woman filled two cups and handed one to Lizzie. "How about I stay here with you for a bit, just in case you need anything else?"

"That's nice of you. Thanks."

Half an hour later, the Salem policeman and his big-city counterpart entered the employees' lounge. "We'd like to ask you some questions, Miss Crane, if you're up to it," Darcy said.

Lizzie nodded. "Okay."

"I saw it all, if you want to talk to me too," the docent said.

"We will. Right now, however, Detective McKinnon and I need to talk to Miss Crane alone."

Darcy pulled up a chair with a back as straight as his own, sat in it, and stared hard at Lizzie. The Boston policeman leaned against a counter, waiting until the docent left to ask, "How are you feeling, Miss Crane?"

"I've felt a whole lot better."

Now that the adrenaline rush had worn off, pain gripped her like an iron fist. As she mentally replayed what had happened—and what might have happened—anxiety rose in her chest. She took a few deep breaths to calm herself, but each inhalation made her back hurt more. *I hope I haven't got a cracked rib,* she thought.

Sergeant Darcy shook his head, but his words seemed to convey more regret than recrimination. "If you'd stayed in Salem, as I asked you to do, none of this would have happened."

"But then I wouldn't have discovered the forged Dürer painting upstairs, in the Dutch Room. If you compare it to the picture in the guidebook, Sergeant, you'll see what I mean. The subject's face is that of Hugh Franklin."

"I don't want to make this situation any worse for you, so I'll try to be quick. I can fill Detective McKinnon in later," Darcy said. "Is this related to what you showed me at the library yesterday?"

"Yes."

"Do you believe the deceased and the man we spoke of are connected?"

"Yes. If you come to the Franklin Gallery this evening, I think you'll find it worth your while. You too, Detective McKinnon." She jotted the address on a piece of paper and passed it to Darcy. As she did, a spike of pain made her wince. Trying to keep her voice from quavering, she asked, "Please, can I go now?"

"Are you sure you don't want to go to the hospital?" Darcy asked, concern softening his ordinarily emotionless, all-business voice.

"I'm sure."

"Is there someone I can call to come fetch you?"

Lizzie gave him the phone number of Alan's home. "Ask for Norman."

Chapter Twenty-Three

"He had two lives: one, open, seen and known by all who cared to know, full of relative truth and of relative falsehood, exactly like the lives of his friends and acquaintances; and another life running its course in secret." — Anton Chekhov

Norman directed a housemaid to see Lizzie to the master bedroom. He told another to bring her tea and two aspirin tablets. He didn't ask what mishap had befallen her, nor did he get in a lather about the unexpected dilemma. Instead, he took charge of the situation like a ship's captain steering his craft in a rough sea. Lizzie found his calm, efficient manner comforting.

"Please don't say anything about this to Mr. Peabody," Lizzie said. "I'll tell him myself."

"As you wish, Miss Crane," he replied, but she sensed the conflict he felt between his loyalty to Alan and his respect for her privacy.

After the housemaids left, she stretched out on Alan's bed and promptly fell asleep. An hour later, she awoke feeling groggy and disoriented. But at least the nap had soothed the fear she'd experienced at the museum. The clock on the nightstand said half past three. As she pushed herself into a sitting position, her muscles cried out in agony. Her back, especially, throbbed where Edward Oliver had slammed her into the stone railing on the museum's balcony.

Edward Oliver. When she first met the irritating, angry young man at one of Roman's parties, he'd struck her as pathetic. She would never have suspected him of participating in an art heist ring or attempting murder. Yet she'd nearly met her death today at that same man's hands. The memory sent a wave of nausea rippling through her body, and she held her breath as the room spun around her.

Finally, her dizziness and anxiety eased. Alan's bedroom resumed its usual colors and dimensions. Lizzie stood up slowly and stripped off her French blue crepe dress. A long rip ran from under the left arm, where the sleeve joined the bodice, down the side to the wide band that circled her hips.

"Drat," she grumbled. "That was one of my favorite frocks."

Gritting her teeth against the pain, she stood with her back to the cheval mirror and looked over her shoulder at the damage her body had sustained. A purple bruise was already spreading from between her shoulder blades down to her waist. She turned around, appalled by her reflection. Another bruise circled her neck, along with deep red scratches made by Oliver's fingernails. The bruise poured like spilled wine over her collarbones and down between her breasts.

"Drat," she said again. *Looks like I'll have to wait for another occasion to wear my sexy new evening dress with the plunging neckline.* Fortunately, she'd brought the floor-length, boat-necked gown that had discreetly concealed her injuries after she tumbled down a flight of stairs at her last stint. She held it against her wounded body and studied herself in the mirror. "It will have to do."

* * *

She fit into the silky golden gown the way champagne filled a crystal flute. To hide the bruises on her neck that the gown didn't cover, she donned an Egyptian-inspired choker made with seven strands of lapis, amber, and malachite beads. Then she checked her makeup a final time before limping downstairs to the parlor to wait for Alan to come home from work.

She sat on the leather Chesterfield sofa in front of the fireplace. The housemaid who'd escorted Lizzie to the bedroom stopped in to see how she was doing. Another brought her tea. At quarter to six, she heard Alan's voice in the foyer and every switch in her body flipped to "on."

When he entered the parlor, she stood and took a step toward him. A stabbing pain shot from her shoulders to her hips. She flinched, and although she tried to hide it, a grimace twisted the smile from her face.

Alan rushed across the Isfahan carpet and grasped her arm. "Lizzie, what's wrong?"

He held her elbow, supporting her as she eased herself back onto the sofa, and then sat beside her. Before she could answer, Norman entered the room. The butler studied Lizzie's face, and she thought she saw him raise an eyebrow, as if trying to ascertain her condition and determine what comment, if any, he should make regarding her health. She met his gaze and touched her finger to her lip.

"Would you care for a libation, sir?" the butler asked Alan.

"What do you say, Lizzie?"

"A splash of whiskey would be lovely."

"Please bring two glasses of Jameson's, will you, Norman?"

"Very well, sir."

After Norman left, Alan asked, "What's happened?"

"A man tried to kill me this afternoon."

"What? Who?" he practically shouted. "We have to telephone the police."

"They know already," she said. "The man's dead."

Taking both her hands in his, he said, "Tell me everything."

Trying to keep her emotions in check, her voice steady, Lizzie told him about the magazine articles. She paused briefly when Norman brought their drinks, then explained her suspicions about Hugh Franklin. She described how Sebastian Amory had forged paintings and how Edward Oliver had stolen the originals from the museum. How Oliver had attacked her and how he'd tumbled to his death.

"I don't know what to say, Lizzie." Alan shook his head, struggling to take in all she'd revealed. "I'm dumbfounded."

"You must be thoroughly exasperated with me."

"Yes, I am," he admitted angrily. "You've got to stop playing detective. It's too dangerous, Lizzie. We have police whose job it is to investigate crimes and they're much better suited for it than jazz singers." He brushed her cheek gently with his fingertips, his tone softening. "I couldn't bear to lose you."

"I'm sorry, Alan. I didn't mean to worry you. But I was afraid Sergeant Darcy would arrest Sid." She took a sip of her whiskey before continuing. "I'm guessing Darcy and the Boston cop, Detective McKinnon, will be at Franklin's opening tonight—Darcy knows the art dealer's in it up to his teeth. Maybe they'll arrest him. I just hope the newspapers don't make a spectacle of it."

"You should've left it to Darcy from the beginning."

"You're right," Lizzie admitted. "What time is it, by the way?"

He glanced at his Patek Philippe watch. "Quarter past six."

"I want to get to the gallery before everyone else arrives and collect my painting."

"Lizzie, you're in no shape to attend an art opening tonight."

"We have to go," she insisted. "If the cops arrest Hugh Franklin tonight, they'll shutter the gallery. All the paintings may be impounded until the case is finished—I might never get the Hopper."

"Aren't you worried that it might be a fake?"

Lizzie shook her head. "No, I think Franklin is more discrete than that. I doubt he'd publicly display a forgery of a living artist's work on the walls of his gallery. Too big a risk that someone, maybe even the artist himself, would realize it wasn't legit." She remembered what Isaac Roman had told her about dealing in stolen art and wondered for the umpteenth time if he too was involved in this scheme. "My guess is Franklin staked out specific pictures his clients wanted—Old Masters and rare, valuable pieces—then arranged to have them stolen by Edward Oliver and replaced with Sebastian's forgeries."

"You think that's what he did with the Dürer portrait?"

"Yes. And that's why Oliver tried to kill me. To shut me up."

Alan sipped his whiskey, eyeing her over the rim of the glass, trying to assess her condition. "I don't know, Lizzie. After all, you've been through… Why don't I go and collect the painting? You can stay here and rest."

"I don't want to miss out on whatever goes down tonight."

"You know that old expression, curiosity killed the cat, don't you? I think you're pushing your luck."

Lizzie smiled sweetly at him, curiosity outweighing her reservations. "But you'll be there to protect me, along with two armed policemen."

"Are you sure you feel up to it?"

"Ab-so-lute-ly." She finished the last of her drink. "This delicious whiskey has already taken the edge off the pain."

"All right then," he said, uncertainty still lacing his words. "Give me time to change clothes."

* * *

The Franklin Gallery glowed with golden light that illuminated the paintings, sculptures, and tapestries inside, tantalizing passers-by. When Lizzie and Alan entered, only a few people were browsing. The staff still scurried about, setting out hors d'oeurves and punch. She steered him toward the Edward Hopper painting he'd purchased for her, but hadn't seen until tonight.

"What do you think?" she asked.

He stared at it for a few minutes, during which Lizzie worried he might regret having spent so much money on a picture of a simple house in a New England fishing village where nothing at all seemed to be happening.

"I think it's marvelous," he said finally.

She wanted to throw her arms around him, but squeezed his hand instead. "Thank you, Alan. You can't imagine how much this means to me."

A man in his fifties of average height, with an unremarkable face and fading brown hair, approached them across the brightly lit gallery. "Are you familiar with Mr. Hopper's work?" he asked Alan.

Alan extended his hand and introduced himself. "I purchased this painting last week for Miss Crane. She knows the artist. We've come to take the picture home."

"Welcome, Mr. Peabody. I'm Hugh Franklin. Miss Crane, I'm delighted that you could come to my gallery tonight and bring Mr. Peabody with you."

Turning back to Alan, Franklin explained, "We like to keep the exhibit intact for the duration of the show. While I appreciate your patronage and your interest in Mr. Hopper's work, I won't be able to release the painting to you until next month."

"I'm afraid that won't do. Miss Crane is on her way to New York, and she wants to take the painting with her."

"If the painting is removed now, a gap will be left on the wall."

"I'm sure you can find another picture to fill the gap," Alan said. The commanding tone in his voice defied argument. "Much as we like this painting, if we can't take it with us tonight we don't want it."

Lizzie watched Franklin's face as he considered the possibility of losing a sale. She wondered if Franklin knew who Alan Peabody was, and suspected he did. It wouldn't be good business to alienate a man of his status, a man who might continue to be a valuable client. A man with connections that could benefit the Franklin Gallery.

"Very well," the gallery owner reluctantly acquiesced.

Franklin reached up to take the painting down from the wall. As he did, the spotlight illuminating it glinted on the buttons of his tuxedo's sleeve. Lizzie noticed the two jet buttons at the cuff didn't match. One was etched with a five-pointed star, the other a six-pointed one.

Lizzie felt her heartbeat quickening, and she struggled to keep her excitement from showing on her face. From the corner of her eye, she spotted Sergeant Darcy, wearing his uniform, enter the gallery along with Detective McKinnon in a cheap black suit, who seemed equally out of place in this sophisticated arena.

Franklin handed the painting to Alan. "Wait a moment, please, while I write a receipt for you."

While Lizzie waited for the receipt, Alan carried the Hopper painting outside and locked it in the trunk of his silver Bentley. She helped herself to a glass of punch and a cracker daubed with *foie gras*. Ignoring the aches and pains caused by Edward Oliver's assault, she slowly made her way around the gallery, staring at the various paintings without really seeing them. *Has Franklin heard about Oliver's death?* she wondered. *Does he know his partner-*

in-crime tried to kill me this afternoon because I figured out their scheme?

A well-dressed couple in their middle years entered the gallery. A few minutes later, three young people who might have been art students followed. By the time Alan returned, more than a dozen viewers were circling the room, including an elderly gent with thick glasses who struck up a one-way conversation with each of the paintings as if they were old friends. By eight o'clock, Lizzie suspected the gallery would be packed with gawkers, art enthusiasts reviewers, reporters, and prospective buyers.

"Here you go, Miss Crane," Franklin said as he handed her the receipt. "I hope you enjoy Mr. Hopper's painting."

"Thank you, I'm sure I will."

She slipped the receipt into her purse and crossed the gallery's polished maple floor to meet Alan. "Everything copacetic?" she asked.

"The painting's safe, if that's what you mean."

Lizzie nodded toward Sergeant Darcy and his colleague. "I need to speak with them. Do you want to come with me, or would you prefer to avoid that?"

"Honestly? I wish you'd never gotten involved in this mess. But since you have, I'd better go with you."

She linked her arm through his as they approached the two officers. After brief introductions, Lizzie asked Darcy, "Did you bring the button?"

The hatchet-faced policeman nodded and held up a glassine bag.

"Good, because the left cuff on the jacket of Mr. Franklin's tux is missing the original button. An unmatched one has been sewn on in its place. I believe you'll find the button in your bag came from Franklin's jacket. And I suspect it was torn from said jacket the night he murdered Sebastian Amory."

"Miss Crane, please wait here while I speak with Mr. Franklin," the Boston officer McKinnon said. "I may need you to come to headquarters with us to give a statement."

"I'm telephoning my attorney," Alan said, gripping Lizzie's arm. "She's not talking to you further without counsel present."

The detective nodded. "Very well."

Leaving them in Darcy's supervision, McKinnon approached Franklin.

Lizzie saw him discretely show his badge to the gallery owner. Saw Franklin's deadpan face break into a series of emotions: surprise, indignation, disbelief, and finally, fear. Saw Franklin summon his manager and speak to him in hushed tones, before the policemen accompanied Franklin out to the street and into a squad car.

* * *

Norman served them a quiet supper of flounder stuffed with crabmeat, wild rice, and asparagus, along with a bottle of oaky chardonnay. Alan had placed the Hopper painting on the mahogany sideboard, so he and Lizzie could admire it while they ate.

"What do you say we take a trip to Gloucester as soon as you're feeling better?" he suggested. "We could use a diversion. Let's visit the places Hopper painted—maybe we can locate this very house. From what I understand, Cape Ann has been a mecca for quite a few noted artists. Winslow Homer, Fitz Hugh Lane…"

"Yes, that sounds swell," she said. "You've been so kind and generous to me, Alan. How can I ever thank you?"

"By being happy," he answered as he refilled her glass with golden wine that matched her silk evening gown. "And by staying out of trouble. When I think about what might have happened to you today…"

"I'm sorry, Alan. Truly, I am. I never meant to worry you."

He patted her hand in what was meant as a reassuring gesture. "It's over now. The cops have caught the culprit. You can relax."

"I'm not so sure. A button and a few magazine articles aren't enough to convict Hugh Franklin of trafficking in stolen art, much less murder. Even the fake Dürer in the Gardner Museum only points to Sebastian's involvement and Oliver's. It doesn't prove Franklin knew anything about it."

She sipped her wine, wondering if Sergeant Darcy and his Boston colleague would manage to dig up more dirt on the gallery owner. If they couldn't produce additional evidence, Franklin would most likely go free. *Then what?*

"I'll call my attorney first thing in the morning. He'll make certain everything's on the up and up. From now on, don't talk to the cops unless he's present and says it's okay. Promise?"

She nodded. "I promise."

* * *

Alan helped Lizzie out of her evening gown. When he saw the bruises that stained her chest and back, he gasped. He started to put his arms around her to protect and comfort her, but pulled back, afraid of hurting her further. Instead, he took her hand and led her to the bed. He brushed feather-light kisses on the back of her neck, along her shoulders, and down her spine, as if his kisses might somehow make her better.

For a while, the wine had numbed her emotions as well as her physical pain. Now, both came rushing back. She burst into tears, something she rarely did, crying uncontrollably. Her whole body shook with heartrending sobs.

"Lizzie, what can I do?"

She shook her head. There was nothing anyone could do. Two young men, both talented artists, had died awful deaths. At each of The Troubadours' stints, someone had died, starting last summer when their saxophonist was murdered. *I feel like an Irish banshee—wherever I go, someone dies.*

Alan gently rolled her onto her side to reduce the pressure on her injuries. Then he lay beside her, touching her as lightly as a sheet while she cried herself to sleep.

Chapter Twenty-Four

"Tis best to weigh the enemy more mighty than he seems." —
William Shakespeare

After Alan left at seven-thirty in the morning for his office, Lizzie went downstairs and ate breakfast at one of the worktables in the kitchen, even though Norman offered to serve her properly in the dining room. Scanning the morning edition of the *Boston Globe*, she spotted an article about Edward Oliver's death, but it provided few details. Thankfully, it didn't mention her. She searched the newspaper further for a write-up about the Franklin Gallery but found nothing. Although she'd hoped to read that the gallery's owner had been arrested, she realized the police probably didn't have enough evidence to hold Hugh Franklin. Even if they had charged him, he would've posted bail and gone free. At least for now.

Lizzie finished a second cup of coffee, then pushed herself up from the table. Aches and pains screamed from every fiber in her body. Slowly, she made her way to the foyer, where the Bakelite telephone sat on a mahogany table, and called her friend Cora Delaney. When the tarot card reader picked up, Lizzie said, "That reading you did for me last week? You were right. Another death. Major deception. Plus, a dangerous situation I should've had the good sense to avoid."

"Tell me about it. I rarely remember what I see in the cards after a reading is over," Cora admitted.

"Have you seen the morning *Globe*?"

"I just started the crossword puzzle. What's up?"

"On page three, there's a piece about a man who fell to his death at the Gardner Museum yesterday. A security guard there named Edward Oliver. He tried to kill me."

"Good heavens! Whatever for? Lizzie, are you all right?"

She answered the second question first. "Banged up but alive. He and Sebastian Amory were partners in a scam to steal paintings from the museum and elsewhere and replace them with Sebastian's forgeries. I figured it out, so Oliver decided to bump me off."

"Oh, Lizzie. I don't know what to say. I wish I could've seen more clearly what was coming."

"I didn't call to blame you, Cora. I just wanted to fill you in. That's not the end of the story, though. Remember Hugh Franklin?"

After a pause, Cora said, "No, I don't think so."

"He's a friend of Roman's. Owns an art gallery here in Boston, very chi-chi. He's involved, too."

"What about Roman? Is he part of the scam?"

"Haven't the foggiest." Lizzie shook her head, even though Cora couldn't see her. "Say, can you do a tarot reading for me over the phone?"

"Hmm, I've never tried that. We can give it a shot, though. Let me grab my cards."

A few minutes passed, during which Lizzie wondered if they'd been disconnected before Cora spoke again. "Well, here's what I see. The Five of Swords suggests an enemy, a fight perhaps, or at least a conflict. Next, the Seven of Swords, which means more treachery and a potentially dangerous situation requiring caution on your part. And then the Three of Swords. Sadness, heartache."

"Swell," Lizzie grumbled. "Just what I wanted to hear."

"But wait a moment. Here's the Knight of Wands," Cora said. Lizzie imagined her friend tapping the card with her long, manicured fingertip as she'd seen her do many times before. "He represents a messenger bringing good news."

"So there's hope?"

"There's always hope. If we lose that, we are lost indeed."

* * *

Red tulips, yellow daffodils, and purple hyacinths blossomed in Boston's Public Garden, promising brighter days ahead. Mothers watched children chase each other, shrieking with delight. Dog owners walked their pets along the park's paths. A young man with a goatee sang and strummed a guitar, hoping for tips from passers-by. He reminded Lizzie of Bert the day she'd first encountered him in New York's Central Park, playing for change that would enable him to eat that night.

If possible, her body ached even more than it had yesterday. But she couldn't bear to sit alone in Alan's townhouse on this beautiful morning while he spent the day at his desk in the financial district, investing his clients' fortunes in speculative ventures. She was still struggling with sadness and regret over the deaths of Sebastian Amory and Edward Oliver—the two had become entwined, Oliver's demise amplifying Sebastian's. For the moment, however, fresh air, sunshine, and nature's beauty soothed her frayed spirits.

She broke off pieces of bread and tossed them to the squirrels that scurried about, chattering as they snagged her offerings. The park's famed swan boats sat ready to ferry passengers across the shallow pond. Beyond the park stretched the Charles River, where young men rowed sculls or glided along in small, cat-rigged sailboats. Suddenly, she sensed a change in the atmosphere around her. Although she couldn't have attributed it to anything specific, the park's peaceful ambiance shifted.

"You put the cops on me," a woman's voice growled.

Lizzie turned to see Thea Gallagher standing behind her. "What are you doing here?"

"Following you." The young woman stepped closer, her eyes burning with rage. Her long hair, blowing wildly in the wind, made Lizzie think of Medusa, a mythological Greek woman whose head was covered with venomous snakes. "Any minute now, the police are going to arrest me for

Sebastian's murder."

"The cops had you pegged from the beginning," Lizzie reminded her. She considered telling Thea that the police suspected Hugh Franklin of killing Sebastian, but decided to hold her tongue. Without more incriminating evidence, the wealthy gallery owner might never be charged, much less convicted.

"At the very least, they'll get me as his accomplice in the forgeries. All thanks to you." Thea lit a cigarette, took a long drag, then blew out a stream of smoke.

"I had nothing to do with the two of you faking artwork," Lizzie said. "I didn't even know either of you existed until eight days ago."

"The coppers might think otherwise after I talk to them," Thea said. "Doesn't it all seem a little too coincidental, the connections between your friend Sidney, Sebastian, and Isaac Roman? Isaac hiring you to perform on the very night Sebastian was murdered?"

"Are you saying Roman's involved in this too?"

Thea puffed on her cigarette and shrugged. "Who knows what Isaac's involved in? Underneath his flamboyance and charming demeanor, he's an enigma."

"What do you want?" Lizzie asked.

"If I go down, I'm taking you with me."

Thea's threat took her by surprise. Trying to sound calmer than she felt, Lizzie said, "Is that so? And how do you plan to do that?"

"Your fingerprints are all over Sebastian's studio. On his paintings too. I'm going to tell Sergeant Darcy you were our partner in crime."

"You'll never make it stick," Lizzie said, but the truth pressed a panic button. She'd even left her prints on the stove where the couple baked forged paintings to make them appear old.

Thea tossed her head and glared at Lizzie, a haughty smirk on her face. "Maybe not. But even so, I'm betting your Beacon Hill sugar daddy won't want to get his hands dirtied in a scandal like this. As I recall, he handles the financial portfolios of a number of high rollers. Bad publicity isn't good for their businesses, you know. Easier to dump a cheap showgirl who's just a trifle to him than get dragged through the rumor mill."

Her words hit Lizzie like a stomach punch.

"It was a nice day until you showed up." Lizzie scattered the last bits of bread for the squirrels, before turning away. "I have nothing more to say to you."

"Enjoy it. Your nice days are numbered."

* * *

When Alan came home from the office, he found Lizzie in his bedroom, packing her suitcases. She looked up at him with tears in her eyes.

"I'm sorry, Alan. I have to go home."

"What's wrong?"

She pulled a beaded dress from the wardrobe, folded it, and laid it on top of several other frocks. "I can't put you and your family through this mess."

"What mess? What are you talking about?"

He cupped her chin in his hand and gently tilted her face up to look at him. Instead, she squeezed her eyes shut, tears running down her cheeks. She pulled away and reached for the risqué black gown she'd worn last Saturday night. The night of Sebastian's murder. She unhooked the dress from its hanger and started to wrap it in tissue paper.

Alan took it from her and hung it back in the mahogany wardrobe. "Tell me what's going on."

Lizzie did. "I feel like I'm running in the shadows, chasing a light that keeps slipping away from me. Just when I think the sun's finally coming up and brighter days lie ahead, darkness overtakes me again."

"But you weren't involved," he said after she finished describing Thea Gallagher's threat.

Lizzie shook her head. "No, but Thea will trump up a story anyway. It will be in all the papers. I'll be implicated in the forgeries, maybe Sebastian's death. The cops might even think I pushed Edward Oliver off that balcony. You'll be dragged into it, too, Alan. The media won't miss a chance to skewer one of Boston's Brahmins."

Alan put his arm around her and guided her to sit on the edge of the four-poster bed. He sat beside her, shifted his arm, and laid his hand on her thigh.

"If you run off to New York now, you'll look guilty," he said.

"But it might divert the press. They'll think you gave me the bum's rush when you discovered my nefarious past." A new stream of tears streaked down her cheeks. "I wouldn't blame you if you did. I've brought trouble to your door. You have your family, your work to consider. You don't need to put up with this sort of muckraking."

"This isn't the first conundrum my family has faced, nor will it be the last. What was it Rafael Sabatini said? 'Only he who is without anything is without enemies.'"

"Then let those enemies be of your own making, not because of me."

Alan pulled a handkerchief from his pocket and dabbed at her tears. He stroked her hair and kissed her forehead. "We're going to have supper together, then we're going to talk to my lawyer. We'll work this out, Lizzie. Trust me."

Chapter Twenty-Five

"Time will bring to light whatever is hidden." — *Horace*

"Miss Crane? There's a telephone call for you."

Lizzie looked up from her crossword puzzle at Penelope, the housemaid for whom she'd come to feel affection during her days in Alan's household. The girl's blond curls and open, innocent face reminded her of Melody. *I miss her so much,* Lizzie thought. *Wouldn't it be swell if she were on the phone?*

"Thanks, Pen," she said as she pushed herself up from the game table in the comfortable second-floor sitting room, where one day she supposed Alan's children might gather to play.

For a moment, she paused while the pain resulting from her ordeal at the Gardner Museum swept over her. As it gradually loosened its grip, she straightened and followed the girl downstairs to the entryway with its oriental carpet, graceful Sheraton furniture, and gilt-framed portraits of the Peabody clan. The telephone's handset lay in wait on a mahogany table.

Lizzie picked it up. "Hello, this is Elizabeth Crane."

"Lizzie, it's Cora."

"Hello, Cora. I'm so glad to hear your voice. Are you well?"

"Yes, I'm fine," the card reader said.

"Do you have more info to share with me? I hope it's better than the last reading."

"No, something more down to earth, but it ties in to what I saw in the cards yesterday. Karl just told me the police took Thea Gallagher in for questioning late yesterday afternoon. She claimed you and Sidney were in cahoots with Sebastian in an art forgery scheme. Thea denied knowing anything about it until after he was murdered. The cops released her into her father's custody."

Lizzie inhaled a deep breath, then let it out slowly. Had the police already searched Sebastian's studio and collected her fingerprints? It came as no surprise that Thea was the enemy Cora had seen in the cards. Yet despite her animosity toward the treacherous young woman, Lizzie couldn't help but worry about how Paul Gallagher would punish his daughter as a result of this latest incident.

"I was expecting that," Lizzie said. "I ran into Thea in Boston's Public Garden yesterday after I talked to you. She threatened to implicate Sid and me. I don't think she believes we had anything to do with Sebastian's death—how could we? She's just trying to save her own neck. For some reason, she's got it in her head that I put the police on to her. But she was a key suspect from the moment she pulled her Lady Godiva stunt in Roman's ballroom the night Sebastian was murdered and made their affair public knowledge."

"The Five and Seven of Swords," Cora said, and Lizzie imagined her friend fingering her rope of pearls like worry beads. "What about the Three of Swords?"

"Thea pointed out that Alan would dump me to keep from getting caught up in the controversy."

After a long pause, Cora said, "You're still in residence at his townhouse, so I guess that hasn't happened."

"No, so far, he's been very supportive. But it's just the beginning. This whole business could get really ugly, and if it does, well, who knows?"

"Still, there's the Knight of Wands… I guess it could represent Alan."

"The messenger bringing good tidings?" Lizzie asked, trying to hide the sarcasm in her voice. "Can you see when that light in the darkness might show up?"

"The cards don't usually tell time accurately," Cora answered, "but my guess is soon."

* * *

Less than an hour later, the housemaid entered the sitting room again, where Lizzie sat in a chintz-covered armchair reading an Agatha Christie novel.

Penelope cleared her throat before saying, "Excuse me, Miss Crane, there's another telephone call for you."

Again, Lizzie followed the girl downstairs to the entrance hall, picked up the telephone's handset, and spoke into it. "Hello, this is Elizabeth Crane."

"Isaac Roman here."

"How nice to hear from you, Mr. Roman. I hope you're well."

Even though only a few days had passed since she left his Salem mansion with all its delights and turmoil, it seemed like months. She wondered how much he knew about all that had happened in that brief span of time. Although her name hadn't appeared in the papers in connection with Edward Oliver's death, surely Roman must have read about the young artist's dramatic fall in the Gardner Museum. She suspected he also knew the police had questioned Hugh Franklin—the two men were friends, or at least associates. Maybe partners in crime. Did he realize that Lizzie had accused Franklin of Sebastian's murder? Had Franklin warned Roman that she might point a finger at her former host, too? Maybe he also knew that Thea Gallagher had claimed Lizzie and Sidney were Sebastian's accomplices. Thea might even have implicated Roman in selling the forgeries.

"I'm at the State House," Roman said. "Can you get away to meet with me for a few minutes?"

A seriousness she'd never heard before lay heavy in his voice. For the first time, the robust, energetic, bon vivant she knew sounded weary.

"It will take me about fifteen minutes to walk down there."

"I'll wait for you on the front steps."

The connection clicked off, followed by the dial tone's buzz. *Why is Roman here? What does he want with me?* she wondered as she replaced the handset in its cradle. If he wanted to book The Troubadours for another stint, he would have phoned Sidney in New York, not her here at Alan's home. But his leaden tone didn't sound like he meant to discuss a new business proposition.

Lizzie glanced in the mirror and smoothed her hair. Then she hurried upstairs to grab her coat and a red cloche hat that made her look jauntier than she felt. On her way out, she told Penelope she was meeting with a friend and would return soon, in case Alan came home from visiting his mother while Lizzie was gone.

Her heels clicked on the cobblestones as she walked along Beacon Hill's narrow streets toward the State House. As she turned onto Beacon Street, the distinguished brick building with its golden dome designed by architect Charles Bulfinch more than a hundred years ago came into sight. She noticed Roman's Isotta-Fraschini parked on the edge of the Common before she spotted its owner.

Isaac Roman sat on the front steps of the building. Dressed in a conservative charcoal gray suit, a lighter, fog-gray coat draped over his shoulders, he propped his elbows on his knees, resting his chin on the heels of his palms. He stood as she approached and attempted a smile, but it lacked the vivacity that usually radiated from him.

Suddenly, Lizzie realized she might be walking into a trap. She shouldn't have agreed to meet Roman alone. At least, she should've told Penelope where she was going and who she planned to see. It wouldn't be difficult for her former host to shove her into his custom-made automobile and whisk her away.

"Hello, Mr. Roman," Lizzie called to him, drawing on her performer's skill to hide her apprehension and present a cheerful image. "To what do I owe this unexpected visit?"

She extended her hand in greeting. He took it, pressing a folded piece of paper against her palm. Lizzie knew instinctively not to acknowledge it.

"Let's walk a bit, shall we?" he said, crooking his arm for her to take.

Together, they walked down the steps, across Beacon Street, and into Boston Common, although the chilly, cloudy day was less than optimal for a leisurely stroll. Lizzie wondered what the few people they passed thought of them. Did they see a well-dressed older gentleman of means accompanied by a pretty paramour half his age? Or a daughter devoted to her distinguished father?

"I regret that you're an unwitting fly who's stumbled into this spider's web," Roman said. "I hope you can believe I never intended any such thing when I hired you and your friends to perform at my home."

"I don't blame you for this absurd mess," Lizzie said. "Still, it's all been such a catastrophe."

This morning, the *Boston Globe* had run an article linking Edward Oliver's death to Sebastian Amory's art forgeries. The newspaper had stopped short of implicating Hugh Franklin in the brouhaha. However, Oliver's assault on Lizzie in the Gardner Museum and his subsequent death threatened to drag her into the spotlight. So far, Alan's attorneys had buffeted her against the worst of it. *How much longer can they protect me, though?* she asked herself.

"On the piece of paper I gave you is an address to a private vault in a warehouse in Chelsea," Roman said. "Hugh Franklin stores his treasures there."

It took Lizzie a few moments to realize what he'd revealed. Stolen paintings, forged artwork, and other precious commodities with questionable pedigrees were stashed in an unpretentious warehouse on Boston's outskirts, awaiting transfer to the highest bidders.

Roman is the Knight of Wands, she realized. "Why are you telling me this?"

"Because you don't deserve to have your life ruined by something that's not your fault."

A golden retriever, hardly more than a pup, broke free from its owner and sprinted across the grass toward them. It stood before Roman, wagging its tail enthusiastically. He bent and scratched its tawny head until the dog's owner caught up with his pet and clamped a leash on its collar.

As the dog and its owner moved away with a cheerful wave, Roman said, "Give this address to Detective McKinnon."

"How will all this affect you?" Lizzie asked.

"That's none of your concern."

Roman stopped abruptly and turned around, guiding Lizzie back in the direction from which they'd come. At the edge of the Common, he approached the Isotta-Fraschini and opened its door. "May I give you a lift someplace, Miss Crane?" he asked.

Lizzie shook her head. "No, thank you. Goodbye, Mr. Roman."

* * *

When Alan returned from visiting his mother, Lizzie handed him the piece of paper Roman had given her and recounted her meeting with the enigmatic art collector. Her former host and possible thief. The larger-than-life man she'd come to think of almost as a friend. Joan Amory's angry words, thrown like darts at Roman in his parlor the day after Sebastian's death, echoed in her ears: "I thought you were a friend."

"Do you think it's legit or a trap?" Lizzie asked.

Alan shook his head. "I don't know."

"If I give this address to the police, they may find enough evidence to arrest Hugh Franklin. But they might also wonder how I knew about this secret vault and its contents. I'd have to tell them about Roman. That info might reinforce their suspicions about my connection to him."

"Do you think Roman's involved too?"

She shook her head. "Haven't the foggiest. He's sticking his neck out to help me. I'm not sure why."

"Lizzie, you have to stop trying to protect everyone else and start protecting yourself." He folded the piece of paper and slipped it in his jacket pocket. "We'll ask my attorney how to proceed. In the meantime, don't talk to anyone else about this. No one. Promise?"

"I promise."

* * *

At five o'clock that Sunday evening, a distinguished-looking man in his mid-forties with a high forehead and spectacles, impeccably dressed in a well-tailored dark blue suit, met with Alan and Lizzie in the townhouse's formal parlor. Alan introduced him as his attorney, Michael Harrison. Lizzie sat on the leather Chesterfield sofa beside Alan, with Harrison in one of the wing chairs near the fireplace. Norman served them martinis.

Alan had already explained Lizzie's situation to Harrison. Now, he handed his lawyer the note Isaac Roman had given her this afternoon.

"What do you recommend we do with it, Mike?" Alan asked.

"I think we have to give this to the police. Otherwise, you could be guilty of withholding evidence." Harrison folded the note. "May I keep this?"

"Yes, of course," Alan said.

"What do you think will come of it?" Lizzie asked.

"I expect the cops will get a warrant to search the vault. If they find stolen art, they'll arrest this fellow Franklin."

"And Roman, too?"

She recalled the private art gallery on the second floor of Roman's mansion and considered that, if Thea Gallagher could be believed, Lizzie was one of the few people to view it. Might that be held against her as evidence of collaboration?

"I don't know, Miss Crane."

Alan took her hand. "Let's not think about that right now. One step at a time."

The attorney sealed Roman's note in an envelope, then put it in his attaché case. "I'll try to arrange a meeting with Detective McKinnon in the morning."

They chatted a little longer while they finished their martinis. Then Harrison and Alan stood, shook hands, and said goodnight.

"Thanks, Mike, for coming out on Sunday evening."

"I won't tell you not to worry," the attorney said, "but unless there's something more that you haven't told me, Miss Crane, everything they've got against you is circumstantial."

"That's all I know," Lizzie assured him. But even as she spoke, she wondered if Sidney still had secrets he hadn't shared with her. "Thank you, Mr. Harrison."

"I'll be in touch, Alan."

Chapter Twenty-Six

"The propensity to truck, barter and exchange one thing for another is common to all men, and to be found in no other race of animals."
— Adam Smith

The next morning, at half past nine, Lizzie and Alan met Michael Harrison in front of the police department. Alan held her arm as they made their way inside. A fresh-faced young officer showed them to a room painted battleship gray, and they took their seats at an oak table beneath a fluorescent light that buzzed like a swarm of gnats. Harrison placed his attaché case on the table unlocked it, retrieving a legal pad of paper and an assortment of handwritten notes.

"You must be honest," the attorney instructed Lizzie. "But don't say any more than you have to—don't volunteer a thing. Let me do the talking. Pay attention to me. If the police ask you a question and I want you to be quiet, I'll touch my index finger to my lips. I know you're probably nervous, Miss Crane, but this shouldn't take long."

Remembering the numerous times policemen had interrogated her during the past several months, she thought *this seems pretty tame, all things considered. At least I have Alan and Mr. Harrison here to guide me.* She wondered how much Alan had told his attorney about the previous murders in which she'd been involved. Would those incidents cast her in a damaging light and hurt her credibility?

The door opened, and Detective McKinnon entered. In the stark electric light, his polished badge pinned on his dark blue uniform shone as a reminder of his authority.

Alan and his lawyer stood.

"Please, be seated, gentlemen," the policeman said in an easy-going voice that might better befit a veterinarian caring for a frightened animal than a big-city cop investigating a murder case. An amiable smile lit up his ruddy, broad-cheeked face. "Good morning to you, Mike. You, too, Mr. Peabody. And Miss Crane, thank you for agreeing to meet with me on such short notice. I gather you're feeling better than when I saw you on Friday morning? You certainly look well."

"Yes, thank you," she said, recalling her first meeting with McKinnon after Edward Oliver assaulted her at the Gardner Museum. She couldn't imagine feeling worse than she had then.

"So, Mike, what do you have for me?" the policeman asked. "Is this going to break the case wide open? Win me Detective of the Year?"

His jocular manner confused Lizzie. The cops she'd dealt with in the past, including Sergeant Darcy, wore their duty like heavy backpacks. No levity. No relaxation. Certainly no humor. Was he trying to put her at ease? Or was this a case of the iron fist in the velvet glove, designed to get her to trust him so he could catch her up in his snare once she let down her guard?

"We have a piece of information we believe to be relevant to the case of Sebastian Amory's death." Harrison lifted the lid of his attaché case again, reached inside, and withdrew the envelope that contained the Chelsea address of Hugh Franklin's secret vault.

"So you said when we spoke earlier." McKinnon reached for the envelope.

Harrison laid it on the table and covered it with his hand. "You and one of Salem's finest, Sergeant Richard Darcy, led art gallery owner Hugh Franklin away from his Newbury Street establishment Friday night. What's the upshot?"

McKinnon held out his hands, palms up. "Hey, Mike, you know I can't reveal that. Police business. It's an ongoing investigation."

Harrison nodded. "I also know you're on to something significant—you just don't realize the extent of it yet. A big fish is nipping at your line, but you don't have what you need to reel it in. If you don't act fast, that big fish might slip away." The attorney tapped the envelope. "This, Detective, is the key that will unlock your investigation."

McKinnon's eyes lit up. He tugged at the lobe of his right ear. "I don't have the authority to make deals, if that's what you're suggesting," he said. "That's for the courts to decide."

"We're not even close to the plea-bargaining stage," Harrison reminded him. "You know, we might be able to avoid that business altogether."

McKinnon rubbed his jaw, as if checking the closeness of his morning shave. "What do you want, Mike?"

"This could be the biggest case of your life," Harrison said, figuratively waving the carrot in front of the policeman. "The case that brings you notoriety, accolades, that promotion I know you've been vying for."

"What do you want?" McKinnon asked again, his tone of voice hardening.

"I want you to leave Miss Crane alone. Her only involvement in this unfortunate situation is to have had the bad fortune to discover the murder victim's body. Since that morning, she's been subjected to repeated questioning by police, been harassed by other more likely suspects, even attacked and almost killed by a person of interest in this case. You, yourself, were called in after said attack at the Gardner Museum on Friday."

McKinnon sighed loudly. "Mike, I can't offer you a guarantee like that. It's not in my hands entirely. I don't even know yet what you've got to trade."

Lizzie shifted her position on her chair, uncrossed her legs, then crossed them again. The volleying between Alan's lawyer and the lawman both intrigued and troubled her. Under the table, Alan laid his hand on her thigh, as if willing her to stay calm.

"All business is about bartering. This is no different," Harrison said. "Would you prefer I talked to someone higher up?"

A dark scowl fell like a veil over the policeman's face. His former engaging personality receded behind a cloud of defensiveness as he silently bristled at the attorney's suggestion. Lizzie realized he wanted to solve this case and he wanted it bad. He glanced at her, then held out his hand to Harrison, palm up, wriggling his fingers. Signaling the attorney to give him the juicy morsel.

Harrison picked up the envelope. He slapped it on the palm of his hand a few times. "Miss Crane would also like you to keep the source of this information confidential."

McKinnon snorted. "You're pushing your luck, Mike."

The attorney removed his spectacles and wiped them with his linen handkerchief. He waited a few poignant moments, then started to put the mysterious envelope back in his attaché case.

The detective held up his hand to stop him. "Gimme."

"Do I have your word?"

Grudgingly, McKinnon nodded. "This better be good."

* * *

Lizzie had promised Alan she wouldn't talk about their meeting with Detective McKinnon or Hugh Franklin's secret vault with anyone—not even her friends. Especially not her friends. So when Sidney telephoned on Tuesday to ask how she was doing and when she planned to come back to New York, Lizzie said simply, "I don't know."

"What's up?" he asked, a hint of concern in his voice. "I hope you're not planning to marry Peabody and move to Boston."

"No, nothing like that," she said. "But I must admit, it's been swell staying here with him these last few days. I've never felt so pampered."

Well, that part's true, at least, she thought. *Fortunately, my name hasn't appeared in the papers, so Sid doesn't know the rest of it. Edward Oliver's death might not even make the news in New York.* She longed to ask Sid if he'd heard anything more from Sergeant Darcy or any of the other players in Sebastian Amory's murder, but thought that might be a breach of her promise to Alan. Instead, she kept the conversation focused on the Village scene and what Sidney had been up to since his timely escape from Salem after Sebastian's funeral.

"That's one thing I wanted to talk with you about," he said. "Yesterday, I heard from a woman named Anne Cabot Lawrence who lives in Newbury-port, Massachusetts. It's only about forty miles from Boston. She said she attended some of our events in Ipswich last August at the Winslow estate. I don't remember her, but maybe you do. She wants to hire us for an event next June."

Images of the elaborate oceanfront estate, where their previous saxophone player had been murdered, flashed in Lizzie's memory. Anne Cabot Lawrence was a longtime family friend of the Winslow family who'd hosted the week-long celebration during which Melody had met her future husband and Lizzie had met Alan.

"Yes, I remember her. I quite liked her, in fact. What's the event?"

"She's getting married. Wants us to play at her wedding reception, maybe a few parties beforehand."

Lizzie recalled the tall, outspoken, athletic woman she'd met that summer on the Winslows' porch one salubrious evening laced with music, booze, and dangerous secrets. At the time, she'd supposed that Anne Lawrence was a lesbian and was surprised now to discover that her assumptions had been wrong.

"Make the deal, Sid."

"You haven't even heard the terms."

"I already know I want to do it. It will be nice to visit Massachusetts again." *If only Melody could come with us, but by then, she'll be married and maybe in a family way.* "Besides, we've spent so much time on Boston's North Shore this year, it's starting to feel like a second home."

"Your wish is my command," he said, and Lizzie thought his tone sounded brighter. "Hurry back, Bearcat. New York is lonely without you."

* * *

By now, Lizzie's bruises had faded to an ugly, mold-colored green. The awful aching had subsided, so that it only hurt when she applied direct pressure to the damaged places. Now, when Alan took her into his bed, she could position herself in such a way that pleasure surpassed pain.

Chapter Twenty-Seven

"When I see a hidden action brought to light, I worship the god of Truth." — Edna St. Vincent Millay

The raid on Hugh Franklin's vault made the front page of Wednesday morning's *Globe*. Lizzie read the article while eating breakfast in Alan's kitchen, thankful that neither her name nor Isaac Roman's appeared in print. She wondered if Franklin suspected that his friend Roman had ratted him out. Did anyone else know the secret location of the gallery owner's treasures?

A kitchen maid refilled Lizzie's coffee cup. "May I bring you anything else, ma'am?" the girl asked.

"No, thanks."

The article didn't say whether the police had arrested Franklin. Even if they had, he'd surely post bail—unless they had enough evidence to charge him with killing Sebastian Amory. The paintings, even if they proved to be stolen or fraudulent, wouldn't be enough to convict him of murder. She wanted to talk to Alan about it—certainly, he'd seen the paper before going to his office this morning.

A housemaid interrupted her thoughts. "Miss Crane, there's a telephone call for you."

Lizzie followed the girl to the foyer and picked up the receiver, delighted to hear Alan's voice on the other end of the line. "You've been reading my mind," she said. "I was just now wishing I could talk to you about Hugh

Franklin's arrest."

"Apparently there's more. I heard from Mike Harrison a few minutes ago. He wants to meet with us this evening. Says he has important news, but that's all he'd tell me over the phone."

"Not even if it's good news or bad?"

"No, he's being rather mysterious."

"Well, then, I'm going to think positive. We're due for something good," Lizzie said. "But I admit, I'll be on pins and needles 'til then."

* * *

The grandfather clock in the entryway chimed eight as Michael Harrison sat down with Lizzie and Alan in the formal parlor, martinis in hand. Behind his spectacles, the attorney's eyes sparkled. Lizzie thought he seemed to enjoy keeping them in suspense.

"It's not out on the streets yet," he told them. He sipped his martini. "This is really excellent."

"The martini or the news?" Alan asked.

"I meant the martini, but I think you'll find the news pretty spectacular, too."

"We read about the raid on Franklin's vault," Lizzie said. "Did they find stolen or forged artwork?"

"They found quite a cache. It will probably take some time to determine how much of it is hot, though."

So Roman was right, Lizzie thought. Again, she wondered if her former employer, for whom she'd come to feel fondness as well as gratitude, would get caught up in the police's dragnet.

Harrison paused briefly for effect, before revealing what had not yet made the papers. "The cops arrested Hugh Franklin this afternoon for the murder of Sebastian Amory."

"Oh my," she said. Although she'd suspected the gallery owner ever since seeing the photos of him in the magazine in Salem's library, hearing his guilt confirmed by the attorney still stunned her.

Alan took her hand. "That truly *is* good news. What brought them to that conclusion?"

"In addition to the cache of goods the cops discovered in Franklin's Chelsea storeroom, they found chloroform in his gallery," Harrison said. "Amory's killer drugged him with it before shooting him. A piece of cloth had been soaked in chloroform and stuck in the victim's mouth, rendering him numb or even unconscious."

"I'd wondered how Franklin managed to overpower Sebastian," Lizzie said. The awful memory of the artist tied to the tree, arrows piercing his torso, gagged with his own purple ascot flashed in her mind. "At least the chloroform may have prevented him from feeling the pain of being shot."

"Why would Franklin have kept chloroform in his art gallery?" Alan asked.

"Mixed with turpentine, it's used as a varnish for paintings," Harrison answered.

Alan finished his drink, and as if by magic, Norman appeared bearing a silver shaker. The butler refilled their glasses, then discreetly removed himself from the parlor.

"The police also found a bow and a quiver of arrows of Navajo design in Franklin's vault," the attorney added. "The arrows matched the ones that killed Amory."

"Why didn't Franklin get rid of the incriminating evidence?" Alan asked.

"Maybe he couldn't bear to trash his collection or let go of something that had special significance to him. Some murderers like to hold on to mementos of their kills, like hunters who hang stuffed animal heads over their fireplaces. But because they can't display their trophies publicly, they transfer reverence to things associated with the hunt, such as the weapons used to slay their prey," Harrison explained with a shrug. "Perhaps he thought he'd never be found out, that he was above the law. You'd be surprised how many people, especially rich, powerful ones, believe they're invincible."

Lizzie took a sip of the icy-cold gin splashed with just a hint of vermouth. The irony of such a bland-looking, understated man as Hugh Franklin choosing to murder his colleague in such a gory, show-grabbing manner seemed a contradiction at first. But perhaps, given his interest in art, he couldn't resist imitating Botticelli's famous fifteenth-century painting—especially since imitation was the team's specialty. Considering that Sebastian had parodied Franklin with the fake Dürer painting, might Franklin have chosen to strike back with this grisly lampoon? Or, maybe the answer lay in the shadows theorized by Swiss psychologist Carl Jung that was the subject of the Franklin Gallery's current art exhibit. If the police didn't padlock the gallery, maybe she'd go back and have another look.

"Why do you suppose Sebastian came back to Roman's house after riding away into the night with Thea Gallagher?" Lizzie asked. "And why would he have agreed to meet with Franklin in Roman's conservatory? Do you think Franklin might have lured Sebastian with a promise of giving him a show at his gallery?"

"Unless Franklin decides to talk, we'll never know," Alan said.

"Well, young lady. It looks like you're in the clear." Harrison held up his glass in a toast. "Here's to freedom."

"Thanks to both of you," she said, raising her glass. "And to Isaac Roman."

"You're the one who figured it out," Harrison reminded her. "You know, you might make a very good detective."

"Oh, no," Alan stated firmly. "Lizzie's detective days are over."

"Most likely, you'll still have to testify in court when Franklin's case is tried. That won't be anytime soon, though," Harrison said.

They chatted a while longer, then Alan's lawyer stood and said goodnight. "You'll probably read about this in the papers tomorrow, Friday at the latest."

"You don't think Lizzie's name will be dragged into it, do you, Mike?" Alan asked.

"Can't say for sure. If so, she'll be billed as the glamorous lady sleuth who cracked the case—"

Alan cut him off. "That's exactly what we *don't* want."

"Don't worry, Alan. We've put money in the right hands."

"So everything's copacetic?" Lizzie asked.

"I think you can sleep well tonight, Miss Crane."

* * *

She lay in Alan's arms, spooned against his body, breathing easily for the first time in nearly a week. Wrongs, she knew, hunkered down in the shadows like angry ghosts until righted and put to rest. Now, perhaps, those malevolent spirits would move on, letting all of them—Sidney, Roman, Joan Amory, even Thea Gallagher—release the past and get on with their lives. Lizzie's last thoughts, as she drifted toward sleep, were the words of the poet Edna St. Vincent Millay: "When I see a hidden action brought to light, I worship the god of Truth."

Chapter Twenty-Eight

"If I could say it in words, there would be no reason to paint." —
Edward Hopper

Easter weekend passed quietly. Although Lizzie had been raised Catholic and Alan Episcopalian, they no longer adhered to the religious formalities of their childhood. Now that he'd become a Mason, Alan had chosen a spiritual path that led in a different direction. But out of respect for his family's beliefs and to please his mother, they attended services Sunday morning at the beautiful Trinity Church in Boston's Back Bay. Lizzie was glad she'd come, for the extraordinary new Skinner pipe organ and the choir's powerful rendition of Handel's "Hallelujah Chorus" brought her to tears.

Afterward, they ate an afternoon dinner at the home of Alan's sister, Judith Peabody Crowninshield, with her husband and three children, two cousins and their wives, and an elderly aunt. Lizzie knew Judith disapproved of her relationship with Alan. His sister hoped her thirty-four-year-old brother would stop his frivolous dallying with unsuitable women—like this beautiful showgirl he'd taken up with recently—marry a lady of their own class, sire children, and settle into a life of respectable domesticity. However, she had no say in the matter. Alan, by virtue of being a man, the firstborn, and head of the family since his father's death, could have forbidden his younger female sibling from engaging in a romantic relationship with a person below her status. Judith, though, had no such power. And so she politely welcomed

Lizzie into her home on this holiest of holy days.

Earlier in the day, they'd visited Alan's bedridden mother. Although Lizzie was pretty sure Mrs. Peabody held the same opinions about Alan's future as his sister did, the older woman had no intention of inciting controversy with her only son at this late date. Maybe, in this end stage of her life, she'd arrived at a more relaxed, less judgmental perspective of what's truly important and what's purely stuff and nonsense, and come to see that happiness is all that matters. For perhaps different reasons, she, too, welcomed Lizzie into her home and gave the couple her blessing, no matter how improper she may have believed their relationship to be.

* * *

On Monday, Alan uncharacteristically took a day off from work. "Let's go to Gloucester and see if we can find the house in your Hopper painting," he told Lizzie.

After breakfast, they drove forty miles north along a winding seacoast road to the three-hundred-year-old seafaring town that had the distinction of being America's oldest fishing community. On the way, they passed the promontory, where a castle that belonged to an eccentric occultist perched high above the rocky shore. Where five months ago a mysterious woman had been murdered during one of The Troubadours' engagements. Where Alan had saved Lizzie's life.

As they crossed a drawbridge that gave them access to the newly completed Stacy Boulevard that edged the city's harbor and entered Gloucester proper, Lizzie gazed out at the ocean. Fishing boats cut through the blue-green water. She tried to imagine the schooners, barques, and other graceful sailing ships— built perhaps in the nearby town of Essex—that once filled this waterway. Eastern Point peninsula, where the artist Edward Hopper painted his first *plein air* watercolor, sheltered one side of the harbor from the full force of the North Atlantic's ferocious storms. On this mild, cloudy day, pedestrians strolled along the ocean's edge, past the recently installed bronze statue of an eight-foot-tall fisherman at the wheel of his ship, looking out to sea. Past the plaques that listed the names of thousands of local fishermen who'd gone to watery graves.

At an art museum in the center of town, Lizzie and Alan found a book that contained pictures of Gloucester painted by Hopper, Fitz Hugh Lane, Winslow Homer, and other artists. While Alan paid a clerk they'd interrupted from her task of dusting the gift shop's shelves, Lizzie asked, "We'd like to see the places Mr. Edward Hopper painted. Can you give us directions?"

"You're only a hop, skip, and a jump away," the clerk answered. "Start on Middle Street, just a block from here. Then, walk up Pleasant to Prospect and on toward Our Lady of Good Voyage Church. Do you have an automobile?"

"Yes."

"Well, then, you'll want to motor out to Rocky Neck and Eastern Point to see the lighthouse he painted." The clerk plucked a tourist map from one of the shelves and handed it to Alan. "Enjoy your day."

"Thanks," Lizzie said. "We will."

* * *

Following the map and the clerk's directions, they strolled up and down Gloucester's winding streets, searching for the houses that had captured Hopper's fancy. The buildings they passed comprised a mix of styles and periods, from handsome sea captain's mansions to the modest wooden homes of fishermen and factory workers. Here and there, they spotted one that seemed to match a picture in the book they'd purchased in the art museum's gift shop. But the book didn't include pictures of all the places Hopper painted during his stays in Gloucester. Lizzie made a game of trying to guess which ones might have been the artist's unacknowledged subjects.

At the top of a hill near the Portuguese church with its twin towers that overlooked the city and the sea beyond, they stopped in front of a three-story clapboard structure of simplified Greek Revival design. A housepainter, standing on a ladder, busily slapped a new coat of green paint on it.

"Excuse me," Lizzie called to him. "Do you know if this is one of the houses Mr. Edward Hopper painted?"

190

Holding his brush aloft, the man stared down at her quizzically. "Lady, all I know is I'm painting it now."

Lizzie laughed and waved at the housepainter as they continued their exploration. Finally, they came to the house depicted in her picture.

"That's it!" she said, clapping her hands together like an excited child. She felt a sudden longing to sit beneath the billowing yellow awnings on the house's second-story porch and inhale the salty sea breeze wafting in from the harbor. To peer out its third-floor windows and watch the ships come in as its long-ago inhabitants must have done.

Built nearly a century ago, the clapboard house with its pretty porches and intricate curving roof made of scalloped gray slate tiles was larger than those of its neighbors and its lines more graceful. Still, the unbiased eye would have considered it an undistinguished structure in need of repair, with peeling paint and slatted wooden shutters drooping beside its arched windows. An ordinary house, where ordinary people lived ordinary lives.

"I think the painting is a rather glorified rendition of the actual subject," Alan said, putting his arm around Lizzie's shoulders.

"Maybe it's like Edgar Degas said, 'Art is not what you see, but what you make others see.'"

As they stood, studying the house, wondering what Hopper found so intriguing about it, the sun slowly emerged from the bank of clouds that had hidden it all day. Golden light splashed the walls of the house. Like melting honey, sunshine slid along the worn clapboards. It shooed away the shadows that only a moment before had covered the building like a winter cloak. It tickled the sagging shutters, stirring them from their humdrum function, and lit up the wavy glass in the tall, narrow windows so that a fire seemed to burn behind them. Now, as Lizzie watched the sleeping house wake up, she saw what Hopper had seen.

It's a metaphor for life, she realized. *Life is a series of ups and downs, sunshine and cloudy skies. We're always sifting through the shadows, searching for the light they temporarily obscure.* Thinking back over the past two weeks and the unhappiness and turmoil that had accompanied them, she reminded herself, *dawn follows night, spring follows winter.*

She slipped her arm around Alan's waist and hugged him. *Love chases away even the darkest shadows. The simplest thing becomes beautiful, a work of art, when gazed upon by eyes that appreciate it. We are all more wondrous than we appear, we only need someone who cares enough to help us emerge from the shadows, so that we can shine.*

A Note from the Author

This is a work of fiction, though it contains real places and people and events that did happen. Except in the case of historic fact, however, if any of my characters resembles an actual person, living or dead, it's purely coincidental. When genuine people or situations are presented herein, it is in a fictional context. For example, aviator Charles Lindbergh really did perform daring aerial exhibitions around the country before gaining international fame for flying across the Atlantic a year after my story takes place. Edward Hopper really did paint houses in Gloucester, Massachusetts and environs in the 1920s. The town of Peabody, Massachusetts really was named for the philanthropist George Peabody. However, none of these notable individuals ever met the characters in my story––although had my characters been real people it's quite possible they would have encountered the famous folks mentioned here.

I have endeavored to convey all events, people, products, technology, music, literature, social norms, fashion, architecture, locations, and other details accurately, in keeping with the period. Many of the places in this story, including the Salem Willows amusement park, the Hawthorne Hotel, the House of the Seven Gables, and the Isabella Stewart Gardner Museum, still exist. Some, unfortunately, such as Salem's train station, have been demolished. The Pequot Mills' buildings have been converted into offices and commercial space.

If any actual house, hotel, restaurant, church, park, museum, store, cemetery, library, or other place mentioned herein still survives, I've been there (with the exception of the interrogation rooms in the Salem and Boston Police Departments, thankfully). I love doing field research and firmly believe in its value when I'm striving for veracity. I lived in Massachusetts for thirty-one years, eight in Salem, seventeen in Gloucester, and six in the Boston area. Much has changed since 1926, when this story takes place. Yet Salem, Massachusetts, remains one of the most beautiful and historically significant cities in America and provides a wonderful setting for my story. If you've never been there, I hope you'll have a chance to visit someday.

Acknowledgements

First and foremost, I wish to acknowledge my fellow authors and friends, Kate Flora and Susan Oleksiw, who cofounded Level Best Books with me to provide a venue where New England's many talented crime writers could share their work. Over the years, LBB's subsequent owners have taken the company to new heights, winning all the important awards in the mystery/thriller field and delighting readers worldwide. I am grateful to Level Best's Dames of Detection, Verena Rose and Shawn Reilly Simmons, for giving me a chance to reach readers who love historical mysteries and to again become a member of the LBB family.

I also wish to thank all of you who took the time to read early drafts of this book and who offered much-needed guidance, insight, and encouragement: Anne Barnhart, Donna Dermody, Betsy Fields, Daryl Herring, Dave Kaczynski, Wanda McLaughlin, Martha Mitchell, Susan Oleksiw, David Remschel, Kay Stewart, Robert Swoboda, Desmond White, and Lenore White. Your editorial advice was crucial in polishing this rough stone and making it shine. Thanks, too, to Debbie Sessions of Vintage Dancer for sharing her expertise in historic clothing.

About the Author

Skye Alexander is the author of nearly fifty fiction and nonfiction books, including three previous novels in the Lizzie Crane mystery series: *Never Try to Catch a Falling Knife, What the Walls Know,* and *The Goddess of Shipwrecked Sailors*. Her stories have been published in anthologies internationally and her work has been translated into fifteen languages. With fellow mystery writers Kate Flora and Susan Oleksiw, she cofounded Level Best Books in 2003. She's also an artist, astrologer, tarot reader, and feng shui practitioner whose first career was doing interior and furniture design and architectural renovation in the Boston vicinity, including Salem, Massachusetts. She now makes her home in Texas.

AUTHOR WEBSITE:
   skyealexander.com

Also by Skye Alexander

Never Try to Catch a Falling Knife

What the Walls Know

The Goddess of Shipwrecked Sailors

When the Blues Come Calling (scheduled for 2025 release)